He swept the injured woman up in his arms . . .

"Put me down," she said through clenched teeth, embarrassment making her voice overly sharp. "I'm fine. There's no need to see the good doctor."

Seemingly reluctant, he set her down and studied her. "You're sure?"

"Of course I'm sure," she snapped, noticing for the first time that he wore a soft flannel shirt that spread over strong, broad shoulders, then tapered down to slim hips covered with coarse woolen trousers so tight she could tell he would have put a statue of a Greek god to shame.

Seconds ticked by. Carriages passed in the street. And the man's concern slowly turned to amusement. His voice lowered and a devilish smile tilted on his lips. "I take it you like what you see?"

Heat rose to cover her face as she realized that, indeed, she was staring at him. She quickly looked away. "Most certainly not!"

The man chuckled. "Now, little lady, didn't your papa teach you not to lie?"

DIAMOND WILDFLOWER ROMANCE

A breathtaking line of searing romance novels . . . where destiny meets desire in the untamed fury of the American West.

Y0-CDN-065

Also by Linda Francis Lee

TEXAS ANGEL

Wild Hearts

Linda Francis Lee

DIAMOND BOOKS, NEW YORK

If you purchased this book without a cover, you should be aware that
this book is stolen property. It was reported as "unsold and de-
stroyed" to the publisher, and neither the author nor the publisher has
received any payment for this "stripped book."

This book is a Diamond original edition,
and has never been previously published.

WILD HEARTS

A Diamond Book / published by arrangement with
the author

PRINTING HISTORY
Diamond edition / December 1994

All rights reserved.
Copyright © 1994 by Linda Francis Lee.
This book may not be reproduced in whole or in part,
by mimeograph or any other means, without permission.
For information address: The Berkley Publishing Group,
200 Madison Avenue, New York, New York 10016.

ISBN: 0-7865-0062-X

Diamond Books are published by The Berkley Publishing Group,
200 Madison Avenue, New York, New York 10016.
DIAMOND and the "D" design
are trademarks belonging to Charter Communications, Inc.

PRINTED IN THE UNITED STATES OF AMERICA

10 9 8 7 6 5 4 3 2 1

For my parents,
Marilyn and Larry Francis,
with love and gratitude

And as always,
for Michael

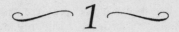

1

RED SATIN. FROM HEAD TO TOE. SHE HAD NEVER BEEN so bold.

Taking a deep breath, she crossed the room to stand before him, her eyes locked with his, her chin held high—her offer unmistakable.

He stood in front of the finely crafted French doors, the gossamer thin draperies pulled back and tied with silken sashes. His eyes were deep and fathomless, providing no clue to his feelings. He did not move or smile, or even tell her to leave. He was quiet and still, seemingly formidable.

Reason demanded that she flee. Some elusive, unfamiliar something that she could not name made her stay. Pride? Perhaps. Though she doubted it was so simple.

The scent of tall grasses and wild prairies drifted in on the breeze, and a clock on the mantel ticked the minutes away. But after what seemed like an eternity he reached out and took her hand. Her breath caught in her throat when he grazed her cheek with the tips of his fingers, barely, softly. Drawing her close, he gently urged her legs apart with his knee, until she felt the warmth of him between her thighs.

Her head fell back. No, she reasoned, her body burning and alive, it wasn't pride at all. It was that finally, she longed to shout, finally she would know.

He traced the line of her neck with the tip of his tongue. His hand slid down her back to the sweet curve of her hips, molding her to him. Relief swept through her when she felt the evidence of his desire, hard against her body. He was not immune. He wanted her—as much as she wanted him. The thought left her light-headed with satisfaction.

A smile tilted on her lips. She reached up and slipped her fingers beneath the neckline of her gown, revealing the gentle curve of smooth, white skin beneath.

The forbidding depths in his eyes were dark, though no longer fathomless. "Your heart is wild, my love," he murmured as he leaned down and nipped at the fine line of her shoulder, "but I'd have you no other way."

With that, cool, dry air whispered against her skin as the red satin finally fell—

"Miss Abigail! Surely not the red satin!"

Then silence.

Abigail Ashleigh's world twisted then wrenched apart. Her heart pounded in her chest. Inhaling sharply, her brown eyes snapped open with a start. She blinked twice, then twice again as her thoughts spiraled down from the images in her mind to collide with the harsh, late afternoon sun . . . and reality. With effort her eyes focused on the scandalized countenance of the proprietress of the General Store.

Heavens above! she groaned to herself. She had been daydreaming, again, with her hand entwined in a bolt of fabric—red satin fabric. She glanced furtively around the store until she remembered that her hand was still wrapped in the bolt. As if burned, she jerked away, the satin color staining her cheeks.

"The satin? Of course not, Mrs. Kent!" Abigail replied with a faint smile, her fingers finding the hardwood button at the top of her white muslin chemisette as if to insure that indeed it was done.

Sighing her relief, Abigail hastily turned her attention to another fabric, her long black skirt sweeping the floor at the sudden movement. She ran her hand over the bolt of serge that lay on the counter next to the other. She bit back disappointment as she stared at the coarse but practical material. Longing filled her, though for so much more than simply the shimmery fabric. But that was absurd, she quickly admonished herself, before she slapped her gloves against her hand, took a deep breath to slow her pounding heart, and pushed the bolt forward. "The serge will do nicely," she said with a firm nod of her head.

Myrtle Kent screwed up her lips and considered the woman who stood before her. Abigail Ashleigh was the oldest daughter of Sherwood Ashleigh, the wealthiest man in town. That she had the intelligence of a schoolmarm, no one could deny. That she had the morals of a saint, everyone admitted. But more than once someone had mentioned the faraway look that was all too frequently found in the woman's eye. For all her intellect could the woman be addlepated? Myrtle was inclined to ask herself. Surely not.

Then suddenly she smiled. Surely not, she repeated to herself. She couldn't recall a single rumor that there was madness in the Ashleigh family. A more stalwart, no-nonsense clan could not be found for miles. The faraway look must stem from the fact that at twenty-nine years of age, Abigail Ashleigh still found herself unmarried. Though if rumors were to be believed, wedding bells would be ringing for Abigail and Walter Jackson very soon. Either way, Myrtle conceded, a twenty-nine-year-old maidenly woman had no business going around in satins and ruffles.

"Yes," Mrs. Kent said out loud, "the serge is perfect." Taking the bolt to the cutting table to measure out the length, she looked up just in time to see Abigail's eyes stray to a roll of perfectly proper, finely crafted ivory lace.

"A bit of lace for you today, Miss Abigail?" she asked, her meandering thoughts instantly replaced by the shrewdness of a born salesperson.

Abigail's eyes snapped back to the proprietress. "No. No, thank you. The serge is all."

"You're sure now, honey? Your dress would be a mite prettier with a bit of lace on it."

"Yes, Mrs. Kent, I'm sure it would be, but the serge is all I need," Abigail added before turning away to put an end to the woman's meddlesome ways. Certainly a bit of lace would make something of a plain dress. But she was no fool. She knew better than to draw attention to herself with a bit of fluff.

The store was crowded with the wares the Widow Kent

peddled to the bustling town. Nearly six hundred miles from any other town of significant size, the General Store was one of the few places El Pasoans and nearby residents could get anything they didn't grow or raise themselves. Bins of flour and locked boxes of sugar crowded the floor. Jars filled with assorted colored jellies lined a shelf in front of a mullioned window. Long rays of golden sun pierced the jars, illuminating the candied fruit that hung suspended inside, before splintering into multicolored prisms.

Abigail reached out and moved her hand through the colored ribbons of light, her mind wandering back to the man in her daydream. Her breath grew short and she felt a strange burning in her throat at the thought that he was only a figment of her imagination. He was not real—and never would be, she had come to believe.

The bell over the door jingled, announcing another customer. Abigail quickly snatched her hand back and pulled on her gloves before turning away from the jellies.

"Lou Smith, what are you doing in here?" Mrs. Kent's words were sharp and unwelcoming.

The little girl stood just inside the doorway, her light brown hair braided haphazardly, her large brown eyes sparkling, and her lips spread in a smile that would melt the hardest of hearts—unless the heart belonged to the Widow Kent.

"Why nothing, Miz Kent. I just came in to see the rainbow is all." Lou eyed the row of jellies. "I did so want to see it."

Myrtle grumbled then bent her head to the task of cutting the material. Abigail could only stare at the child. Some tendril of recognition seemed to wrap around her. Somehow the little girl seemed familiar. But when Lou turned back and met her gaze, Abigail realized she had never seen the child before.

"Hello," Lou said with a small, awkward and outdated curtsy. "Isn't the rainbow so very beautiful?"

Abigail hesitated before she glanced back toward the jellies and colored light. After a moment she smiled. "Yes, it is."

"They say if you follow a rainbow to the very end you'll find a treasure." Lou smiled softly. "I know that must be where the Angel Mama has gone." She shrugged her shoulders. "One day I'll be able to follow the whole way . . . and then I'll find her."

Abigail looked closely at the girl named Lou. Her manner of speech was odd and not altogether childlike. But a mere glance told a different story. The youngster couldn't be more than five or six years old. The thought unsettled Abigail. How could such an obviously young child act so serious? And who was the Angel Mama? But, of course, Abigail didn't ask those questions as she would have liked, she simply said, "I don't believe we've met."

"My name is Lou. I just moved to town with the mama. We've lived in many—"

"Lou Smith!"

Myrtle's irritated bark brought both Lou and Abigail to attention.

"How many times do I have to tell you to stop bothering my customers." The proprietress came around the counter, muttering the whole way, holding the brown paper wrapped material by the string. "Little children with sticky hands and bumbling elbows are the bane of my existence. One day I'm going to up and sell this blasted store and move to Houston to be with my dear sister. She, I'm certain, hasn't had to deal with children in years! Now get on home with you, child."

Lou only smiled, seemingly undisturbed by the angry outburst. "Farewell," she called, her voice like delicate chimes, before she turned, pulled open the door, laughed in delight over the ringing bell, and skipped out of the General Store.

"That child is trouble, I tell you." Myrtle shook her head and handed over the package.

Abigail looked toward the door and watched the bell jingle to a halt. "She seemed nice enough to me."

Myrtle gave Abigail a pointed look. "You don't know her," she stated emphatically. "Mark my words, the child is

a feather-brained simpleton. And that mother . . ." Her
words trailed off with a shake of her head.

"Hmmm," was all Abigail said before she took her package and exited the store.

Stepping out onto the boardwalk, Abigail was just in
time to watch helplessly as Lou tripped and tumbled down
the short flight of wooden steps that led to the hard-packed
dirt road.

"Lou!" she cried, propriety forgotten as she hurried
down the stairs.

Through a cloud of dust, Lou looked up with a crooked
smile. "I guess I failed to be careful."

Abigail shook her head as if trying to make sense of
what just happened. "Are you all right?"

Pulling herself up, Lou sat on the bottom step and
brushed at smudges of dirt and grime. Abigail dropped
down beside her.

"I'm fine," Lou answered. "Yes, indeed. You're awful
kind to ask."

"Good Lord, child, it has nothing to do with being kind. I
was afraid you were hurt. You scared me to death!"

"Oh, my!" Lou swiveled around to look at Abigail,
worry written clearly in her brown eyes. "I'm terribly sorry.
You're not angry are you?"

"Angry? Heavens no!" Abigail reached out and
smoothed the hair from Lou's face. "Only worried," Abigail found herself saying, as though she had known the
child a lifetime.

Lou smiled. "I like the way you talk. It sounds so pretty.
Tell me your name."

"Abigail," she responded, feeling suddenly awkward.
"Abigail Ashleigh."

"Such a pretty name, too." Lou reached up and very
carefully touched a long strand of tightly curling brown
hair that had escaped Abigail's bonnet. "Just like your hair.
I've never seen such hair as this."

Abigail blushed and her smile melted away into the hot
summer day. "Not many have."

"It's so soft and pretty. Don't you love it so?"

Soft and pretty! Love her hair? The words and simple question jarred Abigail. No one had ever called her hair anything close to soft or pretty—unwieldy, unmanageable, a mess, certainly, but soft or pretty, never. And the question: Did she love her hair? She stared blankly at the child. "I've never thought about it." And strangely, she realized, it was true.

She knew her father didn't like her hair. She knew Walter hated her wayward tresses. And her sister merely stared at it and shook her head in dismay—or was it glee, Abigail suddenly wondered. Regardless, she had reflected at great length on what others thought of her hair, but had never considered whether *she* liked it or not. And that bothered her—like so many things had begun to bother her recently.

"You've never thought about your hair?" Lou looked at Abigail as if she didn't believe her.

Abigail chuckled. "Certainly I've thought about it. My family hardly lets me think of anything else," she said more to herself than to the little girl who sat next to her.

"Well, it is so very pretty, just like you." Suddenly Lou sprang up from the steps. "You make me happy, Miss Abigail. I think you will be my new friend."

For a second Abigail thought Lou was going to throw her tiny arms around her and give her a hug. But then the child seemed to reconsider such an act and before Abigail could uncharacteristically offer one of her own, Lou straightened up and said, "I've got to go now. I'm not through with egg-taking."

And with that she skipped away, a wave tossed back over her shoulder, leaving Abigail to wonder about the odd little girl, her odd manner of speech, and to rack her brain to figure out what egg-taking might be.

With a shake of her head Abigail pushed herself up and climbed the steps. She looked out over the town and watched Lou disappear around one of the many low, flat-roofed adobe buildings that lined the roads. There was Holloway's Restaurant, Barkin's Tannery, and the boardinghouse her Aunt Penelope ran for her father.

El Paso Street was busy. Horse-pulled wagons and mule-pulled *caretas* intertwined with pedestrians on the dusty road. Everyone seemed to be going somewhere, though where Abigail couldn't fathom. A quarter mile away in just about any direction brought a person face to face with desolation—vast expanses of nothing but cacti and jagged mountain peaks.

She took a deep breath and started down the boardwalk, making her way home. Her hand strayed to the strand of hair that had escaped her bonnet. The bolt of red satin came to mind. Without warning her feet itched to run and her heart longed to soar. What would it be like to toss care to the wind, throw back her head and laugh up to the skies, her hair wild to tumble down her back, dressed for all the world in red satin? What would it be like to be free and alive?

But her step faltered when she caught sight of Millie McAllister walking down the boardwalk on the other side of the road. Everyone knew Millie was free and alive. The woman's shimmering dress in the middle of the day bespoke her reputation.

Abigail sighed and tucked her hair back inside her bonnet and her brown paper package tightly under her arm, before she continued on her way. She was alive, no question, but being free from the life she led was nothing more than one of her many silly imaginings. She knew she should count herself lucky to have someone as upstanding as Walter Jackson willing to marry her. Certainly her family had despaired that she would remain on the shelf forever.

Yes, she thought as she made her way down the boardwalk, better off safe and well-fed than adventuresome and dead. She nearly snorted aloud at her lifelong motto, but stifled the sound with a sigh.

Despite the midday hour, piano music and laughter drifted along the boardwalk, undoubtedly from the notorious Red Dog Saloon that catered mostly to nefarious clients both day and night. Without realizing it, Abigail's finger tapped the beat against her paper package and her feet took up the rhythm, her perfectly polished black boots alternately peeking out from her skirts with her snappy steps.

The sun was warm on her face and the sky was almost painfully blue. As she drew closer to the saloon the music grew louder—and surprisingly sweet. For the moment she forgot her cares, and her lips nearly spread in a smile . . . nearly. But as it happened, her growing delight was cut short just when she stepped past the shuttered doors of the Red Dog. With considerable force the saloon doors swung open, backsiding Abigail, sending her brown paper package flying through the air and her modestly clad body sprawling across the boardwalk.

"What the hell!"

The blasphemous phrase rumbled through the air as Abigail landed face down, hands spread out to halt her flight. Once she finally made sense of what had happened, she noticed the largest, most sinister looking boots she had ever had the misfortune to lay eyes on planted right in front of her face. What the hell was right, she mused as she looked up and took in the ominous knife strapped to a thigh that looked more like the trunk of a good-sized oak tree than any part of a man's anatomy. And with that she blushed. But the blood from her blush rushed to her feet when two hands took hold of her under the arms and pulled her up at breakneck speed. Her head swam from the force.

She staggered and nearly went sprawling once again when the man took hold of her arm and proceeded to pound the dust from her skirt. But she forgot about possible danger, burning embarrassment, and the total impropriety of the situation, when the man leaned down in his attempts to better pound her garment, and they came face to face.

He had the deepest steel-blue eyes she had ever seen, with craggy lines at the edges that spoke of laughter and the sun. He had a full mouth that must have spent a great deal of time in a smile, a full head of thick blond hair, and a beard and mustache that nearly matched. Despite her five-foot-six-inch frame, when the man finished his pounding and straightened, Abigail had to crane her neck to look the length of him. But crane she did to take in this massive man with granite-hard shoulders and a neck lined with muscles.

Good God, he was huge! And dangerous, she thought suddenly. Her heart hammered at the thought.

"My apologies, ma'am," he drawled, his voice as smooth as molasses and as deep as a bullfrog's croak during mating season. "I didn't see you coming. In the future you'd do best not to walk so close to doors. You're lucky you weren't knocked senseless." His eyes slid over her and he smiled. "Looks like you're none the worse for wear though."

She felt warm all over, and the many scandalous love scenes she had read in the novels she secretly ordered told her it was not due to the sun that scorched the earth. Finding it difficult to breathe, she could do little more than stare at him. "Of course," she finally managed, her voice barely a whisper.

The man's smile vanished and he eyed her more closely then, seeming to reconsider his assessment. "Maybe I should take you over to the doc just in case."

In a flash, the concern in his eyes changed to determination, and he had her swept up into his arms with the obvious intent of taking her to the medical man when Abigail finally found her voice.

"Please, sir, put me down. I'm fine, fine, really fine."

The man either failed to hear or, more than likely, failed to take notice of her protests, for he simply secured her squirming body in his arms as if she weighed no more than a sack of salt, and strode in the direction of Doctor Peters. For a moment Abigail forgot to protest as the unfamiliar feel of a man's arms holding her secure commandeered her mind. She nearly pressed her forehead to his chest as she imagined the man in her daydream, sweeping her up and carrying her toward—

"Feeling faint?"

His words startled her from her thoughts. It took a second for her mind to settle, but once it did, she tensed and squirmed enough that the man was forced to stop.

"Hold still, woman."

"Put me down," she said through clenched teeth, embarrassment making her voice overly sharp. "I'm fine, simply fine. There's no need to see the good doctor."

Seemingly reluctant, he set her down and studied her. "You're sure?"

"Of course I'm sure," she snapped, noticing for the first time that he wore a soft flannel shirt that spread over strong, broad shoulders, then tapered down to slim hips covered with coarse woolen trousers so tight she could tell he would have put a statue of a Greek god to shame.

Seconds ticked by. Carriages passed in the street. And the man's concern slowly turned to amusement. His voice lowered and a devilish smile tilted on his lips. "I take it you like what you see?"

A heartbeat passed before heat inched up her neck to cover her face when she realized that, indeed, she was staring at him. She quickly looked away. "Most certainly not!"

The man chuckled. "Now, little lady, didn't your papa teach you not to lie?"

Her eyes opened wide and she searched her slim repertoire of experience with men to come up with a suitable response. Finding nothing remotely appropriate, she only managed to sputter, obviously providing him with a good deal of additional amusement for he threw back his head and laughed.

Her lips pressed into a tight line. Her shoulders came back. "You, sir, are no gentleman." Then she began to turn away with a huff, but was stopped when he reached out and gently took her arm.

"True," he stated simply, his eyes dancing with mischief. "I've been away for ages, and I think I've forgotten how a gentleman is supposed to act."

Abigail's glance flew from his hand on her arm to the busy street, praying no one was noticing this little scene. "Unhand me!" she hissed, trying to ignore the tingling that spread down her arm, concentrating instead on the hell that would have to be paid if her father or Walter ever got wind of this. "I am not interested in being the object of your attention . . . or your mirth."

His brow suddenly furrowed. He reached down and tilted

her chin until their eyes met. "I'm sorry." His voice grew deep and oddly gentle. He stared at her for what seemed like forever. His eyes grew intense, dark, and suddenly troubled. He took in her prim collar and stiff skirt, and the crease in her brow. "I couldn't resist," he said finally. "It's been so long since I've seen such an innocent."

"Innocent!" she spat, taking refuge in anger rather than let herself think about the look in his eye or the rapidly worsening condition of strange sensations she was feeling as his fingers held her chin.

The intensity of his gaze evaporated as quickly as it had appeared, and he laughed up to the heavens, sending birds from their trees and dogs from their lairs. "Last I heard, being called an innocent wasn't an insult. But maybe things have changed over the last few years." His fingers trailed back to the strand of hair that had once again come free. "Perhaps you could show me what I've been missing," he said, his voice changing with lightning quickness to a caress.

Her lips parted and her breath caught in her throat. She couldn't seem to do anything but stare at him as the unaccustomed feelings finally pressed their advantage. His touch was so firm yet gentle, like nothing she had ever experienced. Not even her wildest dreams could compare to this. And he was like no man she had ever seen. It was not simply his size that set him apart, but his manner, as well. One minute he was playful and laughing. The next, he stared at her with all the intensity of a man who had seen too much. But what, she wondered, had he seen? What had made this man look so fierce but approachable—dangerous but appealing?

"I take it your answer is yes," he nearly whispered when she failed to respond.

His gaze slid over her, shockingly frank in its appraisal—intimate—as if she were no better than Millie McAllister. Her curiosity vanished when common sense and reality came flooding back with a rush. She sucked in her breath as indignation engulfed her, and she wrenched

free of his hold. "You, sir, can think again if you presume
for one second that I would show you anything—ever!"

And with that Miss Abigail Ashleigh turned in a flurry of
stiff skirts and starched crinolines, and hurried down the
boardwalk just as fast as propriety and her tightly laced
boots would allow her to go, the man's rumbling laughter
dogging her every step.

2

ABIGAIL DIDN'T SLOW DOWN UNTIL SHE REACHED THE white picket fence that surrounded the Ashleighs' sprawling two-story clapboard home. Thoughts of the man from the Red Dog plagued her the whole way. Thick blond hair, dark blue eyes. And she wondered what he would look like without the beard and mustache. But she quickly berated herself for being the feather-brained simpleton that Mrs. Kent accused Lou Smith of being, especially since she was thinking such thoughts about someone who so obviously was not a man of refinement and manners. Lord have mercy, he had manhandled her in a way that was improper down to the core. What if anyone had seen? she wondered as she stepped into the foyer and quietly shut the front door. Holding her secure, the unaccustomed feel of his massive arms pressed against her shoulders and thighs, his dancing blue eyes looking down into hers . . .

"Finally!"

Abigail turned with a start, her eyes rounded with guilt, to find her younger, though already married sister standing in the doorway that led to the dining room.

"Really, Abigail," Emma Ashleigh Weston said, her violet eyes snapping with impatience. "We've been waiting forever."

"I'm sorry, Em."

Emma merely shook her head and sighed before she continued into the dining room with a swish of long taffeta skirts, her delicate hand smoothing her inky black tresses. "She's here," she announced to those who waited. "And Grant will be down in a minute."

Abigail stood in a large central foyer with high ceilings, and spacious parlors on either side. Hand-rubbed rosewood armoires filled with books of all kinds, all of which she had read and reread so many times she had them nearly memorized, mixed with flowers and sunshine and soft velvet curtains that were pulled back with silk sashes. Her stepmother, Virginia, had redone the house seven years before when she moved in, causing a ruckus that had left the Ashleigh household in an uproar that lasted a good six months. But Virginia had persevered like a dog with a bone between its teeth until it was done. At the time, Virginia had been newly married and her husband had supported her every move. But that, Abigail thought with dismay, was a long time go. Things had changed considerably in the ensuing six and a half years.

Straight ahead, where Abigail had no choice but to go, through massive double doors, was the dining room and the midday meal. She could see the center of the table through the doors, and knew when she entered she would find her father to the right and her stepmother to the left. It never varied. Nor should it, she hastily reminded herself.

One of the many household servants appeared to take her bonnet and package.

"Thank you, Consuela," she said, trying for a smile, before she attempted to smooth her hair, conceded the futility of the act, then followed her sister.

Three seats remained vacant at the long mahogany dining table. Sun shone through the large stained-glass window above the sideboard, all of which had been shipped to this desert town at a great deal of expense decades ago. Sherwood Ashleigh indeed sat at the head of the table, firmly entrenched behind a newspaper. Virginia Sherwood, a good twenty years younger than her husband, likewise sat at the other end, reading a newspaper as well. Emma was busy arranging herself artfully in her chair. Abigail headed toward her own chair, hoping she could make it without being noticed.

"Abigail!"

Adam Ashleigh, Abigail's young, six-year-old half

brother, skidded to a stop on the highly polished hardwood floor, socks on his feet, shoes in his hand. Sherwood lowered his paper with a scowl. He looked from the boy to his wife. "Virginia, how many times do I have to tell you that boy needs to learn not to run in the house. And why aren't his shoes on?"

Virginia dropped her hands, crunching the paper in her lap. Her silky blond hair was pulled neatly back into a loose chignon and her bright blue eyes crackled with exasperation. "He's standing right in front of you, Sherwood. Why don't you ask him yourself?"

Adam looked back and forth between his parents.

"Put your shoes on, boy," Sherwood said with a scowl, then turned his attention to Abigail.

Abigail tensed, but her step didn't falter as she moved toward her seat.

"Where have you been, Abigail?"

"At the General Store, Father. I bought some material."

Sherwood grumbled. "I'm sure it's too much to think you might have found a bolt or two that would make something of your appearance." His pale gray eyes narrowed and not a single strand of silver-white hair was out of place as he surveyed his eldest daughter. "Though material is hardly all you need. Why is it that whenever I see you your hair looks as though a tornado just touched down on your head?" He turned to Emma. "Look at your sister, here. Always lovely. Emma, why can't you teach Abigail how to do something, if not with her manner of dress, at least with her hair."

"I've tried, Daddy. You know I have," she said with great seriousness as she lowered her head to hide her smile.

Pain stabbed at the back of Abigail's eyes, and it was all she could do to keep her hands demurely in her lap. Adam reached out from his seat next to hers and patted his sister's arm.

"Really, Sherwood," Virginia said, her forehead knotted. "How can you treat your children—"

"Enough, woman. Let's eat."

"Grant's not here, Daddy," Emma said from her place next to her father.

No sooner were the words out than a tall man with dark hair and dark eyes entered. He wore a white cambric shirt, black trousers, and a brown leather vest. His lips were full and his mouth wide and he would have been strikingly handsome had he smiled.

"So, my recalcitrant son-in-law has decided to join us."

Grant Weston looked at his father-in-law. "I didn't realize I had a choice."

Sherwood stiffened and started to rise. Emma reached out and patted her father's arm. "Now Daddy," she soothed, casting a quick, scathing glance at her husband. "Grant has had a difficult morning. He works so hard. You know that."

"Doing what?" Sherwood demanded. "Mucking about in a barn filled with manure. I've said a hundred times he needs to be working down at the bank."

"And I've told you a hundred times I don't want any part of your money." Grant's words were emotionless and indifferent.

"Yeah, but you sure like living in my house, eating my food!"

Grant stilled; his body tensed. His eyes grew unfathomable. "I have every intention of moving out, and if you and your daughter didn't turn your nose up at every place I find, we'd be out of here by now, and you know it."

"Vermin deserve better than the houses you've found! And every piece of land you come up with is miles from town," Sherwood nearly yelled. "If you'd come down to the bank to work you'd earn a decent living and could afford the kind of home my daughter deserves! Mucking around in manure, for Christ's sake! What kind of a job is that!?"

Grant didn't answer at first. He simply stared at the older man. "It's an honest job. I'm my own boss, not running around bowing and scraping to another man. And I do good work. There's not a horse around better shod than one I've done."

"Shoeing horses," Sherwood said with disgust, turning to

Emma who sat quietly staring at her hands. "What do you have to say about this, Emma? You can't be happy about your husband working in manure?"

Emma didn't answer and Abigail longed to kick her sister for not standing up for her husband, especially considering it was Emma who had shamelessly thrown herself at the man seven years before. And she hadn't seemed to mind that he was a blacksmith then.

Glancing from Sherwood to Emma, Grant took a deep breath and Abigail thought he was going to turn around and walk right out the door. But she breathed a sigh of relief when he simply ran a hand through his hair then slipped into his seat.

No one spoke. The only sound came from the clink of silver on china as servants offered steaming bowls and abundant platters of food around the table. The pang of dissatisfaction Abigail had experienced earlier intensified until she had to restrain herself from throwing back her chair to run screaming out of the stifling room. How could she survive another day in this house? she wondered as she had been wondering more often and with more intensity over the past few weeks. And that scared her. What else did she have besides this family? Nothing. And what kind of opportunities were there for unmarried females who had no skills to speak of or education besides what she could garner from books around the house? Millie McAllister came to mind. There *were* no opportunities, she conceded, unless she was willing to sell her affections, which of course she was not!

She was stuck. But soon she would have a house and children of her own, she reminded herself. Unless, like Emma and Grant, Walter let her father convince them to live here. Panic threatened. Her chance at freedom might prove to be nothing more than a life sentence. And that she didn't know how she could manage.

"I have a new friend," Adam said to his father, breaking the silence.

When Sherwood didn't respond, Virginia quickly stepped in. "That's wonderful, dear. What's his name?"

"He's a she! And her name is Lou."

"Not Lou Smith!" Emma said, her burst of sudden, quick anger catching everyone's attention. "I told you to stay away from her, Adam Ashleigh."

"She's nice and I like her," Adam replied, his countenance hurt and wary as he took a bite of mashed potatoes.

Abigail eyed her sister. "I met Lou Smith earlier today," she offered. "I thought she was a sweet little girl."

Emma fumed, and was on the verge of saying something when Virginia carefully laid her fork down on her plate and said, "I didn't realize, Emma, that you were in the habit of telling Adam what he can and cannot do?" Her tone was even, but her eyes snapped with anger.

"Well, someone has to! You certainly don't. If it was left up to you my house would be in shambles by now!"

"*Your* house?" Virginia's voice was tight. "You seem to forget yourself, Emma. This is not simply your house but my house, as well. And I am the woman of the house, at that."

"Only because you lured my father into marriage with your wicked ways!"

Virginia flinched as if struck. Sherwood tossed his fork and knife onto his plate with a clatter. "How is a man supposed to digest his food with such bickering going on? This is *my* house, so quiet your mouths and let me eat in peace."

Virginia's face grew strained. After a quick glare at Virginia, Emma smiled at her father. "I'm sorry, Daddy. The heat makes me ornery."

Sherwood reached across the table and patted his daughter's arm. "I know, princess, I know."

Abigail's throat tightened and she looked away. How many times had this scene played itself out in this house—Emma was always the victor, whether she deserved to be or not. Abigail's mind careened with the unfairness of it all. Her heart was heavy. And as a result, it was a moment before her father's next words registered.

"I still can't believe it. Monday. She wants to leave Monday," Sherwood was raving. "I told her, I said, 'Penelope, it's already Friday. How in the world am I going to get

someone to take your place by Monday?' And do you know
what my ungrateful sister said to me?"

No one asked. Everyone knew there was no need.

"I'll tell you what she said. She said, 'Too bad.' Too
bad! After all I've done for her. Practically gave her that
boardinghouse. Did I interfere? No! Where could she have
made a better living? And now she is up and moving back
to Saint Louis to live with Medora. My sisters," Sherwood
lamented with a shake of his head, "think they can sit up
there in Missouri and sip tea and do nothing . . . all with my
money!"

"Penelope is getting on in years, Sherwood," Virginia offered, her voice stiff.

"At the very least she could have given me some decent
notice."

"As I recall, every time she has tried to give you notice
you have found some excuse to make her stay."

"Whose side are you on, woman?"

Virginia sighed. "Your side, dear, only your side. But
you have often complained about Penelope's managing of
the boardinghouse. Perhaps this is all for the best. You'll be
better off finding someone else."

"What the hell am I supposed to do in the meantime?"
Sherwood practically shouted. "Run it myself!?"

"I'll run it!"

The room grew silent. Sherwood Ashleigh slowly turned
his wintry gray-eyed stare on his eldest daughter. "You?"

Abigail nearly shrank back from her father's scathing
glare, but she held firm. The words had popped out of her
mouth before she could think. But as soon as they were out
she knew it was perfect. Running the boardinghouse might
be the only opportunity she would ever get to do something
with her life—her only opportunity to get out of this house.
So she took a deep breath and raised her chin in the face of
her father's disbelieving stare.

Emma laughed. "You run it, Abigail? How absurd. You
don't know how to do anything but read books. Besides, we
all know that Penelope runs a house filled with men!" She
hesitated. "Though I suspect that would hardly be a prob-

lem for you. You're lucky to get my castoffs. And we all know the only reason Walter wants to marry you is to get at Father's money."

"Emma!" Virginia snapped.

"Now, now." Sherwood stepped in, still staring at Abigail. "Enough of this bickering."

Her father didn't deny Emma's words and Abigail nearly pressed her eyes closed against the growing pain behind them. But still she held firm. After all, it wasn't like she hadn't heard the same sentiment a thousand times before since Walter Jackson had begun courting her six months ago. "Father, I can run the boardinghouse."

Sherwood eyed his daughter and seemed to consider. "As your sister has already pointed out, you don't know the first thing about running anything, daughter, much less a boardinghouse."

Abigail started to protest.

Sherwood held up his hand to silence her. "When was the last time you made a bed? Or cleaned a floor? Or made a meal?"

"Fath—"

"You've had servants catering to your every whim since birth." Sherwood snorted. "Had I only been so lucky. But no. I've had to work for everything I own. But you better believe had I been lucky enough to have a rich father I would have appreciated everything he gave me. But not this lot. The more I give, the more everyone wants."

"Father!" Emma broke in. "You know I appreciate all you do for me."

Sherwood smiled at Emma.

Abigail nearly groaned out loud. "Father," she said, surprising herself along with everyone else when she persisted. But an unfamiliar burning determination made her bold and willing to use whatever tactics it took to gain her chance. "You forget all my summers in St. Louis with Aunt Medora. Certainly you'll agree she doesn't have servants and—"

"Damn right she doesn't!"

"Sherwood!" Virginia reprimanded.

"Don't Sherwood me, woman! I pay for the roof over my sister's head along with the clothes on her back. I'll not be paying for servants as well."

Abigail sighed. "Father, the point is, while in Missouri, I helped Aunt Medora with everything from . . . from ironing to cooking."

Her father looked as though he didn't believe her, and with good reason, Abigail conceded, for if truth be known she truly didn't know the first thing about running a household. But how hard could it be to learn? Guilt surged. She hated having to lie. But how else would she ever get a chance? "I can do it, Father," she stated quickly before she lost her nerve.

Virginia looked down the table and studied Abigail. A slight, barely perceptible smile curved on her face and her eyes sparkled with what looked like approval. She turned to her husband. "You can't make Penelope stay, Sherwood. And I think Abigail would do a marvelous job."

Glancing at her stepmother, Abigail could hardly believe what she heard. She never would have imagined gaining support from her. In the seven years Virginia had been married to her father, Abigail had never done more than exchange pleasantries with the woman. The thought suddenly embarrassed her.

Emma fidgeted in her seat, her skirts rustling as she looked on in disbelief when her father did not immediately object. Sherwood studied Abigail as if seeing her for the first time.

"All right, missy," he finally said, stroking his chin. "I'll give you a chance. Until the end of November. That's a little more than a month. But one mistake and you're finished. Am I understood?"

"Of course, Father."

Emma gasped. "This is so outrageous and . . . and unfair!"

Sherwood glanced at her. "Would you like to run the boardinghouse, Emma?"

"Well, uh, no," she said, clearly disgruntled. "But . . ."

"No buts. It's the biggest headache I own, and I'd sell it

if I could. But there's not a buyer to be found, and since Penelope seems determined to leave I need someone else to run the place. If Abigail thinks she can do it, who am I to stop her. And like I said, if she doesn't do it right . . ." He shrugged his shoulders, his message clear.

"Father," Abigail said before she could think better of it. "What if I do well?" Her chin inched up higher, and her eyes suddenly looked more green than brown. "Are you willing to give me the boardinghouse if I can make it work? After all, you said it causes you nothing but headaches."

Her father's eyes widened slightly then narrowed in turn. "A little backbone, eh, Abigail," Sherwood stated, rubbing his chin.

"Father!" Emma said, throwing her napkin down onto the table. "This conversation is ridiculous. Abigail has no business running a boardinghouse, much less a boarding-house full of men. What will people say?"

"I'm Sherwood Ashleigh, the largest landholder in the area, not to mention the sole owner of the only bank within six hundred miles. They'll not say a word if I say it's all right. And I say it is."

"And what about giving it to me if I do well," Abigail persisted, her heart pounding in her chest at her daring.

Virginia leaned forward in her seat. "It's true that you have done nothing but complain about that place since I married you, dear."

Sherwood glared at his wife before he chuckled and turned back to Abigail. "All right, daughter. If you make it work, I'll give it to you."

"This is too much," Emma gasped, jerking up from her chair.

Abigail nearly jumped out of her seat and flung her arms around her father, but just at the last second she got hold of herself. "Thank you, Father," she said calmly instead, trying to hold down the shout of joy that threatened just beneath the practiced surface of strict propriety.

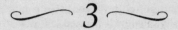

3

"I'll miss you."

Abigail hugged her aunt, the skirt of her pale gray dress catching in the early morning breeze.

"I'll miss you, too, dear. But you'll come to visit with the rest of the family, won't you?"

"I don't know. I haven't thought that far ahead." Abigail squeezed her aunt's hands. "But I suspect I'll have my hands full with the boardinghouse this year."

Penelope Ashleigh held her niece at arm's length. "I can't tell you how much I appreciate you taking over for me. And I'm sorry you've had such short notice. I haven't had a chance to show you around as I should have. I've done nothing more than write up a list of things I do every day—or at least I think I did." She seemed to consider, then shook her head and smiled. "I'm so forgetful these days, but I've been in such a rush and all." Penelope's eyes darkened and her lips pursed. "But you know your father. I was afraid if I didn't make this stagecoach he would change his mind . . ." Her voice trailed off. "I do hope you'll be all right."

"Don't you worry. I'll make out just fine."

The Ashleigh family stood in front of the stage depot on Overland Street. Only Grant wasn't there. Everyone had kissed and hugged and were waving good-bye as the stagecoach pulled away when Abigail pulled back her shoulders and smiled. As much as she would miss Penelope, she could not help but be excited about her new life. Yes, her new life. It felt wonderful, and she had to stop herself from twirling around in the street as excitement bubbled within her. Instead, she simply turned around to say her good-byes to her family so she could make her way to the boarding-house.

But she had gotten no more than a hand in the air to wave when she saw him—big and tall, raw strength and energy shimmering about him, as handsome as the day he ran her down.

Abigail stopped so suddenly that Virginia nearly ran into the back of her.

"What is it?" Virginia asked.

"That man. Who is he?"

"Where?" Virginia peered down the length of Overland.

"No, over there. The . . . tall man with the buff-colored hat, walking this way."

"The one with Millie McAllister?"

Abigail looked closer, then stood up straight. "Yes, that one," she said heatedly, not having noticed Millie at first.

"Why, I don't know, Abigail. I've never seen him before. He must be new in town."

Emma joined them just then. "Who's new in town?"

Before Abigail could stop her, Virginia gestured toward the man.

Emma pulled her shoulders back, her snug-fitting bodice of lavender silk pulling tight. She smiled, showing perfect white teeth. "New in town, indeed. And well worth looking at."

"Emma," Virginia admonished. "You're a married woman. What if your father were to hear you talking like that?"

Casting a quick, sly glance at her stepmother, Emma said, "I would have thought by now you'd know I'd never let my father hear something like that." A giggle escaped her lips as she tossed her head and returned her attention to the newcomer.

The man approached. Millie caught sight of the women then reached over and took the man's arm. He looked down at Millie and for a second Abigail would have sworn he seemed surprised. But if he was he didn't pull his arm away. Obviously, Abigail snorted to herself, the woman's attentions didn't bother him at all—him or half the other men in town, if rumors were to be believed.

Today his mud-covered boots and tight-fitting pants were replaced by a cambric shirt and woolen trousers—ordinary attire that looked anything but ordinary on the man. Mesmerized, Abigail watched the muscles work with each step he took. He walked with a grace that belied his size—smooth and sleek, no wasted energy. He would have seemed predatory, she thought suddenly, if it hadn't been for the stunning smile that spread on his lips. Indeed, he truly was well worth looking at as Emma had none too demurely pointed out.

When he saw Abigail his step hesitated for a second before amusement danced in his eyes and he tipped his hat. "Morning, ladies," he said when he came to the three seemingly dumbstruck women on the boardwalk, though his eyes never wavered from Abigail. He seemed on the verge of stopping altogether. Abigail couldn't breathe. What would he say? Would he embarrass her in front of her family?

Her concern, however, was short-lived. He must have realized that Millie was still clinging to his arm and he did nothing more than cast Abigail a dashing grin, then continued on his way.

Emma's smile faded as she watched the couple disappear down the street. She glanced at her sister. "Easy on the eyes, maybe. But from the women who seem to draw his attention I'd say he's no better than a handsomely clad, no-good drifter." Then she turned on her dainty heel in a swirl of sashes and silk and walked toward the family carriage.

Mortification over the man's perusal as well as her sister's words made Abigail want to melt between the cracks in the boardwalk and disappear. Though why the obviously despicable man's attention should faze her or, after all these years, Emma's barbs would bother her, she couldn't fathom. Especially when faced with the excitement that loomed no more than two blocks away in the form of the two-story boardinghouse. Yes, she thought, taking a deep breath, her adventure was really going to happen. The

cloud of dust marking the departing stage was proof
enough of that. She'd not let that man or her sister ruin it
for her.

Virginia stood quietly next to her. Abigail realized she
had yet to thank her stepmother for coming to her aid in
getting the chance at a new life. "I've been meaning to
thank you for helping me with father."

"Nonsense," Virginia stated, waving the comment away.
"You deserve it, and everything I said was no more than the
truth. Besides, I think you'll do a wonderful job."

Abigail's lips quirked in a wry smile. "Let's hope so."

Suddenly they both laughed, their gloved hands unexpectedly catching in a grasp of friendship. Abigail looked at
her stepmother. "I find myself wondering if we haven't
wasted the last seven years."

Virginia squeezed Abigail's hand. "Thank you," she
said, her voice oddly strained. "Perhaps we can spend the
next seven making up for lost time."

"I'd like that."

"Good," Virginia responded with a nod before her voice
grew firm and in charge once again. "Why don't we drop
you off so you can get started."

"That's all right. The day is glorious and I think I'll
walk." She started away, then stopped. "Hopefully once I
get settled in you and Adam will stop by."

"You can count on it."

"Virginia!" Sherwood bellowed from the carriage.
"What are you women yammering about? I've got business
to attend to. I don't have all day to waste like you do. And
for that matter, it seems to me that Abigail doesn't have
time to waste either."

Virginia and Abigail looked at each other, and for one
insane second Abigail thought they would burst out laughing again. But the moment passed and Virginia hurried
away to the waiting carriage.

Abigail turned on El Paso Street, her skirts carefully
gathered against the dust and dirt on the road, and walked
up two blocks. As always, the streets were busy. Though
she had lived in El Paso her whole life, she knew very few

people well. Certainly she knew who most everyone was, but none to call friend. She truly hoped Virginia would come by the boardinghouse.

The town was filled with both Americans and Mexicans. The men for the most part all looked the same, dressed in simple shirts and coarse trousers, though not a single man would be found without a six-shooter on his hip after dark. The women, however, were varied in their dress. Americans wore stiff dresses with petticoats and crinolines that could be found back east, while the Mexicans wore deliciously soft, loose-fitting skirts and blouses that were sure to show ample amounts of bronzed skin.

When Abigail passed the Red Dog, she blushed as her recalcitrant mind dredged up the memory of being held by that man—that man who consorted with women of lesser reputations, she reminded herself sharply. No doubt he was in the saloon right then, throwing back liquor and doing who knows what to that woman. She looked straight ahead and quickened her step.

The boardinghouse was on the plaza at the corner of El Paso and San Francisco streets. A thick vein of the Rio Grande, known as an *acequia* that served as an irrigation ditch, sliced through the southern edge of the grass and tree-lined area filled with merchants hawking their wares and women strolling their babies.

Unlike her father's clapboard home, the boardinghouse was made from native materials. Thick adobe bricks with sun-bleached pillars and beams made up the entire building. When Abigail entered the house it was empty. Large white tiles covered the floor. The walls were painted white, brightening the high-ceilinged rooms. The second floor, she vaguely recalled from past visits, consisted of three decent sized bedrooms while the downstairs was made up of the front parlor, kitchen, dining room, and a sitting room that had been turned into a bedroom for Penelope. Now it would be hers.

Pulling off her bonnet, she took a second to realize she would have to hang it up herself. Not a good start, she admonished herself.

Despite her aunt's hurried departure, the house was im-
maculate. Fresh beeswax gleamed on the solid oak furni-
ture and not a single speck of dust clouded any surface.
Abigail went to the back of the house to the kitchen and
found a full supper already prepared, with a note informing
Abigail that all she had to do was heat it up. She wouldn't
have to try her hand at real cooking until tomorrow. Thank
goodness for small favors.

She walked about the house and determined as best she
could that everything was in order. The day was crisp and
clear and the thought of sitting back and sipping on a cup of
tea and simply savoring the moment sent Abigail searching
through the cabinets for tea leaves. When she didn't find
any, she decided to run across the street to the General
Store to purchase some.

"So it's true!" Myrtle Kent exclaimed after watching
Abigail arrive from the boardinghouse.

"If you mean that I'm taking over for my aunt, yes, it's
true. Now if you will be so good as to measure out a quarter
pound of tea I'd be most appreciative," she said in her
sternest voice.

"Well, certainly I'll get you some tea. But tell me, does
your father approve of this?"

"Mrs. Kent, of course my father approves. Do you think
for one second I would be there if he didn't?"

"I suspect you're right. And if your father doesn't have a
problem with it I don't suppose anyone else should either."
Myrtle scooped tea from a tight-lidded canister then poured
it into a small burlap bag.

The transaction was made and Abigail turned to leave.

"Now don't you be a stranger," Myrtle called after her.
"Maybe in the afternoons we can visit. You know Penelope
and I visited just about every day. I'll miss her."

"We'll all miss her, Mrs. Kent."

Escaping the confines of the store as quickly as she
could, Abigail tried to hold on to her excitement. All she
needed was the town busybody coming over for afternoon
tea and crumpets on the pretense of friendship. One un-
dusted highboy or one unpolished floor and it would be all

over town. Not that she thought she would have an un-
dusted highboy or an unpolished floor, she quickly added to
herself. It was just that if she was going to make mistakes,
which undoubtedly would happen, she wanted to make
them in private.

She closed the door with a little more force than was
necessary. The glass rattled and she jumped. And then it
happened. Once again. Like a recurring nightmare. She
plowed right into the man who seemed to plague her every
step like a scourge. Though thankfully this time she remained on her feet and was not tongue-tied over his awe-
some size and devastating good looks. This time she was
mad from the get go.

She shook off the huge hand that steadied her. "When
are you going to learn to watch where you're going?" she
demanded.

He stared down at her, at first surprised, then amused.
His blue eyes crinkled at the corners, making him look for
all the world like an oversized schoolboy, she thought un-
kindly. Though if truth be known, her heart skipped a beat
and she had the crazy longing to reach up and trace the
creases with her fingers.

"You really don't have to go to such trouble to meet me,
ma'am." His grin broadened. "All you have to do is ask."

Abigail's eyes narrowed then grew incredulous as his
meaning sunk in. "Ask!" The word came out as a high-
pitched squeak. "All I have to do is *ask*?"

She was working herself up into a lather of righteous indignation when he leaned back against a post, tipped his hat
back with one finger, then crossed his arms on his massive
chest and said, "I'm really an accommodating type, especially when I'm being asked to accommodate such a pretty
little lady like you."

Her sharp retort was well on its way to being spoken
when it caught in her throat at his words. Pretty! He had
called her pretty! This man with steel-blue eyes and sandy
blond hair thought she was pretty? Abigail stood stiff and
still, embarrassed, angry, and oddly pleased at the same
time. Her daydream loomed. She nearly smoothed her hair
until she realized what she was doing and she got all the

madder, drowning out any other emotion. "Me? Want to meet you! Your lack of manners is only equaled by your conceit. For you, sir, think too highly of yourself!"

She turned on her heels, slapping at his hands when the long folds of her dress caught in his legs and he tried to steady her. With a humph she stomped off, his deep, rumbling laughter once again following her the whole way.

Rather than go home and fume, she all but marched through the plaza in hopes of dissipating her anger. A number of curse words she hadn't even known she knew came to mind. She would have blushed had she not been so out of sorts. The man had called her pretty and she practically swooned at his feet. Now she knew it. She was losing her mind. She had turned into a weak-kneed, moon-eyed, swooning mess of femininity at one kind word from a less than admirable man. And from the laughter that had followed her, he probably had been making fun of her anyway. Swooning! Heavens above! She would not have it!

When she had walked for a good twenty minutes and her blood still boiled, she gave up and returned to the house. If she ever saw that man again she'd . . . she'd what, she wondered. "I'll show him a thing or two," she barked at the empty house. Though what exactly she would show him she had no idea.

Tossing the tea and her reticule aside, Abigail found a pan and filled it with water from an earthenware pitcher. She stared at the stove for a good long while, wondering how in the world she could make it work, before she gave up, poured the water in a glass, and drank it down in one long, unladylike swallow. She'd deal with the stove later.

Taking a deep breath she closed her eyes and told herself to forget the audacious man. Really! He was an ill-mannered heathen, and in the future she'd make an effort to avoid him. It was just plain bad luck that she had run into the man as often as she had. But her luck would change. Hadn't she already proven that by the very fact that she was here in the boardinghouse? Already she felt better.

Once a modicum of calm had returned, she searched for the list of duties Penelope had said she left. Finding nothing that resembled such a thing, she picked up the list of boarders her aunt had left for her.

ELDEN WINERIDGE—paid through end of the month
HARMON DAVIS—paid through end of the month and next
NOAH BLAKE—paid through end of the month and the
    next two

A quiver of fear ran down her spine. Not because she was afraid of the men, but because the enormity of what she had taken on was beginning to sink in. She hadn't even been able to light the stove! And now the three nameless and faceless boarders had names. By the end of the day the names would have faces. And it was her responsibility to run this place and run it well or the only chance at freedom she was ever likely to get would be snatched away from her so fast she was certain it would make her head spin. She had to make it work. She couldn't afford to fail.

Her father's knowing look loomed in her mind. Her sister's disparaging laughter rang in her ears. Wouldn't they just love it if she were to fall flat on her face. Especially so soon. Oh, how pleased her sister would be. And her father. He certainly would not be surprised. He had made it clear her whole life that he expected little of her talents. More than likely if she had managed to look decent while she was growing up he probably would have left her alone altogether.

Abigail pressed her eyes closed. She could not fail. She had to prove to her father that she could do it. And as soon as the boarders arrived she would have to make them feel confident that she knew what she was doing. She couldn't afford to lose.

And so she tossed her bonnet on the bed in her new room, took a deep breath, straightened her person, then returned to the kitchen to deal with the meal Penelope had so thoughtfully prepared.

Lighting the stove didn't prove any easier now than before. As a result, heating up the food didn't go as smoothly as Abigail would have liked. In fact it didn't go at all. But, she reasoned to herself, cold roast beef wouldn't hurt anyone. Besides, it was hot outside. Cold food would be a welcome change.

No sooner had she finished setting the food on the table than she heard the front door open and shut. Her first boarder entered the dining room.

"Evening, ma'am. I reckon you must be the new landlady." His eyes darted back and forth between his hands and her face before he seemed to remember his hat, then grabbed it off his head, revealing a shock of carrot-red hair. His hesitant smile of pleasure revealed straight though overlarge teeth and his painfully pale white skin was covered with freckles.

"Good evening," Abigail said with a proper smile. "I'm Miss Ashleigh. And who might you be?"

"Oh, yeah," he chuckled. "I'm Harmon Davis, ma'am, Miss Ashleigh."

The door opened and shut once again, bringing her second boarder down the hall and into the dining room. He stopped suddenly when he caught sight of Abigail. "Are you the new landlady?" he asked, not caustically but none too friendly either.

"Yes," Abigail responded simply. "I'm Miss Ashleigh."

"Elden Wineridge."

Elden Wineridge was only a few inches taller than Abigail and was obviously a man who took pains with his appearance. His brown hair was neatly trimmed and his mustache was perfectly waxed. He looked at her only a moment longer before he walked to what was obviously his chair at the table, pulled it back, and sat down.

Abigail didn't move. She wasn't sure if she should chastise the man for his lack of manners or simply follow suit and sit down. Simply sitting won out when she came to the conclusion that this was no social setting and it was not her place to teach this man etiquette. She merely had to provide him with three meals a day and accomplish the long list of other duties that Penelope had supposedly written down. No, this was no social setting.

Elden reached for the green beans without saying a word, much less saying grace.

"Mr. Wineridge," she said, deciding social setting or not, he should have the common decency to wait until all had arrived. "Not everyone is here yet."

Elden looked at Abigail as he served himself. "If you're referring to Noah, who knows when he'll be here. Five minutes, ten, not at all?" He reached for the platter of beef then scowled when he realized the fare wasn't hot. He started to protest, but was cut off.

"He's right," Harmon volunteered, seemingly unconcerned about the cold supper. "Though Noah's only lived here a couple of days, Miss Penny had taken to leaving him a plate of food on the counter. He doesn't keep a regular schedule."

"Well, if that's the case," she said, thankful an explanation about the food had been avoided, though eyeing a forkful of beef that was halfway to Elden's mouth, "I suspect we should say grace."

Elden stopped, sighed, then put the utensil down. With a tight smile, he bowed his head.

"Lord make us truly thankful for what we are about to receive," Abigail said. "Amen."

"Amen," Harmon and Elden offered before each dug into their meal without another word.

Abigail took a deep breath then let it out slowly. So far not so bad. She might just make it after all, she thought.

But just as Abigail cut the first bite of her aunt's roasted beef, she heard the front door open, then slam shut. The house seemed to shake from the force. Not a heartbeat later she turned her head to a resounding hello. Her eyes opened wide. Her fork fell from her fingers to clatter on the plate before it bounced off and dropped to the floor. Good God, how could this be? Surely there was some mistake. But there he stood as if he belonged, proving her wrong, his massive frame filling the doorway, his wide, seemingly ever-present smile slashing across his face—the ill-mannered heathen who had knocked her down.

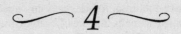

4

Noah Blake stood perfectly still and took in the sight of the woman he had run down outside the Red Dog Saloon. Shock, surprise—he couldn't quite determine what he felt at finding her here. He did know, however, that she made him smile. Not because she was an exceptional beauty. She wasn't. But pretty, most definitely—that is when her face wasn't marred by a scowl, which seemed all too often if the few times he had run into her was any indication. But when she smiled, or stood oddly breathless as she had for a few seconds the day before, she was lovely in a way that made him think of spring flowers and long grasses. And her hair—gloriously wild brown hair that shouldn't be forced back into an eye-squinting bun like a wild mustang kept in a tiny stall meant for a dapple mare. She would be beautiful if she would let loose—even just a little. Then just as had happened in front of the Red Dog, he had the sudden thought that it was a waste. And he was a man who hated waste.

He chuckled silently to himself. But waste or not, this prim and proper little landlady was no concern of his.

"What are *you* doing here?"

Abigail's sharp words brought Noah out of his reverie, and Harmon's and Elden's heads up from their meals to look back and forth between their new landlady and the new arrival. The ensuing silence echoed uncomfortably against the whitewashed adobe walls.

A grin tugged at Noah's lips. "I live here," he said finally.

Pressing her hands against her skirt, her shoulders tense,

Abigail stared at him, her eyes wide with disbelief. Then she groaned. "Don't tell me you're Noah Blake."

"None other." His blue eyes crackled with amusement. "And you must be Abigail Ashleigh, Penny's niece."

Abigail longed to wipe the insufferable smirk right off his face with a slap. Her hands fisted in the napkin to keep them still as her mind tried to come up with a civilized answer to what she should do. Demand that he leave? Leave herself? How could she possibly stay in the same house with this . . . despicable man?

Their eyes locked, mischievous blue with furious brown.

"Are we going to eat, Miss Ashleigh?" Elden asked, his voice laced with sarcasm. "Or are we going to just stare at one another all night?"

Heat suffused her cheeks, and she bit back the retort that uncharacteristically sprang to mind. She knew that Elden Wineridge, who had already shown he cared little for etiquette, would not have hesitated one second in proceeding with his meal whether others had joined him or not, had he not simply wanted to antagonize her. "By all means," she said, her voice sharp. "Let us continue."

Noah sat at the other end of the table from Abigail. He started to tuck the red napkin in his shirt collar, but seemed to think better of it after glancing at his landlady over a red rose in a vase at the middle of the table. With a sigh he laid the napkin in his lap, then served up a mountain of food on Penny's delicately flowered china. A long green string bean fell off the edge onto the crisp white linen tablecloth. Just as he reached over to so indelicately return the bean to his plate, he noticed his landlady's stare.

"Something piqued your interest, Miss Ashleigh?"

Noah's voice rumbled down the table and half a second passed before Abigail realized she was yet again staring at the man. Without a word she quickly looked away.

"I didn't think so," he said with a chuckle.

Silver clinked on china as the foursome quietly ate their meal. The roast beef stuck in Abigail's throat and she wondered if she would be considered rude if she excused herself and went to her room to think of a way out of this situation—or find a way to calm her pounding heart. More than likely, Noah Blake would chuckle and give her that knowing look, and assume she was leaving because of him, which of course she was. But she would not give him the pleasure of knowing for certain, she swore, stabbing a green bean with conviction.

"So, Elden," Noah said between bites. "How's everything at the U.S. Customs office?"

Elden glanced up quizzically. "Fine, Mr. Blake," he said, before he returned to his meal.

"How about you, Harmon? Make any big sales recently?"

Harmon sat up in his seat and beamed at the attention. "Well, as a matter of fact, I expanded my route and found a lucrative little market in Mesilla." He blushed and bowed his head.

"Good, good," Noah practically bellowed and reached over to slap Harmon on the back. "Hard work and perseverance, I always say."

Elden sneered. "And luck."

"Luck?" Noah considered. "I don't doubt it, but I've always been inclined to think that the harder you work and the longer you persevere, the luckier you get."

"Is that how you've been so successful?" Harmon asked. "They say you're a tremendously successful trapper even at a time when not many people can make a livin' trappin' anymore."

Abigail watched with something close to amazement as Noah Blake grew uneasy, and perhaps, she thought, angry.

"Shouldn't believe everything you hear, Harmon. Contrary to what everyone is saying, trapping is still alive and well," Noah replied, before he quickly turned his attention to the head of the table. "And what about you, Miss Ashleigh?"

Abigail jerked in her seat, knocking the table, sending a glass of plain, room temperature water splashing across the table. "Oh my word," she cried as she jumped up. "Just look at what you've done!"

All three men started in their seats, though only Noah

had the presence of mind to reach out with his napkin to staunch the flow. "What did I do?"

"You . . . you startled me!"

"Good Lord, woman, I'd hate to see what you'd do if I jumped up and yelled 'Boo.' "

This got a chuckle from Harmon. Even Elden smiled.

"Why you . . . you . . ."

"I what?"

He what, indeed, she asked herself. As was fast becoming typical of her encounters with this unbearable man, Abigail was unable to come up with a reasonable response. So she simply narrowed her eyes and glared, only to receive a hearty laugh for her efforts.

Elden scraped his chair back from the table, his eyes snapping with anger. "I hope this evening's meal is not an indication of the way things are going to go around here."

Abigail's hands flew to her chest. "What's wrong now?"

Elden scowled. "Fluttering about . . . spilling things . . . a man wants to eat in peace, Miss Ashleigh!"

Harmon shifted in his seat. Noah's brow furrowed.

"And cold food?" Elden added with a raised eyebrow. "Are we going to be eating picnic-style from now on? Well let me tell you, I don't pay good money to eat cold meals."

Noah pushed back his chair to stand, and tossed his wet napkin down onto the table. "Wineridge, quit your belly achin'. It's her first day for crying out loud."

"No, Mr. Blake," Abigail said, her hand held out to ward off further words. "Mr. Wineridge is right. There's no excuse. And I apologize. I assure each and every one of you that in the future things will be no different from when my aunt was here."

"It better not be," Elden grumbled, before without so much as a thank you or good-bye, he quit the room. His quick footsteps resounded down the hall, then up the stairs to his room before they heard his door slam shut.

Abigail stood without moving, her hands clasped together, staring at the empty doorway.

Noah shook his head. "That boy needs to be taught a lesson. Not a day has gone by since I moved in last week that

he's not complained about something." His voice softened.
"Don't let it bother you, darlin'."

His soft kind words and sweet endearment were unexpected. Her forehead knotted and she knew she should
chastise him for his improper familiarity. But when she
looked up and found those steel-blue eyes leveled on her,
the words stuck in her throat.

"He's been that way the whole time I've lived here, too,"
Harmon offered as he added his efforts to mopping up the
water.

Abigail quickly turned back to the table and gathered the
wet napkins, myriad emotions cascading through her mind.
She would have preferred that Noah Blake stayed obnoxious. Anger and shock seemed easier to deal with than the
strange hammering against her ribs she was experiencing
now. "Thank you for your help, gentlemen. I can do the
rest," she stated, wanting nothing more than to be left alone
with her thoughts. "I'm sure you have better things to do
with your evenings."

But before anyone could move the front door opened
then slammed shut. What now? she wondered desperately.

"Abigail!"

"Oh, no," she whispered as angry footsteps pounded
down the hall.

"There you are!"

"Walter," she said, trying for a smile. "You're back."

Walter Jackson stood in the doorway, still dressed in his
traveling suit after four long days of journeying between
small towns on bank business. He had moved to the area
eight years before and had worked for her father since he
arrived. No sooner had he started his first day at the bank
than he began courting Emma Ashleigh. It had lasted no
more than a few months before she dropped him flat. His
interest in Abigail had blossomed only six months ago,
seven and a half years after he had met her. Certainly not
love at first sight, or even second sight for that matter, Abigail thought with the crazy feeling she was going to laugh.
She knew she should be grateful for his attention. However,

there were times, such as this, that she wished she had never caught his eye.

"Just what do you think you're doing?" he demanded, his slick good looks harsh with anger.

All traces of humor vanished and she scrambled for words to placate Walter's ire.

"Now, Walter. Let's not be foolish here."

"Foolish!" Walter barked, unaware of the tension that began to surface in the room. "If what I have been told is true, and from all appearances it seems to be, then you're the only one around here being foolish!"

Noah stepped forward, the ever present grin suspiciously gone. "I'm afraid I can't allow you to talk—"

"Now, now, now," Abigail piped in, hurrying toward Walter, casting a quick, pleading glance at Noah. "Why don't we just go out on the porch and talk about this."

Walter glared across the room before he allowed himself to be ushered outside. "Who is that man?"

"Just a boarder, Walter. No one to concern yourself with."

"Why haven't I seen him before?"

"Apparently he just moved to town."

"Well, I don't like him."

Abigail had to bite her tongue to keep from saying that Noah Blake didn't seem to like him either. "You don't even know him, Walter." Though why she found herself defending the man she couldn't imagine. But that seemed to be the way with her. Always smoothing things over. Never wanting anyone to be angry.

"And I have no intention of getting to know him either. I know a bad apple when I see one," he added.

Abigail pulled the thick cottonwood door shut behind them. The sun was down but the moon had yet to arrive.

"Now, are you going to explain yourself, Abigail?"

For one fleeting second Abigail wondered why she should have to. But it passed quickly, and she knew she had to make this man whom her father respected and expected her to marry understand. "I'm taking over for my Aunt Penelope."

"I can see that, Abigail! The question is, why?"

Looking down, Abigail ran her hands over the pleats in her skirt as she gathered her courage. "Because I want to do something with my life, Walter."

"Being my wife isn't good enough?"

His question was stilted and stiff and she knew she had insulted him. The familiar sound of cicadas called in the distance. She had always loved the sound, so peaceful and reassuring that life was safe and unchanged. But this night, suddenly finding herself living in town, she also heard the sound of piano music, no doubt from the saloon, bringing home the fact that her life had been set on a new course. She had to believe it was for the best.

"Walter, you've never proposed," she found herself saying.

His spine stiffened. "What do you mean, Abigail? You know I have every intention of marrying you. Next you'll be telling me that at your age you expect me to get down on one knee and declare my love."

She wanted to say yes, please, tell me that indeed you do love me, that everything I hear is untrue. But she didn't. Instead she simply said, "Nothing is set, Walter. While you say I know your intentions, perhaps you mean my father knows your intentions. Furthermore, no one has asked me what *I* want," she said boldly, yet again surprising herself.

Amber lamplight illuminated the porch. Walter peered across the distance that separated him from Abigail. "What are you talking about? You don't want to marry me? Is that it?"

Abigail sighed. "That's not what I'm saying," though suddenly she wondered if it wasn't. "It's just that at least for now, I need to do this. Please try to understand."

"Understand! Why can't you understand? What does it look like when the woman I am supposed to marry is running a boardinghouse—full of men! What will people think?"

Her eyes narrowed. How dare he, she longed to shout. What did he think she was going to do—go crazy with the men in the house? He should know her better than that. The tight hold she had kept on her tongue loosened and before she could think better of it, she said, "Anyone with a lick of sense will know I'm working hard and doing something besides sitting around being waited on hand and foot. Everyone else can go straight to—"

"Abigail!"

She sucked in her breath. Good Lord, what had she almost said? What was happening to her? she wondered in dismay. Wayward dreams. Errant thoughts. And now nearly a profane tongue. Where was it all coming from? she wondered. She had no idea—no idea where the sudden urge to fight, as if fighting for her life, had come from. And it scared her—not only because she didn't know its source, but because she seemed to have no control over it. Her breath came out with a sigh. "Perhaps you should go home."

Walter stared at her, his slicked-back brown hair glistening in the light, his brown eyes boring into her. "I'm not certain where this tone of voice has come from, but I'll have you know I don't like it. As far as this boardinghouse business goes, we will see what your father has to say about it in the morning after I've had a chance to talk with him," he said before he turned on his heel and banged down the steps.

Her knees felt weak. Never had she stood up to the man, or to anyone for that matter. Part of her wanted to run after him and beg his forgiveness. But another part, a part she didn't know existed, wanted to shout for joy. Yet again, she wondered where it came from.

She sank down onto the top step as she suddenly realized that Walter might talk her father out of their arrangement. But no, she reasoned, surely her father wouldn't go back on a promise. If there was one thing Sherwood Ashleigh prided himself on, it was his ability to keep his word. He might not make it easy, but he would let her continue to try her hand at running this place.

Suddenly more exhausted than ever before, she returned indoors and grimaced when she remembered the dishes. Her grimace, however, turned to a groan when she found Noah sitting at the table, smoking a pipe.

"Could you do that outside?" she snapped.

He scraped back his chair and gathered up an armload of plates, the pipe clamped firmly between his teeth.

"Mr. Blake, there is no need for you to help with the dishes. And please do your smoking outside."

Still he ignored her, taking the dishes to the kitchen, smoking the whole way.

Abigail sighed, too tired to argue, then followed with an armload of her own.

"I'd like to think that Walter fellow is an ornery brother of yours or an obnoxious cousin," Noah stated simply.

Silence.

Noah turned slightly and seemed to take her measure as he set his pipe aside. Abigail grew uneasy under his scrutiny but doggedly continued to scrape the dishes, willing the man to disappear. Noah, apparently, had no intention of going anywhere, he simply stood there, waiting, expectantly.

"What are you getting at?" Abigail asked finally, the words blurting out.

"He's not some kind of . . . betrothed, now is he, Abigail?"

"Miss Ashleigh, to you, sir. Furthermore, my personal business is none of your affair."

She glanced around the kitchen before she spotted a bucket. "That should do," she muttered to herself. She poured cool water in a bucket, rolled up her sleeves, then dipped a plate inside.

Noah's attention shifted to her efforts. "Haven't you ever washed dishes before?"

Her hands stilled. "Why do you ask?"

"You didn't heat the water."

Abigail stiffened. "Heat the water?" She glanced between the plate that was not coming particularly clean in her hands, the stove, and Noah Blake. Her forehead wrinkled as she considered, before a smile spread on her lips. This oversized heathen might have his uses yet, she thought with glee. "Of course! We have to heat the water. And would you be so good as to light the stove for me?"

Noah studied his new landlady for a good long while. Abigail started to fidget, afraid her plan would fail. And sure enough she was certain it had when finally he turned and walked outside. Her shoulders slumped only to quickly straighten when he returned moments later with a bundle of wood and proceeded to the stove.

With Abigail nonchalantly watching over his shoulder, Noah had the big iron contraption blazing with heat in no time.

"Ah! That wasn't so difficult as long as you know what you're doing," she chimed.

Noah looked back at her, his brow tilted suspiciously.

"I mean, uh, see, you were able to do it and you should be proud. Very few men can do such things."

"If that Walter is any indication of the type of male company you keep, then I can imagine how they all seem useless."

"Walter Jackson is hardly useless, Mr. Blake." But she was barely listening to Noah or herself. She was repeating the steps to light the stove over in her head again and again like the rosary until she felt certain she would not forget.

Once the water was heated, they washed and dried the dishes side by side without a word. Gradually, Abigail forgot about the stove and Walter, and became aware of the hard-muscled forearms next to her. Noah had rolled up his sleeves and the blond hair on his arms was wet up to his elbows—the very arms that had pressed against her back and legs when he had held her. She recalled the tightly fitting pants that had clung to him like a second skin.

"So, this Walter fellow is your fiancé?" he asked again.

Red flooded her cheeks. The plate she was drying bobbled in her hands. "No!" she stated with a vehemence born of embarrassment over having been thinking of male parts. "I mean not yet . . . or not officially. And I thought I told you it was none of your business."

"True enough. But I find it hard to sit back when a man

comes barging in and berates a lady. That man is no gentleman."

Abigail puffed up like a blow fish. "Like you'd know a
gentleman if he jumped up and bit you in the face!"

Noah stared at her, nonplussed, before he threw back his
head and laughed. "Always full of surprises, aren't you?
You might lie down like a door mat for that lightweight
Walter or even Elden Wineridge, but there's a wildfire in
there somewhere that's going to leap out one day and if
you're not careful, darlin', someone's going to get burned."

The words made her gasp, then she fumed. "How dare
you speak to me in such a manner! Walter Jackson is a
finer man than you will ever be." She tossed the drying
towel on the counter and pierced him with a hateful look. "I
don't like you, Mr. Blake. But since I can't kick you out as
you've paid in full for the next two months, fourteen days,
and three and a half hours, I suggest we make the best of a
bad situation and stay out of each other's way."

Pulling his hands out of the water, he retrieved the towel.
He eyed her coolly as he dried his arms then rolled down
his sleeves, all without saying a word.

Abigail longed to run, but stood her ground. She'd not
act the coward.

His lips tilted in a smile. "How can you not like me,
sweetheart?"

"My name is Miss Ashleigh!"

"Darlin', you don't even know me."

"Are you deaf? You'll not call me . . . anything but—"

"Miss Ashleigh," he finished for her. "I know, I heard.
But you don't look like a Miss Ashleigh."

He took a step forward.

Despite her resolve to remain firm, Abigail took a step
back, her heart banging against her ribs with the force of a
hammer to anvil. "Stay away from me, Mr. Blake." Her
next step brought her up against the counter. "I've heard of
your type."

Noah's smile broadened. "What's my type, darlin'?" he
asked, his voice deep and seductive, his eyes straying to her
lips as he reached out and ran his fingers down her arm.

The pulse in her neck beat wildly. Her palms grew moist. She should run—far away and never look back. Instead, she stared at his mouth—full and wide with perfect white teeth. What would it feel like if he pressed his lips to hers?

Her voice was breathless when she finally answered. "The type that sweeps a woman away with breathtaking smiles and sweet words, then breaks her heart when he's had his fill."

He leaned down so close that his face was scant inches from hers. "You don't know me at all . . . Miss Ashleigh," he whispered.

She could feel his breath—warm and heady, rich with tobacco. He was going to kiss her. She could feel it. The gentle touch of lip to lip. Moist and soft. Turning to a demand. Her eyes fluttered closed.

"But in the next few months," he added as he brought his hand up to wipe a streak of soap suds from her forehead, "you'll have plenty of time to learn." His hand fell away and he straightened.

It was a second before she realized that he had stepped back. There would be no kiss. The heady feel of his fingers drifting across her skin vanished. The seductive moment slipped away like dry leaves on a windy day. Disappointment surged. No lip on lip, or pounding demand . . .

Her mind jerked. Her eyes snapped open and mortification consumed her. Embarrassment turned to irrational anger.

"For now," he added, seemingly unaware of her resurging anger, "I'll bid you good night. I have people waiting." He turned toward the door.

"Like Millie McAllister, I suppose," she snapped, her tongue acting independently of her mind.

He stopped in his tracks and hesitated. He ran his hand through his hair, pushing it back from his forehead. Glancing back over his shoulder, he looked at her with one raised eyebrow and the widest boyish grin she had ever seen. "It warms my heart to think you care."

Abigail bit back a curse. "Don't fool yourself, Mr. Blake. I could care less who or *what* you keep company with."

Noah laughed, a deep hearty sound that filled the house. "I can see we're going to get along just fine . . . darlin', and don't you forget it." Then he reached over, grabbed his hat from a peg on the wall, and strolled out of the house, whistling the whole way.

"Argghhh!" she growled once the door slammed shut. "We are not going to get along, Mr. Blake. And don't you forget that!"

～ 5 ～

Abigail woke slowly. The room was dark and unfamiliar. The bed felt strange. The ceiling was different. And she couldn't quite grasp the change.

Only moments later, however, it came to her. The boardinghouse! When she realized where she was she threw back the covers and swung her legs over the side of the bed. It hadn't been a dream! Excitement bubbled up. She was at the boardinghouse, starting a new life. No longer was she standing on the fringe of life watching others live. She was living. Glorious, glorious life.

But then her excitement wavered when the image of unlit stoves, Elden Wineridge, Walter Jackson, and—please dear Lord, she beseeched the heavens, let it have been a nightmare—Noah Blake unmercifully leapt into her mind. But she knew with a heart-wrenching certainty that her prayers weren't to be answered—Noah Blake was all too real. "Ugh," she groaned out loud. But then she pushed thoughts of the man, the others, and her less than stellar beginnings from her mind. She had no interest in ruining what she knew was going to be a marvelous day.

She dressed quickly, purpose coursing through her veins. It was time to fix her first meal. Breakfast. Uncertainty snaked through her, but she shrugged it off. How hard could it be?

The house was quiet when she took her candle and walked out of her room. Stepping out the back door in search of wood, she filled her lungs with early morning air. The sky was still dark, though fast turning shades of purple and blue. She could linger all morning, simply watching the sun rise. But that would get her nowhere fast.

In the kitchen she dropped the wood inside the stove, found a match, and struck the pad in her attempt to start a fire. She followed the steps Noah had taken meticulously, willing the tinder to catch, alternately berating then cajoling the seemingly fickle flame. It took awhile, but finally it caught, though not before she had nearly scorched the eyebrows right off her face. But it was done, and that was all that mattered.

The only items she found in the cool box to make her meal were a few eggs. There weren't many, but she would make do. After a search she found a pan and utensils and a loaf of bread, but no other food stuffs except a big sack of oats. Eggs and bread would have to do for now.

Cracking eggs, she decided some minutes later, was harder than it appeared. She had fished out most, but not all of the tiny, elusive pieces of shell from the bowl of yolks when she gave up and poured them into the pan that had been sitting on the hot stove the whole time. The batter hit the metal with an angry hiss, and before Abigail could put down the bowl and pick up a spoon to stir, the smell of burned egg sizzled through the kitchen.

"Oh, no," she wailed, thankfully thinking to grab a towel before she took hold of the searing hot handle to pull the pan away. Her efforts, however, were in vain. The lumpy mass had already turned an awful shade of dark brown. And the smell. Lord have mercy! So much for the eggs.

She looked around the kitchen, her finger pressed against her lips as she considered. Her gaze fell upon the burlap bag filled with oats. Surely she could boil water, she thought to herself, and what more could a person possibly need to make oatmeal than hot water and oats. They'd have breakfast yet, she determined with a small burst of pleasure over her quick ability to formulate a new plan.

When her boarders entered the dining room sometime later, Abigail was sitting in her seat, a picture of propriety, her hands laid in her lap, bowls of oatmeal at each place.

The men sat down and eyed the fare before them.

"Oatmeal?" Harmon ventured.

"Why of course, gentlemen. What better way to start the day than with a hearty meal of oats."

Noah looked back and forth between the oatmeal and Abigail.

Elden eyed the gray mass. "Growing up we called it mush."

Harmon took a bite and grimaced. Noah followed suit and covered a choke with a cough before taking a long swallow of water.

"This . . . ah . . . fine meal," Noah began with one raised eyebrow, "doesn't have anything to do with the smell that brought me out of a deep sleep like a soldier, now does it, Miss Ashleigh?"

Abigail glared at the man before she threw him a sickeningly sweet smile. "I can't imagine what you're referring to, Mr. Blake. Perhaps the fact that you didn't return from who knows what den of iniquity until well past one in the morning left the stench of debauchery in your nose."

Elden and Harmon stared at Abigail with wide-eyed amazement. A slow lazy smile spread on Noah's lips. "I didn't realize you waited up. Had I known, darlin', I would have come in and said goodnight."

Abigail's mouth fell open in disbelief. Come in! To say goodnight! The indecency!

Seconds passed in total, painful silence as Abigail snapped her mouth shut, sucked in her breath, and stared at Noah Blake. It came to her then in a blinding rush that she hated him. With all her heart. The cad!

She sat straight and silent, searing him with a withering glance so cold and venomous that even her sister would have been hard-pressed to duplicate it. But then she forced a smile. She would not lower herself to this hideous man's level. "Eat up, gentlemen," was all she said, her serene demeanor doing little to cover the blood that boiled just beneath the surface.

Harmon took a bite, then swallowed with effort. "Maybe a glass of milk would help get this . . . help eat . . ." He blushed then gave up trying to explain. "Could I please have some milk?"

"Milk?" Abigail asked, her brow furrowed.

"You know," Elden's irritating voice broke in. "The white stuff."

Her mind raced. She hadn't seen any milk in the cooler. "I'm afraid we don't have any, Mr. Davis. But rest assured," she said with a reassuring smile, "that this evening I'm going to prepare a sumptuous meal that will more than make up for the lack this morning."

Noah sat back and grinned. "Oatmeal steaks, perhaps?"

Harmon covered a snort of laughter with his napkin. Elden grimaced at his bowl. Noah had the audacity to wink at her, then took hold of his spoon and proceeded to shovel oatmeal until the bowl was all but clean. She should have expected the man to eat with all the delicacy of a hog come to trough.

Once the men had left for the day, Abigail said a small prayer of thanks, then took out a stack of cookbooks she found in the pantry. The day had yet again come up bright and beautiful and she decided to take the books out onto the front porch. Contentment washed over her as she sat in a wickerwork chair to peruse the pages.

The sounds of the street frequently dragged her attention away. She waved to Mrs. Holloway of Holloway's Restaurant, and Mrs. Peters, the doctor's wife, as they strolled along the plaza. She even managed a heartfelt hello for Mrs. Kent when she glanced to the right and saw the woman step out on the walk to sweep in front of the store. It was so very different to sit on the porch and watch the town come to life than to stroll amongst the very same streets during the day while running errands. And she liked it. Very much.

She had started on the second cookbook when she saw Millie McAllister walking down the steps from her room above the Red Dog Saloon. Long strands of blond hair hung loose from her chignon to curl perfectly around her oval face and down her back, her bonnet swinging in her hand. On the boardwalk she seemed to move across the wooden planks as regally as a queen. She held her shoulders back and her chin high, her eyes straight ahead, her hips gently swaying, ignoring the women who whispered behind their hands when they saw her approach.

A wagon rolled by and the driver stood on the floorboards and waved his hat. "Miss Millie, don't you look a sight for sore eyes this mornin'!"

Millie smiled. "Why aren't you the sweetest thing a girl could want to see this fine morning, Mr. Conway."

Mr. Conway whooped to the skies and Abigail rolled her eyes and returned her attention to the cookbook. But scant seconds later she peered over the top of the pages, intrigued in spite of herself, as Millie continued down the boardwalk.

Without knowing she did it, Abigail's chin lifted a notch and her shoulders came back. But when Millie looked in her direction, Abigail quickly dropped her glance back to the book of recipes.

Once Millie had disappeared down the street, Abigail decided she could put off washing the dishes no longer. With every intention of returning, she pushed out of her seat and left the books on the porch. Her step hesitated. Glancing over her shoulder to where Millie had disappeared, Abigail raised her chin, pulled back her shoulders, then took a step, hips swaying, only to catch her foot in the hem of her dress and trip through the doorway.

She felt her face color and she quickly glanced about to see if anyone had witnessed her graceless bit of stupidity. Finding no one paying any particular attention to her, she hurriedly made her way to collect the oatmeal bowls.

Just as she pulled out the wash bucket, someone knocked at the door. Smoothing her skirt, Abigail left the kitchen to find Lou Smith on the front porch glancing through the cookbooks. When she saw Abigail, a smile broke out across her face.

"Miss Abigail! What are you doing here? Where's Miss Penny?"

"My aunt has gone to St. Louis and I've taken over for her."

Lou considered this information. "I will miss Miss Penny

so very much. Gertrude and me do walk to Miss Penny's every morning. Early before the sun peeks out. Today Gertrude was feeling poorly and I had to leave her at home. That's why I'm late. Miss Penny always gives us a sweet. But she makes me put them in my pocket until the sun is full up before we can taste them."

"Oh," Abigail looked around, confused. "I don't think I have any sweets."

"That's all right. I'm late anyhow. I wouldn't be expecting any. And though I will miss Miss Penny terribly, I feel so very happy that I will see you every morning."

"Every morning?"

"Of course. I do a good job taking eggs. Everyone says so." Lou screwed up her lips in consideration. "Everyone, that is, except Mrs. Kent."

"You bring eggs in the morning?" She gave this some thought. "I see. That's why I found so few in the cool box." Relief washed over her. That was one mystery solved, though as well as she could cook them it hardly would have mattered if she'd had ten dozen. Now if she could only determine where to get the milk. But her relief died a quick, unmerciful death in the next second.

"Oh, no, Miss Abigail." Lou studied the older woman as if she had grown two heads. "I don't bring eggs to you. You give me eggs that I take to the parts hereabout. I know people are going to be mighty angry this morning since I'm late. But I promise to tell everyone it's my fault. Don't you worry about it, Miss Abigail."

Worry? Me? she thought with a frustrated shake of her head. She looked around as if someone might overhear. "I hate to ask this Lou, but where do I get these eggs from to give you?"

Lou's eyes opened wide. "From the henhouse, where else?"

Where else indeed. And then suddenly Abigail became aware of the distant sound of clucking and squawking from somewhere at the back of the house. She realized she had been dimly aware of the racket for some time now, but had paid little attention since she never imagined it had anything to do with her. Snatching up her skirts, she flew through the house, Lou at her heels, then out the back door. Following the noise, she came around the corner to stop dead in her tracks, her mouth agape with wonder. For there it was.

"Good Lord!" she cried. "It's a henhouse!"

"Like I said, Miss Abigail, Miss Penny has me take eggs to all the folks around here. And from the sounds of those chickens, they got some eggs to be taken. Hopefully it's not too late."

Abigail squeezed her eyes shut for a moment. "Lou, dear, do you know how to . . . take eggs?"

"Well, sure. Miss Penny puts them in my basket—"

"No, I mean, take them away from the chickens."

"Oh! Hmmmm. I don't know. I've never tried. But it doesn't seem so hard."

"Good. Tell me what to do," Abigail said with determination, not to be undone by a flock of fowl.

Lou considered. "I guess you just go in there and take them away."

"That's it?"

"I guess."

That morning Abigail had pulled on her favorite pair of linen walking shoes. She rarely wore them, but today seemed special. It was her first full day as a woman of means—or at least as one who meant to have means one day. For a second she thought she should run back to the house and change.

"You better hurry, Miss Abigail. Those chickens don't sound like they're a bit happy."

Abigail wavered before she made her decision. She walked up the ramp to the henhouse in her favorite shoes and carefully pulled open the door. The rush of feathers and wings, pecking beaks and scratching claws that hurled out the door, nearly flattened her. Lou squealed and headed for the house, the chickens close behind her.

"Haven't you fed them, Miss Abigail?" she called from the relative safety of the back door.

Fed them? She didn't even know she had them! How

was she supposed to have fed them? Good Lord, what had she gotten herself into?

Turning back to the henhouse, however, she was determined to persevere. First she'd get the darned eggs, she muttered to herself, then she'd feed them. She groaned at the thought that the oatmeal bowls still sat unwashed in the kitchen. Not to mention that she had yet to plan the sumptuous meal she had promised. And the sun seemed to be charging through the sky with all the swiftness and determination of a pit bull terrier.

The stench that hit her when she ducked and ventured inside the henhouse made her head swim and her stomach roll. But that was the least of her concerns when she saw the beds of straw filled with crushed eggs. Ruined. Every one of them. She pressed her fist against her forehead and squeezed her eyes shut.

"Miss Abigail!" Lou's voice traveled across the yard, up the ramp, and through the door. "What are you doing in there? You're awful quiet."

Abigail dropped her hand to her side and shrugged to the now empty henhouse. Nothing to do but keep going, she thought to herself, refusing to let her confidence falter.

Exiting the henhouse, the fresh air partially revived her. "I'm afraid our neighbors will have to go without eggs today."

Lou wrinkled her nose. "Smashed up, huh?"

"Yes, smashed up."

"I reckon everyone's already had their breakfast by now anyway, and most people have an egg or two left over from yesterday for their cakes and biscuits."

Cakes and biscuits! People made cakes and biscuits? Didn't they buy them at the mercantile? In her mind's eye she searched the nooks and crannies of the General Store, but couldn't for the life of her remember a single cake or biscuit within the four walls. She had never given much thought to where eggs and cakes and biscuits came from— in fact she had never given it a thought at all.

Embarrassment surged through her when she realized what an absurd excuse of a woman she truly was—she who just that morning thought she would become a woman of means. She clenched her fist. Well, she would. She would learn about eggs and cakes and biscuits, she promised herself with conviction. And in the meantime, perhaps she could buy some from . . . she shrugged her shoulders . . . from someone.

Abigail shook her head as she waded through the fowl until she came to the back door. "I'll get the eggs tomorrow, first thing."

"Fine," Lou said as she turned to leave. "And I'll get here early like I'm supposed to. I'm sure Gertrude will be well by then."

Abigail started to ask who this Gertrude was when Lou stopped all of a sudden. The sound of a bellowing cow broke through the ruckus. She looked back at Abigail. "Did you forget to milk Alberta, too?"

Abigail stood stock still, afraid if she so much as moved a muscle she'd scream. "Good-bye, Lou. I'll see you tomorrow."

"No, not tomorrow, Miss Abigail," Lou said with a shake of her head. "This afternoon, when I bring you your bread from Mrs. Lewis."

Bring her bread? Alberta's irritated bellows and the chickens, agitated flurries pressed in on her. Suddenly, she felt surrounded and inadequate. What else didn't she know? she wondered as she leaned back against the wall. What other surprises did she still have to face? She needed to find that list Penelope said she left.

Alberta got milked, but only because Abigail waylaid a young boy named Pepe who happened to be passing by. He told her he didn't have time, until she ran inside and returned with a silver piece she had in her reticule. Suddenly Pepe had time. She wasn't certain who got the better part of the deal, suspected it hadn't been her, but had no time to bargain with the boy because she still had to feed the chickens and come up with some kind of a meal for supper—not to mention those doggoned oatmeal bowls that still had to be cleaned. And Good Lord, what was she going to do about the mess in the henhouse? She knew for a fact she'd not set her derrière down in there if she were a chicken.

In the small barn where Alberta was kept, Abigail found a barrel of grain and a mound of straw. Filling a small bucket with grain, she returned to the fowl and scattered the contents on the ground. Once the livestock was appeased, she removed the egg-covered straw from the henhouse and replaced it with fresh straw. Feeling disproportionately proud over an absurdly small accomplishment, she made her way back to the house. With straw sticking out of her hair she glanced down at her feet and found that her linen walking shoes were covered with feathers and something suspiciously slimy. Ugh! After fruitlessly trying to clean the linen, she shrugged her shoulders and told herself she didn't like the shoes anyway.

Standing at the kitchen counter in her woolen hose, her shoes tossed out the back door, she was ready to do the dishes—only to find the fire had died out. She hung her head, and for a second she considered simply throwing the dishes out along with her shoes. Surely there was an extra set of crockery around here somewhere.

But that, she finally conceded, was out of the question. She couldn't get in the habit of throwing everything away. Sooner or later, someone was bound to notice that things were missing. She gave a snort of laughter at the vision that loomed in her head of some startled soul coming upon a heap of perfectly good but dirty goods. With that, she went about the laborious process of lighting the stove once again, every now and again giggling at the idea of that startled soul and heap of goods.

The sun had journeyed well into the sky when she finally had the last bowl dried and put away. Abigail stood back and eyed her accomplishment with pride. Now, to think about supper. She returned to the front porch, sat back down in the chair, and picked up another cookbook. Down the street she could just make out the corner of the bank. A twinge of concern came over her at the memory of Walter saying he was going to speak to her father. Thankfully, she hadn't seen hide nor hair of her supposed betrothed, and she knew like she knew her own name that had Walter been triumphant, he would have been at her doorstep within minutes after the bank opened. Apparently she was safe, at least for a while.

The sun felt good on her face and she leaned her head back and relaxed. Just for a moment, she told herself as she slipped into a deep, dream-filled sleep.

Thump, thump, thump, thump.
Abigail murmured in her sleep.
Thump, thump, thump, thump.
The noise pressed in on her, disturbing her dreams. Gradually she woke, her eyes fluttering open to find Harmon and Elden standing on the porch, Harmon bent over at the waist, Elden stiff and still, both men peering down at her as if they weren't quite sure what to do.

Abigail leaped out of the chair, startling the men. "Oh my goodness! I must have dozed off for a second." But then she noticed the sun that was setting on the horizon, and realized with a sinking heart that she had been dozing for a good deal longer than a second.

Her boarders only seemed to notice her shoeless feet. Harmon blushed. Elden rolled his eyes then went inside the house with a bang. Harmon followed. She hurriedly gathered the cookbooks off the ground and had her hand on the doorknob when she heard her name called, loudly, from the upper regions of the house.

"Yes, Mr. Wineridge," she called up the stairs.

Elden leaned over the banister just as Noah walked through the door behind her. For someone who supposedly didn't keep regular hours, she thought, Noah Blake managed regularly to be underfoot.

"Miss Ashleigh!" Elden called. "My bed is unmade!"

"Your bed?" She had never considered. Consuela always made her bed at home. Her breath came out sharply through her teeth. How many times did she have to be reminded she was not at home?

"And my clothes. Not a single shirt has been washed.

Today *is* wash day, is it not, Miss Ashleigh?" Elden persisted.

Abigail took a deep breath. Wash day? Was there such a thing as wash day? she wondered. Apparently so, from the look on Elden's face.

"And what about supper? I don't smell anything but dirty clothes and . . ." Elden leaned over the railing and looked meaningfully at her skirt, "chicken refuse!"

"All right, Mr. Wineridge, I concede that this day has not been altogether successful." She heard Noah snort behind her, but she continued. "I've just had a rough start is all and I'll have everything smoothed out by tomorrow. In fact, I'll do wash first thing in the morning. For now, why don't all of you go over to the restaurant for supper. Tell Mrs. Holloway to send me the bill."

Elden grumbled as he trudged down the stairs, Harmon close behind him.

A knock sounded at the door. Noah pulled it open to find Lou standing there, carrying two loaves of bread in her basket.

"Mr. Blake!"

Noah picked her up and twirled her around. "There's my girl," he said as he set her down. "I haven't seen you all day."

"I've been busy. Gertrude's sick and I've been tending her."

"She's going to be all right, isn't she?"

Abigail noticed the concern in Noah's eyes and felt a stab of something that made her feel strangely alone and empty. And she wondered yet again who this Gertrude could possibly be.

"Oh, she is going to be just fine." Lou turned to Abigail. "I've brought the bread." Her face reddened and she glanced at all the adults who stood around before she looked back to Abigail, her voice lowered to a near whisper. "But Mrs. Lewis said you have got to pay since I didn't bring her any eggs."

Heat suffused Abigail's body. She felt pinpricks of sweat bead on her face as the crowd of people stared at her.

"Perhaps you could tell Mrs. Lewis I'll get her the money tomorrow."

"I don't know, Miss Abigail. She was awful mad that she didn't get any eggs. I don't think I'd much like to go back over there and tell her I didn't get her any money."

Abigail forced a smile and tried to put from her mind the fact that three men were watching her with great interest. She had given the only money she had brought with her to Pepe to milk Alberta. She'd have to go to the bank to get more, and it was closed. "Then I'll go over and talk to Mrs. Lewis myself."

Just then they heard someone coming up the steps to the porch. Everyone turned.

"Walter," Abigail said, cringing inside. "What are you doing here?"

This time as Walter arrived he had a smile on his face. Taking his hat from his head, he said, "I didn't realize I needed an invitation." Then he caught sight of Noah. His smile hardened, but remained. He forced himself to turn away and noticed for the first time Abigail's disheveled appearance. With his shirt stiffly starched and his pants perfectly pressed, his hard smile faltered to a grimace when his perusal took in her feet. "Abigail! Where are your shoes?"

She shifted uncomfortably and tried to lose her feet in the folds of her skirt. "It's a long story."

But long or short, Walter was not listening, as just then he turned and his attention locked on Lou. Lou's smile disappeared and she took a tiny step backwards.

"Have you two met?" Abigail asked, uncertain.

Lou opened her mouth to speak, but snapped it shut when Walter smiled and said, "No, never seen her."

Noah's eyes narrowed as he studied Walter. At length, he pulled a coin from his pocket. "Here you go, Lou. Why don't you take this over to Mrs. Lewis."

"Oh, no," Abigail interjected. "I couldn't let you do that."

"Do what?" Walter frowned.

Abigail grimaced. Perhaps, she thought quickly, it was best to cut her losses and move on. "Nothing, Walter." She nodded her reluctant thanks to Noah then said, "Lou, if you'd go on over to Mrs. Lewis's, I'd be thankful." Then she quickly turned and walked down the hall toward the kitchen.

"Abigail!" Walter practically shouted. But then he seemed to restrain himself physically. "Abigail," he repeated, his voice suddenly reasonable as he followed her down the hall. "What's going on around here?"

Noah took in the situation. He noticed Abigail's stiff walk and Walter's blotchy face. Noah hesitated, feeling the need to throttle Walter Jackson. He couldn't abide a man like him. They were all the same. Selfish and unkind. And they generally preyed on sweet innocents like Abigail Ashleigh. He shook his head. But who was he to interfere in her life? She certainly wasn't straight out of the schoolroom, and she had a father and family to take care of her. Like she had said herself, she was no business of his.

"Come on, men." Noah motioned to Harmon and Elden. "It's Tuesday. They'll be having chicken and dumplings over at Holloway's."

The front door slammed shut and Abigail hoped Walter had gone, too.

"Abigail!"

No such luck.

His footsteps came down the hall. She glanced at the back door and wondered if she could make it. She'd go somewhere. Anywhere. Just so long as it was far away from the boardinghouse on the corner of El Paso and San Francisco streets. Her good cheer and optimism had deserted her. Suddenly she felt old, so very old and tired.

"What has gotten into you?" Walter asked from the kitchen doorway. His anger was starting to rise. "No shoes on, your hair is a mess, you smell like livestock, and that Mr. Blake seems to be paying your debts. To whom do you owe money, Abigail?"

Abigail sighed. "Mrs. Lewis. For the bread. Tomorrow I'll stop by the bank. I'll need to have some money on hand for different things."

"What kind of things?"

"I don't know, Walter," she snapped, her patience at its end. "All kinds of things. And why are you so full of questions?"

"Because—"

"Because you don't trust me!"

"I never—"

"You didn't have to. Accusation is written all over your face." She waited for his heated response and was surprised when it didn't come.

"Now, Abigail," he said, his voice surprisingly calm and reasonable. "You're tired—"

"You're right! I *am* tired!" Her mouth opened to tell him she was tired of him, but she stopped. She dropped her head into her hands. She'd had a rotten day and she realized she was taking it out on him. He didn't deserve her wrath. She was to blame. "I'm sorry, Walter. It's been a long day."

His stance relaxed. "That's all right, Abigail."

He took the few steps between them until he stood next to her chair. After a moment's hesitation he laid his hand on her shoulder. It was all Abigail could do not to jerk away.

"Why don't we just forget all this foolishness and return home. I'll take you myself. No one is going to think less of you."

Her fist clenched in her lap. "Have you talked to my father?"

Red seared his face. "Well, yes, actually."

"What did he say?"

Walter shifted his weight. "He said we'd have to just wait and see," he told her, the anger in his voice growing with every syllable.

Her head snapped up and her eyes blazed. "Wait and see? What? Wait to see if I fail?"

"Well, look at you," he said with a meaningful glance over her person.

She gritted her teeth and held back the words she longed to speak. Her family and Walter hovered like vultures, waiting for her to flounder. And as she looked around her, she conceded that their expectations were held with good reason. "I think it's time you should go, Walter."

His hand fisted at his side. His lips thinned. "What are you saying?"

"I'm saying that you should go home. As I said, it's been a long day and I'm tired."

Walter stared at her long and hard, all traces of calm and reason gone. With measured movements, he placed his hat on his head. "If that's what you want, Abigail, then I'll bid you good night." He started to go but stopped. "I hope you're not planning to change your mind about the Saturday Social."

Abigail groaned silently. She had forgotten. She wished she hadn't been forced to remember. She hated Saturday Socials. She hated having the fact that she had no friends and that no one wanted to dance with her thrown in her face every third Saturday of the month. But her father held great store in the family attending such community functions. She had no choice but to go. "Of course I'm going, Walter."

"Fine," he said stiffly. "I'll stop by to escort you to the church."

When she didn't respond, he turned on his heel and strode from the house.

He was angry and she knew she should care. But she didn't. She was merely thankful she was finally left in peace.

6

B<small>ANG</small>!

Abigail jerked in her sleep, grumbled, rolled over, then burrowed deeper into the feather bed.

Bang! Bang!

Her dreams shattered and she came out of the bed like someone had hollered fire.

Bang!

Her heart pounded and her knees were weak as her mind tried to comprehend the noise. On tiptoes she crept out of her room, went to the back door, lifted the curtain, and peered out the window into the semi-darkness.

Lou! What was Lou doing there and what was that noise?

Bang!

Abigail screeched and jumped as the door reverberated beneath her fingers, but her heart quickly plummeted to her feet when she remembered the eggs. Lou was there for the eggs!

Throwing open the door, she gasped and stepped aside just in time for a goat to barrel past her. Lou's brown eyes widened. Abigail gaped. And the goat seemed as surprised as anyone to find itself inside.

"Gertrude!" Lou cried. "Come back here!"

Abigail slumped against the door. "So this is the cause of all that racket. The infamous Gertrude, banging down my door." With a smile, she realized Noah Blake had been so very concerned about a goat! The traitorous thought that he couldn't be all that bad if he cared about little children and animals crossed her mind. But her legs were weak from fright, the cool early morning air was making itself felt, and she was starting to shiver. She thought about it no more.

After much pleading and prodding, Gertrude was once again standing on the back porch.

"Hold on to that goat, Lou, and I'll go change."

Pushing away from the door, Abigail noticed Lou's suddenly despondent countenance.

"What's wrong?"

"You don't like Gertrude. I know she was bad and all, but if you hadn't opened the door just then, she wouldn't have come flying inside like she did. She's terribly sorry."

A quiver of uncertainty ran down Abigail's spine. One minute the child was so happy, then the next so afraid of being in trouble. Having so little experience with children, Abigail wasn't sure if this was normal or not. "I don't . . . dislike Gertrude."

"But you're mad, I can tell."

"Heavens, no. I'm not mad. The noise just gave me a fright is all." She reached down and smoothed Lou's hair. The child perked up a bit, but not entirely. Abigail eyed Gertrude. Quickly, she reached out, gave the goat a few pats on the head then said, "There, see, I'm not angry with Gertrude. Now, let me go put on some proper clothes and we'll go get those eggs."

Abigail pulled on the oldest pair of clothes she owned and was thankful she had retrieved her linen walking boots from the refuse heap, for they had just become her linen egg-taking boots. She smiled at her cleverness and was relieved to find her confidence restored after a good night's sleep. No, she was no failure, she told herself. And she would show her family yet.

With a small lantern, she hurried out the back door and made her way up the ramp. She hesitated at the top.

"You can do it, Miss Abigail."

Lou and Gertrude waited expectantly in the yard, not too close, Abigail noticed, though who could blame them after yesterday's debacle.

Taking a deep breath, Abigail pulled open the door, only just an inch or so. No squawking or chickens trying to cannon out the door. Another few inches allowed her to peek inside. All was peaceful which was fine with Abigail—fine, that is, until she realized every chicken was sound asleep and sitting on its new bed of straw.

"How am I supposed to get the eggs, Lou? The chickens are sitting on them," she hissed through the early morning darkness.

"Real quiet like, maybe you could slip your hand underneath and pull them out."

"Put my hand underneath the chicken?"

"I suppose so. Unless you have a better idea."

Abigail frowned, wishing she hadn't spent so much of her life with her nose in a book—or if she had, at least the books should have been about taking eggs and cooking meals.

"You'd better hurry, Miss Abigail."

With no help for it, Abigail gritted her teeth and went inside. She found a peg to hang the lantern on before she carefully shut the door behind her, then stealthfully approached the fowl. With infinite care she reached out, her head turned away, her eyes squinted, her nose wrinkled, and slowly put her hand into the straw. Inch by inch, her fingers crept forward. Sweat gathered on her brow. She felt as if at any second her hand would come out the other side. Where were those darned eggs? Farther and farther her hand went, until finally she felt something warm and smooth. Curling her fingers around it, she eased her hand back out. An egg! She nearly squealed with her success.

She went faster the next time and when her fingers came to an egg, she stood up in her excitement at the same time she pulled free. The chicken came to life in a squawk of noise and flying feathers. Abigail jumped back and the next thing she knew the slimy feel of egg yolk oozed between her fingers.

And things didn't get any better from there. By the time she came charging out of the henhouse, the chickens close behind her, her hair had been pecked free of its pins and her hands and cheeks stung.

"Oh, Miss Abigail, you do look a sight."

Abigail dropped down onto the ramp, her skirt billowing, her ankles showing, but she didn't care one whit for propriety.

"I take it you didn't get any eggs," Lou stated.

Abigail wasn't sure if she wanted to laugh or cry as she held up one measly egg which Lou carefully but quickly took away as if afraid it would be broken, too. With a wry smile, Abigail dropped her head into her hands, only to groan with dismay when she felt egg yolk cover her forehead. And when she jerked her head up she found none other than Noah Blake standing on the back porch.

"What are you doing there?" she demanded.

Lou pivoted so fast her braids swung out perpendicular to the ground. Gertrude bleated a welcome, hurried to his side, and nudged his hand.

"Sorry, Gertrude. I don't have anything for you today." He chuckled. "I didn't realize I'd be seeing you this morning."

"Mr. Blake." Lou walked forward, shaking her head. "We've had a bit of trouble."

"I can see that."

"We've had no trouble!" Abigail interjected.

Noah only smiled before he sauntered down the steps and approached Abigail. She was certain he was going to make fun of her predicament and she steeled herself against the impending onslaught. But when she met his dark blue eyes they were void of mirth.

"Are you all right?" he asked quietly, bending down in front of her.

His concern left her speechless. She felt a stab of longing more poignant than any of the others she had experienced in the past. She didn't understand it. She didn't understand what this man made her feel—this man who laughed and teased, who was kind to little girls and goats. He was nothing like anyone she had ever dreamed about. No courtly manners or romantic proposals. He was raw and dangerous, his devilish smiles and suggestive comments were proof enough of that . . . but still he alternately made her furious

then stole her breath away. Truly he was the most dangerous kind of man of all.

When she failed to respond, he pulled out a handkerchief
from his pocket and she knew she should protest when he
reached up and wiped her forehead. Their eyes met and
held. The feel of his hand holding her head still while the
other gently cleaned the yolk away, made her warm all
over.

The black sky was rapidly fading to purple and blue with
a hint of orange to mark the impending dawn. The yard was
quiet, even the chickens had simmered down.

No one spoke and her mind wandered. She studied his
face. His forehead was high and his eyes were as blue as
ever. His nose was straight and surprisingly aristocratic for
a man who could scare a grizzly bear with his mere size.
Despite herself her glance slid to his lips. But that was all
she could see, for the rest of his face was covered with his
beard and mustache.

"Have you always worn a beard, Mr. Blake?" she asked
unexpectedly.

His hand stilled before he smiled, wiped one last time,
then put her at arm's length. "No, not always. Mainly just
when I'm up in the mountains trapping. It's mighty difficult
to get a decent shave out in the wilderness. Not a barber to
be found for miles." His lips tilted on one side. "But now
that I'm back, if you'd like, I'll run right down to the barber. Just for you, darlin'."

Red flooded her cheeks like a tidal wave. "Well, I . . ."
she stammered and puffed. "I never . . ." She scrambled to
her feet, nearly knocking him on his backside. She stood
before him, feet spread wide, her arms akimbo. "Why is it,
Mr. Blake, that you get such pleasure from taunting me?
And how many times do I have to tell you it is Miss Ashleigh to you?"

"Like I told you, you don't look like a Miss Ashleigh or
even an Abigail, for that matter." He studied her. "Abby,"
he said simply, then smiled. "You look like an Abby."

Her lips pursed despite the sudden weakness in her knees
and the pain in her heart. As a child she had always longed

for a short, endearing nickname. Most everyone had one. Emma had Em. Sherwood had Wood. Even Virginia was called Jenny sometimes. But Abigail was always Abigail. Not that she would be called anything but Miss Ashleigh by this ill-mannered mountain man, she reprimanded herself.

"Yes, Abby," he confirmed.

"Mr. Blake—"

"Noah."

"Mr. Blake," she emphasized. "We have gone from Miss Ashleigh, seeming to bypass Miss Abigail or even Abigail in the process, until we have somehow arrived at Abby. We are going in the wrong direction."

Noah smiled. "No, darlin', we're going in the right direction," he said, his voice rumbling quietly through the early morning dawn as he pushed up from the ground then reached out to caress her cheek with one long, strong finger.

She held her body very still. Her countenance grew pained. "Do you think I'm so unworthy of respect and decency that you can touch me at will and call me anything you like?"

His brow furrowed and he dropped his hand. The return of her mutinous stance left him unexpectedly wishing for that faraway look in her eye that he knew was always just below the surface of her haughty facade. "Hell, you have it all wrong. I'm just playing with you. I meant no disrespect." And it was true. The thought of this woman thinking he would intentionally hurt her was unacceptable. He liked her. He hadn't given much thought to why he liked her. He wasn't that kind of man. She simply made him feel good whenever he was around her. He only teased her to make her laugh and smile. "I apologize."

He watched as she studied him and he knew she was trying to determine if he was teasing her again or not.

"Uh hum," Lou interjected awkwardly.

Abigail's head snapped around.

"Why don't you and Gertrude go out to Mr. Roberts's farm," Noah interjected smoothly. "If you hurry you can get some eggs and have them delivered before anyone knows any different."

"But Mr. Roberts is mean."

"He's not mean, sweetling, just ornery. Tell him I sent you and he'll give you the eggs."

"Well all right," she muttered, not altogether convinced this was true. "But if he yells at me I'm going to kick him in the shins."

"He won't yell at you. Now get a move on or everyone's going to be having oatmeal for breakfast."

Abigail grimaced. They certainly would be having oatmeal for breakfast, she thought. She watched Lou skip away, Gertrude trotting alongside. "Thank you," she said grudgingly once Lou had disappeared around the side of the house.

Noah turned back to her. "It's nothing. Roberts owes me a favor or two."

"Then I guess I owe you a favor now, too." With a shake of her head, Abigail didn't wait for a response. "Now I must get inside to see about breakfast."

She worked fast and furiously in the kitchen and just as the sun cleared the horizon, Abigail set four bowls of oatmeal down on the table. Her chin jutted forward a notch as soon as she heard the first grumble of dissatisfaction.

"Oatmeal," Harmon said simply.

Noah almost laughed out loud when Elden opened his mouth to speak, the narrowed eyes hinting that he wasn't on the verge of offering his compliments, and Abigail gave him a look that dared him to say a thing.

Elden grumbled then grabbed his spoon. They lapsed into silence. Abigail took a bite and absently gazed out the window while she ate. Elden was the first to finish and push back from the table.

"I hope your efforts with the wash are more successful than your cooking," he said, before he pulled his hat from its peg and slammed out the front door.

"Wash," Abigail half groaned. Her eyes met Noah's questioning gaze. "I love to do wash," she added with a tight smile before quickly looking away.

Harmon departed next, leaving Noah and Abigail alone in the house. Noah helped carry the bowls into the kitchen, but neither one spoke.

"I'll be about town all day," he said finally. "Why don't I check in to see if you need some help?"

Abigail stiffened. "I don't need you to stop by, Mr. Blake, and I certainly won't need your help."

The sudden sound of a bellowing cow filled the air. Alberta. Abigail's shoulders slumped.

"Are you sure?" he asked quietly. He started to reach out, but dropped his hand to his side when she jerked away.

"Of course I'm sure," she snapped, before she set the bowls down, gathered her skirts, and headed for the back door. "Good day, Mr. Blake."

Abigail was forced to engage young Pepe's services once again when she couldn't get a drop of milk from the disgruntled Alberta. And she had to pay the boy on credit. She shook her head in dismay as she began totaling her debts. But she'd deal with that later. First she had to feed the chickens then get busy with the wash.

As it turned out, if egg-taking was considered a disaster, washing clothes was a certified catastrophe. But still she was not to be deterred. Soaping them was not so very difficult, but rinsing the shirts and socks and, dear Lord, unmentionables, seemed impossible. When finally she determined they were as clean and soap-free as they were going to get, she wrung them out and hung them to dry.

Now to deal with the house. Mopping and polishing were not even a consideration. Straightening and making beds would have to do for today. She still had to figure out how to cook a meal. When sheets were finally tucked and bedcovers smoothed as best as she could smooth them, she hurried downstairs to wash the bowls. And already it was well into the afternoon. The wash had taken her longer than she had hoped.

The scorching desert air dried the clothes within hours. Never having taken clothes down, Abigail was not altogether certain how they should feel. But even with her lack of experience, she conceded that stiff as a board was not good. In fact, they seemed a little on the crusty side and smelled strongly of soap. Maybe ironing would help, she thought with a smile. And ironing she had seen done!

She found an iron in the pantry and stoked up the stove. After setting the iron on the burner to heat up, she flipped through yet another cookbook in hopes of finding something easy to cook for supper. Finding nothing with an ingredient list of less than a half-dozen items, most of which she was unfamiliar with, she decided that as soon as she finished ironing, she'd run down to the restaurant and purchase something from Mrs. Holloway. She wondered for a moment if the woman could keep a secret. Secretive or not, she felt the plan was inspired, despite her mounting debts. She knew she wouldn't have a chance to get to the bank today, but tomorrow, as soon as it opened, she'd get some money. What she would tell her father, she had no idea.

Mindful to use a towel, Abigail carefully picked up the iron and carried it over to the first shirt she had laid out. She decided to start on the back, and no sooner had she set the iron down than the smell of seared soap and material sizzled through the air.

"Good Lord, what have I done?" she cried as she stared down at the perfect imprint of an iron on the back of one of Elden Wineridge's best linen shirts.

She glanced at the pile of ironing left to be done and knew she couldn't quit now. She could only pray that Elden wouldn't notice his shirt until she had time to replace it.

With the next shirt, she waited until the iron had cooled, and with surprising ease, she proceeded from shirt to shirt until each one was done.

Folding was not easy as stiff as they were, but eventually the task was done, just as the front door opened and slammed shut. Abigail glanced out the window and noticed how late it was. And she hadn't yet run down the street to purchase her meal. Maybe it was only Lou with the bread, she thought. But her hopes were dashed when she came out into the foyer and came face to face with Elden.

"Mr. Wineridge, you're home early."

Elden shook his head and glanced toward the kitchen. "Does this by chance mean what I think it means?"

"Well," Abigail equivocated with a shrug of her shoulders. "That depends on what you think it means."

The man practically growled. "That we are having oatmeal for supper, Miss Ashleigh."

Harmon and Noah chose that very moment to step through the door.

"Well, it is good for your digestion," she offered with a lame smile.

Elden sucked in his breath. "Miss Ashleigh—"

"Careful, Wineridge," Noah said.

Both Abigail and Elden turned to look at him, then Elden pursed his lips and strode from the house, never having even taken off his hat.

Harmon smiled apologetically. "I think I'll just run over to Mrs. Holloway's myself."

Abigail watched the door bang shut. Gradually she became aware that Noah was watching her.

"I suspect you want another thank you for coming to my rescue like some knight in shining armor! Well you can forget it," she snapped. "I didn't need your help this morning and I certainly don't need it now to deal with my boarders. So go play Sir Lancelot somewhere else!"

He didn't respond, but merely continued to stare at her. It was the look she remembered all too well from the day he ran her down. And like that day her breath caught in her throat and she longed to ask him what he saw, what he was thinking. But of course she did no such thing—she simply grew more uncomfortable by the second. "What do you want?" she finally demanded.

He shook his head then put on his hat. "I don't know, Abigail. I surely don't know." Then he was gone, the door slamming in his wake.

Thursday and Friday proved no better than the rest of the week. By late afternoon Friday Abigail's nails were ruined, her hands were raw, her feet ached, and the house that had been unaccustomed to dirt and dust was fast becoming well acquainted with the ravages of time. It wasn't that she didn't try. Good Lord, a dust rag was never far from her fingertips—she had even taken to carrying one around with her at all times. But the desert sand had the most insidious way of sneaking in through every crack and crevice to ruin all her hard work as soon as she was done.

Her debts were paid, but only after borrowing the money from Virginia. She had hated doing it, but she couldn't come up with an alternate plan. Walter had asked too many questions when she went to the bank. She knew her father would have done the same. And she wasn't about to let on that she had gotten herself into a mess. She had received enough money from her stepmother to continue to pay Pepe for his labors until she had time to learn how to milk the cow herself. But she'd learn. Just as she was learning how to gather the eggs. Sort of. She grimaced. The feel of egg yolk was becoming all too familiar. But less and less of it each day.

She sat down at the kitchen table for the first time since morning. She took a deep breath and smiled. She was finally making progress. Proof was in the oven right that second. She was cooking her first real meal. Already the house smelled of seasoning and home cooking. Her boarders could hardly find fault with her this day.

That evening, Noah came in first. They had exchanged no more than a few stilted pleasantries since their uneasy encounter on Wednesday. Abigail was uncomfortable and had spent entirely too much time trying to figure out what he had meant when he said he didn't know what he wanted from her. Just the thought made her feel strangely alive.

"Afternoon, Miss Abigail," he said, hanging his hat.

She had given up on Miss Ashleigh, telling herself Miss Abigail was better than the Abby he had said he would use. A twinge of disappointment plagued her, but that was ridiculous. She surely did not want to be called Abby by this man. "Good afternoon, Mr. Blake. I trust your day was a pleasant one."

He sat down at the small table next to her. "Pleasant indeed."

His tone was polite but indifferent, and though she knew she should be pleased that he was finally acting as the gentleman he should, she longed to see his playful smile or hear his laughter-filled words.

He pulled out a newspaper. "Smells good in here."

"Does it really?" she asked quickly. "It's my first . . . I mean, it's a roast. I bought it from Mrs. Holloway—uncooked," she added quickly, wanting him to know that she was cooking the meal herself.

With that, a smile hovered on his lips, and her heart soared.

"I'm sure it'll be a fine roast. Elden should be pleased."

Before she could stop herself, she snorted. "I doubt that."

"Hello, all," Harmon said as he came into the kitchen. "Smells mighty fine in here. Elden should be pleased."

Abigail met Noah's amused glance, and she held back a smile.

"We can only hope," Noah responded.

But all hopes and good cheer were dashed when the front door slammed shut.

"Miss Ashleigh!" Elden's sharp, angry voice reverberated through the house.

Abigail's smile evaporated into the late afternoon sunlight. "Oh dear, what now?"

Noah visibly tensed.

Harmon shifted uncomfortably. "Maybe he had a bad day."

"Miss Ashleigh!"

Elden Wineridge came to stand in the doorway, his jacket in his hand, his tie suspiciously gone along with his collar. After a moment, Abigail realized the bright red on his neck was not due entirely to his anger.

"My shirt is *filled* with soap! I have a rash, Miss Ashleigh, and it doesn't stop at my neck!"

Abigail blushed. "I guess my washing was not quite as successful as I had hoped."

"Nor your ironing," he added, before turning to display the perfect brown imprint of the iron.

A tiny, desperate groan sounded as Abigail held back the

sudden burst of tears that threatened. "Oh, dear. I'm so sorry," she whispered.

"You're sorry?"

Noah pushed up from his seat and Abigail knew she should tell him to mind his own business. But just then she was afraid to speak, afraid that if she opened her mouth she would no longer be able to hold back the tears.

"Elden, I think it's time you and I had a talk," Noah said, his voice tight.

"Noah," Abigail managed.

But her thoughts were swept away when Harmon blurted, "What's that smell?"

A heartbeat passed before Abigail leaped to her feet. "Heavens above! The roast!"

She ran to the stove and threw open the door. But it was too late. A wall of smoke poured out, filling the room. Waving the smoke away, she grabbed a thick towel and reached in and retrieved the roast.

The pan was heavy and she dropped it on the stove top with a bang, only to stand there and stare at the charred remains of beef. Noah came up behind her with Harmon close by. Only Elden remained at the door.

"I suspect it will be good for the digestion," she offered quietly, her throat tight, her eyes burning.

"Digestion, Miss Ashleigh?" Elden demanded. "Like the oatmeal which I have eaten more of in the last week than in my entire life! No thank you. My digestive tract has had enough. As have I. I'm leaving, Miss Ashleigh, for good. Tonight. And not a moment too soon."

Abigail didn't move. She stared at the roast without seeing. Harmon grimaced apologetically, then turned away and headed for the door. "I think I'll just go on over to Mrs. Holloway's."

Noah stared at her bowed head. He reached out and touched her shoulder.

"Please just go away," she whispered.

At first she thought he wouldn't go. He neither spoke nor stepped away. His hand was warm and gentle on her shoulder, secure, strangely filling her with strength. And just when she would have damned all else and turned into his comforting embrace, his hand dropped away and she heard his footsteps retreat until the house was filled with nothing more than the sounds of Elden Wineridge packing his bags. Minutes passed while she stared at the charred beef, until Elden pounded out of the house. Her breath came out in a jagged rush when the door finally slammed shut.

She wrapped her arms tightly around herself and pressed her eyes closed. Her gasping sob was cut short when she stuffed her hand in her mouth. No, Abigail Ashleigh, you will not give in. Taking a deep breath, she walked with measured steps to the back door, longing for air.

The fading sun cast the sky in shades of red and orange. She sank down onto the bottom step and stared off into the distance.

"Are you okay?"

She swung around and found Noah leaning against the railing, smoking a cheroot.

"I thought you went with Harmon," she snapped.

"I changed my mind."

"Well, change it back and leave me alone."

He tossed the cigar into the dirt then crossed the porch and came down the steps. His strong hands pressed against his thighs as he eased himself down next to her.

"I told you to leave me alone," she repeated, her voice tight.

"I know," he said, his voice like gravel. "But I can't stand to see a pretty lady unhappy." He reached out and turned her chin until she faced him. "Are you going to be all right?"

She stared at him, and she could feel the tears well up and burn. She swallowed hard, but didn't reply.

"If you're so unhappy," he began, "why don't you just go on home?"

Abigail snorted in response. "You sound just like Walter."

Making a teasing show of being outraged, Noah said, "Heaven forbid I should sound like that fop."

A sob mixed with laughter, a quick burst and sputter of sound, but she held it back, trying to turn away.

His fingers tightened upon her chin, holding her captive, but his voice was gentle. "If you're determined to stay, then you'll find another boarder. One a whole lot easier to please than Elden Wineridge, I might add."

She half laughed half sobbed. "That's right, someone who doesn't mind burned food and stiff clothes." And then, like the dam finally gave way, the tears coursed down her cheeks and her body racked with sobs.

With a gentleness that belied his size, Noah pulled her close and absorbed her tears.

"Oh, Noah," she cried. "What am I going to do? Elden's gone. Harmon looked envious when he watched Elden announce he was leaving, then turn on his heel and do just that. I'm sure Harmon will be the next to leave. Even you, with guts of steel, are sure to get fed up with my cooking."

"I think I should be insulted," he said with a soft chuckle as he held her close. He let her cry until her tears trailed off and her body relaxed. "And I'd think you'd be thrilled if I left, besides." His teasing laughter rumbled quietly through the night, his hand running over her back to soothe her. "In fact, I've wondered more than once if you're not really a French chef in disguise and are doing all this just to get rid of me."

She pulled back, dashed her tears, and looked into his eyes. "It sounds like a great plan," she whispered, "perhaps I should give it a try."

His finger traced the line of her jaw. He took her hand and brought it to his lips, turning it over until his kiss pressed into her palm. "You'd do well to slip Harmon better fare secretly, however. With my guts of steel, as you so indelicately put it, I could last a good long while on worse. Harmon, I think, has a different breed of stomach altogether."

His breath shimmered against the tender skin of her wrist. Her breath caught in her throat. The simple touch startled her and the intimacy that she had never imagined left her breathless. "Ahhh," she began, trying to make her mind formulate a sentence. "A minor problem then."

He kissed her wrist. "And what is that?"

She reveled in the feel, forgetting where she was, or for that matter, who she was. "I can't seem to produce better fare."

He smelled of rich tobacco and his breath was like velvet against her skin. Sensation shimmered down her body, flooding her with yearning, intense yearning that centered in the core of her being, but for what she yearned she wasn't sure. At that moment she only cared about forgetting. Reaching up she pressed her fingertips lightly along the side of his face, amazed at the feel—at once so hard and smooth, until she came to the beard, then oddly both coarse and soft.

A chuckle rumbled in his chest as he leaned down and kissed her forehead. "A promise."

Her mind stumbled over propriety at his words. "What?"

"I promised . . ." he whispered as he kissed her temple, "to shave . . . just for you."

Her fingers stilled and her breath caught. The soft pliancy of her body gradually gave way and she stiffened. What was she doing? she wondered desperately. How could she have let him touch her? She leaped up and her boot caught in the hem of her skirt. She nearly tumbled to the ground, but Noah reached out and steadied her.

"Abby?" He spoke her name as a question. "What's wrong?"

"Don't touch me!" she cried, frantically pushing him away. "I am not that kind of woman."

Noah's brow furrowed, his grasp holding her tight. "You mean you're not the kind of woman who can talk and laugh, and take comfort from a friend?"

Their eyes met and held. Confusion etched his brow as he studied her. He wanted to ask her why she cared so much for propriety, especially when faced with the obvious fact that it was like chains around a spring flower. He had lived his life saying whatever was on his mind and living life to the fullest. And while certainly he had seen stiff peo-

ple before, never had he seen one so ready to burst with
life. The sudden urge to set her free, to break the chains that
strangled the life from her, washed over him like a dangerous, unsuspected river current, and nearly swept him away.
But he held his ground, he retained his stance against an act
that would undoubtedly prove his undoing.

"Let go of my arm, Mr. Blake."

He held on for a second longer as if he wouldn't let her
go, before he finally released her and she fled through the
back door.

7

UGLY. THERE WAS NO OTHER WORD FOR IT. WELL, PER-
haps short on looks, unattractive, plain, or unsightly might do,
but all in all, it amounted to the same thing. She was ugly.

Abigail stared in the mirror and sighed. Not that this was
news to her. She had spent her entire life aware of the fail-
ings of her looks. But this night, for reasons she had no interest in studying too closely, she wanted to look her best.

Boiling water had been the only household skill she had
managed to master, well, she conceded, mastered might be
an exaggeration. Nonetheless she could do it, and she used
it to her advantage and had taken the first full bath she'd
had since leaving her father's home. Her eyes ran the
length of her bathed and coiffed reflection. Even with a
bath, however, her best was not too good.

She was tall and skinny with no curves in any of the right
places, unlike the two oversized melons her sister had
strapped to her chest, she thought, alternately shocking herself then making herself laugh. But she sobered quickly
enough when she noted her own plain brown eyes, overly
wide mouth, and of course, wild brown hair. She had spent
the better part of an hour trying to tame the unruly mass
into some semblance of a stylish chignon. Unfortunately, it
looked no different than when she got up and simply pulled
it back. No wonder no one was surprised that she could get
no man except Walter Jackson. And if rumors were to be
believed, he probably would have courted her if she had
warts and green skin.

Turning away from the mirror she gathered her gloves

and reticule. Walter would be there any minute to escort her to the town's Saturday Social.

She ran her hand over the fine beige calico dress with its tiny brown floral print. The flowers made her feel feminine and dainty. It was one of her favorite frocks and it made her feel just a tiny bit better. A smile surfaced at the thought that her linen walking shoes she normally wore to the social would never be worn to such a function again. Just the idea of the looks on people's faces if she came in with chicken feathers and refuse covering her footwear turned her smile to a bubble of laughter. All the townsfolk would be horrified, but too afraid to say something to Sherwood Ashleigh's daughter. All, that is, but the irreverent Noah Blake.

Noah Blake. Despite herself, she felt a shiver of anticipation at seeing him that evening. She wondered what he would wear. Would he smell of fine cigars? Would he laugh and smile? She pressed her hands to her breast. Would he ask her to dance?

Her heart seemed to stop in her chest. Of course he wouldn't ask her to dance, she admonished herself. And if he did, she'd say no! More than likely, he would taunt and tease her and make her blush with mortification as was his habit. But then a thought came to her from out of nowhere—he wouldn't embarrass her in front of others. The thought startled her. She had no idea where it came from, and more importantly, why she felt so confident it was the truth. But she did feel confident, and it left her strangely comforted.

Walter arrived at exactly seven o'clock. Elden had moved out and stayed out. Harmon had gone to Mesilla on business and wouldn't be back until the following week. And an unusually quiet Noah had told her that morning after his bowl of oatmeal that he would be gone the rest of the day, not to bother with supper on his account.

Abigail had asked him if he would be at the social before she could stop herself. A hint of his old smile flickered on his face. "Of course, darlin'," he had responded in his most impertinent way.

She blushed at the memory.

"Come on, Abigail." Walter's voice cut through her thoughts. "We're going to be late."

He took hold of her arm and led her down the front steps to the road, pulling her along at a brisk pace.

"Walter, please slow down. I'm having trouble keeping up."

With a mutter, he slowed his gait.

"Walter, what is wrong?"

He let go of her arm with a jerk. "What's wrong? I'll tell you what's wrong. Your dress, your shoes, your hair. Couldn't you at least have tried to do something with your hair? You know how your father hates it when you come looking like you do." His voice was a whine. "Now, we'll have to spend the first hour placating him. Why can't you be more like Emma, for Christ's sake!"

The words hurt more than they should have. She had lived her whole life trying to be more like Emma. But still it hurt. And never before had she wanted to be more like Emma, or at least pretty like her sister. While growing up their mother had always said that God had seen fit to bestow Emma with stunning good looks and Abigail with a kind heart. Abigail had worked hard during her life to accept God's will. But this night, just for a little while, she would have given every inch of her kind heart for an ounce of Emma's stunning looks. "I'm sorry, Walter," she said simply, then turned away and headed down the street. They walked the rest of the way in silence.

The townsfolk gathered in El Paso's one and only church once a month to dance and sing—to step away from the hardships of life and simply enjoy. Abigail entered on Walter's arm and they strode directly to a group of seats where her family always gathered. Walter walked through the crowd of people and accepted their greetings and attentions as if they were nothing more than his due. Abigail had always hated that about him, but this night it seemed worse than usual. But if she was truthful, she realized, Walter wasn't acting any different. The difference was in her.

The realization left her feeling alone. She did not know how to go back to her old life—and of course she didn't want to. But with the way things were going, she didn't seem to be able to make her new life work. She seemed to be sitting on a precarious line between two worlds, belonging to neither. An aching sadness filled her.

Pews were stored and the pulpit was replaced by Hank Hall and his band of musicians. Refreshments were spread out on a long table, and just about every resident of the small town was in attendance. Everyone, it seemed, but Noah Blake. Disappointment surged, but then Abigail quickly chastised herself. She should be glad the boorish man was not there.

Walter's scowl evaporated the second they came to her family. "Mrs. Ashleigh, you look lovely this evening," he said, stepping away from Abigail to lightly take her stepmother's hand.

"Mr. Jackson," Virginia said simply.

"And Miss Emma. You're looking a picture of beauty as usual."

Emma raised her fan to her face and looked at him with a simpering smile. "Mr. Jackson, you know I'm a married woman, have been for six and a half years now."

"Of course, Mrs. Weston. And if your husband will indulge me, I hope he will allow me to dance with you this evening."

Emma's smile diminished somewhat. "I'm sure he won't mind."

Walter shook Sherwood's hand and they talked a few minutes about bank business before everyone settled down to enjoy the evening activities.

"Where's Adam, Virginia?" Abigail asked.

Virginia looked around. "Somewhere around here."

"Running wild," Emma added.

Virginia pursed her lips.

Pushing away from the table, Sherwood stood and said he was going to get some punch, but not ten feet away he was waylaid by the Widow Kent.

"Where's Grant?" Abigail asked, distracted, praying that Myrtle Kent wasn't telling tales out of school.

Emma's smile faltered before it grew harsh. "He's working."

"Tonight?"

"Yes, Abigail, tonight. He's a busy man with a great deal of work to do and can't just put everything aside to dance and sing."

Virginia and Abigail exchanged a subtle, curious glance before Abigail said, "I'm sure he's very busy. Maybe he'll be able to join us later."

Emma surveyed around the room, rolled her eyes, then looked back at Walter. "I guess you'll have to do. I want to dance."

Walter didn't bother to ask Abigail if it was all right. He simply smiled his delight, and ushered the younger Ashleigh daughter out onto the floor.

Virginia shook her head. "Are you all right?"

The ache and sadness began to dissolve, replaced by a slow burning anger. Abigail turned her gaze away from Walter and her sister, and looked at her stepmother. With effort she forced a smile. "Of course, I'm all right. I don't like dancing anyway." She glanced over at the refreshment table, where no one stood. All she wanted that second was to be alone. "I'm going to get some punch. Would you like some?"

Virginia studied her stepdaughter closely. "No, thank you," she said finally. "I'm going to say hello to Jane Thurgood."

No sooner had Abigail made it to the relative safety of the punch bowl than her father appeared at her side. And from the look on his face, it appeared she wasn't safe after all.

Noah strode up the front steps of the Methodist church, his hands deep in his pockets. A lazy lick of blond hair fell forward on his forehead. Hesitating at the doorway, he pushed the strands back before his fingers trailed down over his cheek and jaw. It had been years since he had shaved, and the nighttime air felt foreign on his skin.

He thought of Abby and wondered what her reaction

would be. A reluctant smile pulled at his lips when he thought about how she would react when she saw him. She would be intrigued first, then sure enough, embarrassment would scorch her cheeks. He shook his head. Such a waste of life, and he could no more imagine why she was the way she was than the man in the moon. Had Walter Jackson stifled the life in her? he wondered. Certainly the idiot didn't help matters, but he could hardly account for such deeply ingrained unease in the woman. And that bothered him. But then his smile melted into a hard line. Being bothered about Abigail Ashleigh was no different than being bothered by a pup left to drown. Nothing more. And if the woman wanted to be stiff and stuffy, who was he to say differently.

His thoughts were filled with the dichotomy of Abigail Ashleigh when he pulled open the door. Music and laughter washed over him, banishing his sudden, foreign disquiet. He stepped in unnoticed and stood back to survey the crowd. From the looks of the group, the evening should prove a gala event. He was just about to step away from the wall when a familiar voice met his ears followed immediately by one he did not recognize.

"What's going on over at that boardinghouse, missy?"

"Well, Father—"

"Don't you 'well, Father' me. I heard you ran off Elden Wineridge."

"But—"

"No buts, Abigail, it looks to me as though you don't know the first thing about running a boardinghouse. Just as I suspected, I might add. But being the giving man that I am, I gave you a chance. Against my better judgment, even against all of Walter's caterwauling over his injured pride. Good Lord, I've been getting it from all directions."

"But, Father—"

"Evenin'."

Abigail and Sherwood turned to the sound of the voice. For a moment she forgot her father. Her eyes opened wide as she took in the sight of Noah. Her hand came to her cheek. The dangerous mountain man was gone entirely. He stood beside her, his beard and mustache gone, and he was

dressed in a black frock coat over a fine white linen shirt
with a white satin cravat. Underneath the coat he wore
thigh-hugging gray trousers and a beautiful embroidered
blue waistcoat that matched the color of his eyes. His hair
was swept back from his forehead then fell to graze the top
of his collar. And suddenly the shimmery anger and aching
loneliness overwhelmed her. She wanted to look away. She
wanted to run free, escape the bickering and pretense of her
family. She wanted Noah Blake to step forward and offer
her one of his mischievous grins and make her laugh. God,
she wanted to laugh. But she said nothing, and it was Sherwood who finally spoke.

"Who are you?" her father demanded.

Noah eyed the older man with cool reserve. "Noah
Blake."

For the first time Abigail could remember, her father
looked disconcerted.

"You're Noah Blake?" he asked, his tone more suspi-
cious than disbelieving.

"None other."

Sherwood quickly recovered himself. "Well, sir, I'm
Sherwood Ashleigh, town banker. Pleased to make your ac-
quaintance."

"Then you must be Miss Ashleigh's father. Let me tell
you what a fine replacement you have chosen to take over
for Miss Penelope." He looked at Abigail with a countenance so angelic that he was nearly unrecognizable. "Miss
Ashleigh, I must extend my compliments once again on
that unbelievable roast you served last evening. Mmmm.
Such a cook as I have never seen."

Abigail blushed and looked out the window to the night
sky. "Thank you, Mr. Blake," she mumbled, her voice
strained.

Sherwood looked doubtful as he glanced between his
daughter and Noah Blake. "Fine meal, you say?"

Noah had actually never said "fine," Abigail realized, so
he hadn't actually lied.

"'Fine' does a poor job of conveying the extent of Miss
Ashleigh's culinary skills," Noah went on.

Abigail nearly groaned out loud. Indeed, "fine" did a *very* poor job of conveying the extent of her culinary skills, she thought ruefully to herself. But she couldn't help but fill with amusement over the look on her father's face.

"Hmmm," Sherwood murmured, seeming to consider.

"You seem surprised," Noah stated.

Incredulous was more like it, Abigail almost added.

Noah pulled back his shoulders. "You shouldn't be. Your daughter has an unmistakable flair in the kitchen. Some day you should let her show you her talents."

"Well, Abigail. I guess stranger things have happened. And as long as the boarders are pleased . . ." His sentence trailed off and he shrugged his shoulders. "In fact, Mr. Blake, I had planned to come by tomorrow and extend my welcome to our fine town. The mayor was just telling me about the huge success your last trapping expedition was. As I said, I'm the town banker and I'd be happy to look after your money."

Noah's countenance hardened. His amiable compliments about Abigail disappeared. "I'll keep that in mind," was his only response.

Sherwood shifted uncomfortably, clearly at a loss for how to proceed. Apparently determining not to press, he glanced at Abigail. His eyes narrowed. "I'll check in on you tomorrow to see how things are going."

Neither Abigail nor Noah spoke even after her father had departed. They stood at the refreshment table, neither aware of the ruckus all around.

He watched her take a deep breath then exhale sharply, her eyes locked on her father's retreating back.

"You overheard, didn't you?" she asked without turning back to look at him.

"A little."

Her breath came out with a snort. "I guess I owe you thanks once again."

"What for?" A devilish grin tilted on his lips. "I told him nothing more than the truth."

"Yes, you did a remarkable job of making me look good

without actually lying. 'Fine' certainly does do a poor job of describing my culinary skills."

Noah's smile broadened to reveal his straight white teeth.

"Atrocious, abominable, dreadful, non-existent might have done the job quite readily." Abigail raised her brow, glancing over the crowd without seeing. "Unless my charred roast was a bigger hit than I realized."

"I've always been partial to shoe leather," he said with a chuckle.

In spite of herself she laughed and shook her head. "You're impossible, Mr. Blake. You know that, don't you?"

"Of course, I do, Miss Ashleigh. But admit it. If I wasn't around to liven things up, your days would be awfully boring."

"My days are many things with you around," she said, her voice suddenly breathless, "but certainly boring isn't one of them."

"You wound me, deeply. Especially after you haven't even mentioned, much less complimented me on my clean-shaven face."

Her fingers found the top button of her dress. She hadn't turned back around to face him, didn't plan to either, until he was gone. He was massive and undoubtedly fine looking with his beard, even handsome enough that Abigail found herself doing silly things just by looking at him. But now— without the beard and mustache—she never would have imagined. Striking, breathtaking. Both sounded entirely too dramatic, but they were true. She didn't have to turn back to him to remember the strong chiseled jaw that had been unexpectedly revealed.

"I can't imagine why you ever grew a beard in the first place." She found herself saying the words she had been thinking out loud. And she cringed.

"Good looking, you think?" he teased boldly and took the few steps that separated them.

The aching that had receded back to manageable proportions resurfaced. Teasing, laughing—loving. What she would give to have those things in her life. She took a deep breath. She would be a fool to wish for something she could not have. And she was no fool. With that, Abigail pulled her shoulders back and turned, intent simply on ignoring his response and excusing herself.

"Mr. Blake! Miss Ashleigh! What a fine surprise it is to see you." Lou Smith joined the pair and smiled appreciatively as she took in Abigail. "And don't you look just the prettiest thing alive." Then she did a double take over the sight of Noah. She took a deep, awestruck breath. "Mr. Blake," she breathed. "You're beautiful, too!"

Noah laughed, the sound rumbling through the hall and down Abigail's spine.

"Why, thank you, sweetling. But I'm not half as pretty as you and Miss Ashleigh."

Lou reached out to take his hand. "You promised to dance with me."

"But what about Miss Ashleigh? We can't just leave her standing here all alone."

Lou looked pained. "Oh, no, never. She can dance with us, too."

Abigail blushed under Noah's intense stare. "No, no, the two of you dance. I was just leaving anyway."

Lou smiled her delight and hurried out onto the dance floor.

Noah hesitated. "I really did promise her a dance," he said as if perhaps she didn't believe him.

"I'm sure you did." And before she knew what she was saying, she surprised both of them by adding, "And I'll be watching. I'm sure it will prove amusing." Then before Noah could stop her, she turned and fled.

"What were you doing talking to that man?" Walter's words were low and seething, surprising Abigail with their vehemence.

Without thinking, she glanced back over her shoulder, though certainly it didn't take long to realize who he meant. "Noah Blake?"

"Oh, so it's Noah now."

"Good heavens, Walter," Abigail said in exasperation.

"No, it's not Noah, it is Mr. Blake . . . but why should I have to explain—"

"Well, don't tell me the young couple is fighting."

Abigail and Walter turned to find Sherwood not two feet away, a questioning tilt to his gray brow.

"Mr. Ashleigh," Walter enthused, his withering glare replaced by a dashing smile.

The change was so quick and unexpected that it left Abigail feeling disconcerted.

"Never, sir," Walter answered quickly. "Miss Abigail and I were only discussing that new fellow."

"Noah Blake?" Sherwood asked with a speculative glance at Abigail.

"Yes, sir, Noah Blake. And I can tell you I'm not too certain about the man." Walter took Abigail's hand possessively, his chest puffed out with importance.

Sherwood's eyes narrowed. "It doesn't matter what you think, Jackson."

Walter's puffed up chest deflated, and his mouth fell open.

"From all accounts, the man's got money. Money that should be in my bank."

Forcing a smile, Walter nodded his head. "Of course, sir. You are absolutely correct."

"Good. Now get on it right away." Then Sherwood seemed to reconsider. "No, don't bother. I'll see to it myself."

"But that's my job!"

"Your job is to do what I tell you, Walter, and don't you forget it."

Red seared the younger man's face. "Of course—" He started to say something, but was cut off when Sherwood turned away and went to the table where Virginia and Emma waited.

Instantly, Walter whirled around to face Abigail. "Now see what you've done!"

"Me?"

"Yes, you." His momentary kindness when her father was near fled. "If you hadn't gotten all involved with that boardinghouse business you wouldn't have made me look like a man who can't keep his betrothed happy and content with the life that I am going to provide her."

The selfishness of his accusation stunned her. But suddenly she found that she didn't care. She didn't care about Walter or Elden or her father. She had the crazy notion to laugh up to the heavens. She wanted to listen to the music and savor the evening. "Let's dance, Walter!"

Walter stammered and stuttered, but did not resist altogether when Abigail grabbed his hand and pulled him out onto the dance floor. They moved stiffly through the steps, Walter berating her whenever she stepped on his toes. But she only laughed and smiled and gracefully accepted his admonishments even when it was he who stepped on her.

Noah danced with Lou and before he could get away, every little girl in the place begged for a chance. He whirled them around and made them feel like princesses. And when he was done, he made the rounds, bellowing his good cheer and backslapping the men who had become his good friends. Everyone seemed to love him, the more outrageous his comments, the more they circled around him. He was full of extravagant compliments for the ladies, and teasing jokes for the men. And they all loved it.

But before the older contingent of ladies could start making demands on his dancing skills, he slipped into the nearest chair to give himself a well-deserved rest. The chair, as it happened, was right next to the Ashleighs' table.

Abigail's heart hammered, and she wondered if he would ask her to dance. Walter fumed. Sherwood smiled. And Emma forgot his indifference of a few days before and asked him to dance. Abigail's heart plummeted. She didn't stand a chance against her sister.

"Why, Mrs. Weston, I would love to. But this dance is promised to your lovely sister." He turned to Walter. "You don't mind do you, old boy?"

Walter stammered. "Well, I . . . I don't know . . ."

"Nonsense," Sherwood piped in. "Walter doesn't mind a bit."

Walter barely suppressed his anger with a tight grin. "Of

course not, Mr. Blake. I don't mind if you dance with *my* Abigail." His emphasis on *my* made everyone at the table look at him curiously.

Only Noah paid him no mind. He pulled Abigail from her chair and led her onto the dance floor.

"Didn't your papa teach you not to lie, Mr. Blake?"

Noah laughed, remembering he had asked her the very same question when first they met. "When did I lie?"

"I never told you I'd dance with you."

"Oh that," he said, dismissing the untruth with a shrug. "I had to say something to avoid the clutches of that she-wolf sitting at your table."

Shock made her gasp and it was all she could do not to laugh. "Mr. Blake, really. That's my sister you're speaking of."

He looked at her closely, his blue eyes growing dark. "Unlucky you." Then his smile returned. "Anyway, you told me my dancing was sure to amuse you. My male pride demanded that I prove you wrong."

His eyes flickered with devilment and before she knew what he was doing, he pulled her into his arms and spun her around in a series of twirls. Surprise made her laugh and her laughter floated up to the rafters. She couldn't remember a time when she'd had so much fun—felt so free and alive. But just at the end of the twirls, when her mind finally had the chance to catch up and tell her she was doing something she had no business doing, she tripped. But Noah was there. He absorbed her gracelessness by pulling her so close that anyone watching, and there were quite a few who were, couldn't tell.

They looked into each other's eyes, everything around them forgotten—for the moment. They went to a place where they had never been before—a place replete with both tranquillity and heart-stopping excitement. It felt so right to be in each other's arms, and peace washed over them—as if finally they had come home. But at the same time, it was as if their hearts pounded some primordial beat, as old as time. Peace and desire. Wholeness and wanting. At length, he loosened his hold and looked down into her eyes. Seconds passed before they became aware of the ruckus that ran through the crowd.

Millie McAllister had entered, clad in a red velvet gown, low cut, with a fitted bodice, tight-waisted, and hiked up to reveal an indecent amount of ankle.

Abigail, along with every other woman in the place, scowled. Noah merely shook his head and smiled. "Millie," he said with a chuckle.

"I'd say your choice of . . . friends is telling."

Noah laughed in response. "I'd say your choice isn't much better."

They both glanced toward the table where her family sat.

"If you are referring to Walter, he is a fine, upstanding man."

"He's an uptight bore, Abigail Ashleigh, and you deserve better."

His words disconcerted her, expressed the very idea that had begun to creep into her mind. Her good humor vanished. "If I want advice," she snapped, "I'll ask for it. Until that time I'll thank you to keep your ill-formed opinions to yourself."

"You're angry because you know I'm right."

He pulled her so close she could feel his hard muscles pressed against her. "I'm angry, Mr. Blake, because you're about to snap my torso in two. Get your big mangy paws off me!"

He released her so quickly she nearly fell. Steadying her, he grumbled. "You are the orneriest and most pig-headed woman I have ever met. And now I'm inclined to rethink my initial opinion and conclude that you and Walter Jackson deserve each other."

Without waiting for her to respond, he steered her back to the table then turned on his heel to walk away. He hadn't taken more than a few steps, however, when he heard a voice so similar to Abigail's but so very different for its anger and animosity.

"You're acting like a schoolgirl, Abigail, making a fool of yourself over that man. Blushing and carrying on on the dance floor like you were nineteen instead of twenty-nine. My word, what a sight."

He heard Abigail's pained gasp, but when he turned around, against his better judgment, to defend her, he was stopped and further enraged when her father, ignoring the younger daughter's hateful words, said, "Since you apparently are quite the cook, Abigail, why don't we have Sunday supper at the boardinghouse tomorrow evening. Then you can impress us all with your culinary talents. Maybe then I can put my mind at ease that the other reports I have received are unfounded."

Emma smiled into her fan, then turned away.

Abigail glanced between her sister and her father, her look of embarrassment and pain quickly turning to panic. Instantly, Noah forgot his anger in the face of what he knew would be a disaster if indeed Abigail was forced to cook for her family. Her eyes suddenly found his and they seared him with accusation.

"Damn!" he cursed under his breath. "What the hell am I going to do now?"

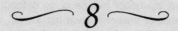

8

"WHAT'S ALL THAT NOISE?"

Noah glanced down the street toward the boardinghouse. "I don't know, but I suspect we're about to find out."

Millie came to an abrupt halt, pulling on Noah's arm. "I don't know about this. I'm not so sure this is such a good idea."

"Of course it is. She needs the help. And you said you wanted to meet her," Noah pointed out.

Millie grumbled. "Well, I guess you're right. Besides I owe you one after you took care of old Riley Tucker."

With a shake of his head, Noah took Millie's arm and forced her to look at him. "You don't owe me anything, you understand. No one deserves to be treated the way Tucker treated you. You deserve more than you're getting out of life."

Unexpected tears sprang into her eyes before she quickly dashed them away. "Thank you for that."

"I'm serious, Millie. You shouldn't be living above the Red Dog."

"And where do you propose I live?"

"Now that Elden's moved out there's a vacant room at the boardinghouse."

"I can't live there," she responded quickly.

"Why not?"

"Don't be dense! You know as well as I do decent folk won't have a thing to do with me." She looked away. "And even if I could move in there, how do you suppose I would pay the rent."

"You could get a decent job."

"Doing what?" she shot back.

"Tending store, doing wash, there have got to be plenty of things a woman can do around here."

Millie shook her head. "You've been living up in the mountains too long, Noah. Even if there was a job I could do, not a single respectable person in town would hire me. Face it, I'm a soiled dove and the whole town knows it."

Anger rolled over Noah. "Then I'll pay for your room and board."

Millie sighed and a soft smile lightened her face. "You're a good man, Noah Blake. But I can't let you pay my way. I've got to make it on my own. You're not going to be around forever. Besides, I'm saving my money. I have plans."

"Plans? What kind of plans?"

"I'm not ready to tell anyone yet, including you." She hesitated. "But when I am I might take you up on your offer of help. I suppose I'll have to leave El Paso when I'm ready to start a new life. And I'll need help to do it."

"Where will you go?"

Uncertainty flashed through her eyes. "I don't know yet."

"Well, let me know. Anything you want. Just say the word."

Millie reached out and squeezed his arm. "You're going to make some lucky girl a fine husband one day."

Noah grunted. "Not on your life, woman. Marriage isn't for me," he said with conviction before they continued down the road.

The noise only got louder as they approached the boardinghouse, confirming Noah's suspicions. Someone was banging pots and pans, and slamming cabinets with enough force to wake the dead. Abigail, it appeared, was angrier about her predicament than he realized.

Once inside the house, Noah and Millie came to a dead stop in the doorway of the kitchen at the sight that greeted them. The fire in the stove was hot enough to melt metal, and flour filled the heat-scorched air. Abigail stood at the counter, her hair wilder than Medusa's, beating within an inch of its life a mound of what Noah could best determine was supposed to be dough. Her face was marred with a scowl so fierce that Millie took a step back toward the front door. Egg yolk splattered Abigail's apron and chicken feathers fanned out from the soles of her shoes. She was not a pretty sight, Noah conceded, but endearing, so endearing in fact that he had the crazy notion to take her in his arms and kiss the flour right off her nose.

The thought surprised him, and didn't make him a bit happy. But then he conceded that just like his concern for Millie, his concern for Abigail was parental as well. Somehow the thought didn't ring true, but he disregarded it altogether and chalked his churning stomach up to heartburn and his pounding heart to getting on in years—despite the fact that he was only thirty-five years old.

Abigail finally noticed she had company and turned on Noah with all the rage of the virago she resembled.

"YOU!" she cried and slammed a pot down with a resounding bang.

Noah's eyes opened wide and Millie stepped farther back into the hallway, well out of sight.

"How dare you show your face in this kitchen after the mess you have gotten me into!"

"Good morning to you, too, Miss Abigail," Noah stated with a smile, stepping forward.

"Don't you good morning me, you . . . you . . . oversized . . . troublemaker."

"Now, Abby, I was only trying to help."

"Help!" Abigail screeched. " 'Miss Ashleigh,' " Abigail mimicked in a voice surprisingly reminiscent of his, " 'let me tell you again what an unbelievable roast you served last evening.' Your *help* landed me in the unenviable position of having to perform the very task that I have so abysmally performed for the last week. I ran Elden Wineridge off with my 'fine' abilities. Now I have to prove to my father that I am indeed capable of doing the very things I am so very incapable of doing. I had hoped I would at least have the chance to learn. A few days. Maybe a couple of weeks. That's all. Then my father could have come over and seen for himself what a good job I am doing. But no," she cried, banging yet another pan. "You had to go and ruin it for me!"

Like a mad woman she threw back her head and laughed, and Noah wondered for a second if he should call the doctor.

"But you're probably only too pleased about this turn of events. By this evening, I'll be finished and forced to move home." Her voice caught and her lip wavered.

Noah took a step forward and just about reached out to her when Millie bustled into the room. "Miss Ashleigh, no one is going to make you move home," Millie stated with conviction. "I'll be happy to help you. We'll cook and clean, and no one but you and me and," she glanced at Noah, her look scathing, "this oversized troublemaker will have to know."

Abigail's eyes opened with surprise and what Noah thought for a moment was delight. "Millie!" she gasped. But no sooner had her delight appeared than it was gone and her lips set in a firm line. "Why thank you, Miss . . . McAllister, isn't it. Your offer is most generous, but I couldn't allow . . . accept . . . really I . . ." her voice trailed off. Abigail watched as the sweet generous look in the woman's beautiful blue eyes filled with pain, then went blank. After all the years of being ostracized and ridiculed by her family, Abigail couldn't believe she had done the very same thing to another—no matter who or what she was. She thought about the woman's reputation and she cringed at the ruckus that would be caused if her father or Walter were to show up unexpectedly. But then she looked again at Millie's closed expression. And before she could think better of it, she said, "Really, I would be most appreciative if you could help me out of this predicament I find myself in." She finished with a quick glare at Noah.

Millie's face filled with uncertainty, but when Abigail offered the woman a smile of friendship, her face melted with a smile of her own. "Where should I start?" she asked, pulling her gloves from her hands.

Abigail glanced around the kitchen and shrugged apologetically. "I'm not sure exactly."

"Millie, you start in the parlor," Noah stated, quickly taking charge. "Abigail, you start by making the beds." He glanced around the kitchen. "I'll cook."

"You?" the women said in unison.

A smile sliced across Noah's lips and he nodded his head. "Yes, me, my fair ladies. And it will be a meal your father will not soon forget," he said, rubbing his hands together.

"This should prove interesting," Millie laughed as she picked up the cleaning implements that sat in the corner and headed for the parlor.

Abigail stood dumbfounded, uncertain what she should do. The boardinghouse was a disaster, her family would be there that evening, and she had a woman of lesser reputation cleaning her parlor and a mountain man cooking her meal. All she could think to do was thank her lucky stars.

"You'd best get a move on, woman."

Noah's voice boomed through the kitchen and before Abigail could think, much less respond, he swatted her on the rear, bringing a surge of embarrassment so fierce to her cheeks that she did nothing more than sputter, then turn and flee to the upper regions of the house.

Abigail was wrestling with a cotton blanket forty-five minutes later when Millie stuck her head in.

"Miss Ashleigh, I've run out of soap and can't seem to find any more."

"Soap?" Abigail considered. "I don't think there is any more."

Millie eyed the rumpled bed. "You say your family is coming over this evening and you're trying to impress them?"

Abigail followed her gaze. "Not very impressive, right?"

Millie patted Abigail's arm. "Why don't you run over to the mercantile and get some soap. I'll finish up in here."

"Oh, I couldn't let you do that."

"Sure you can." Millie smiled. "Think about your family."

Abigail sighed. "One day I'll repay you for this kindness."

Millie waved the words away. "Go on. Get the soap."

Abigail returned with the soap to find Millie, already finished with the upstairs, vigorously scrubbing the dining room floor.

"Oh, heavens, let me help." Abigail took an extra brush and sank down beside Millie. "I'm embarrassed that you're doing this."

"Don't be silly, Miss Ashleigh."

Abigail's glance caught Millie's. After an awkward smile Abigail looked away, followed Millie's lead, and attacked the floor with a good deal of energy.

The women worked in silence, the only sound coming from the scrubbing of the floor and the sweet melody marked by an occasional curse coming from the kitchen.

"I hope he knows what he's doing," Abigail said.

Millie laughed, a free open pleasant sound. "I suspect he does. That man knows just about everything there is to know about survival."

"You must have known him for a long time."

"Couple years is all. Met him in Santa Fe two years back. He told me El Paso was a growing town, told me to come this way. I did. Here I am."

Abigail felt as though a knife had been thrust into her heart. Noah Blake obviously cared for Millie a great deal. Though why she should care, she admonished herself, she had no idea.

"Well now," Millie said, pushing back on her heels. "Looks like this floor is as clean as it's going to get. Why don't we start on the windows."

"Windows?" Abigail asked with surprise.

Millie studied Abigail closely, then reached over and touched her. "Don't you worry. You'll learn. It just takes time."

Abigail looked down at the slender hand on her arm. The touch and the obvious sentiment of friendship and caring behind it were so unaccustomed to her that she could only stare. Not knowing what to say, Abigail forced a smile and simply said thank you.

"Well, daughter, I have to admit, I was skeptical."

Sherwood Ashleigh leaned back in the chair at the head of the table. Virginia sat to his right, Walter to his left. Emma sat between Walter and Grant. Adam sat next to his mother, with a vacant chair next to him that Sherwood had motioned for Abigail to take. He insisted that Noah take the foot of the table.

Noah, however, had insisted otherwise. He practically forced Abigail into the seat at the foot, while Sherwood could do nothing more than silently take Noah's measure. In the end, Sherwood had laughed and said he liked a man with convictions as Noah took the chair next to Adam who had to scoot over as far as possible to make enough room.

"Like I said," Sherwood repeated. "I didn't believe you could do it. Granted, I've had better mashed potatoes. And the roast was a little on the dry side. But all in all, it was better than I expected."

Abigail choked.

Noah straightened in his chair and his brow furrowed. "I can't say that I've ever had a finer meal, Mr. Ashleigh. Done to perfection, I think I'd say."

Abigail's choke turned to a spurt of laughter quickly cut off at the thought of what might happen if her father found out she hadn't cooked the meal after all.

"I think it's a fine meal, as well, Mr. Blake," Virginia added, turning to Abigail. "You have done a wonderful job with the boardinghouse just as I knew you would. Everything looks wonderful."

"I don't know what all the fuss is about," Emma said, her voice impatient. "How hard could it possibly be to cook a roast, mash potatoes, cut up green beans, and butter bread. She didn't even make rolls."

"It takes a fine turn of the hand to make a light loaf of bread," Noah stated, clearly disgruntled.

"Mr. Blake, there is no need to defend Abigail. We are all well aware of what she can—and cannot do," Sherwood said, leaning back in his chair and studying his eldest daughter.

Abigail looked down at her hands, but not before catching sight of Noah's disgruntlement changing to something else. Anger, disbelief? She wasn't sure.

Adam stepped into the sudden, uncomfortable silence. "This house is great!" the six-year-old enthused. "It has a cow and chickens and all kinds of things! Father, can we get a cow?"

"A cow!" Sherwood scoffed. "You don't need a cow, boy. Hell, I've given you just about everything else. Now you want a cow."

"Not for me," Adam stated. "For all of us. Father," he added, his eyes round with amazement. "Cows squirt out milk! Just think of the money we could save if we got our milk for free!"

"You calling me cheap, boy!"

Adam sat back at the sharp tone.

"Sherwood," Virginia snapped, placing a gentle hand on her son's shoulder.

Noah watched the proceeding with something close to amazement written clearly across his face. Grant shook his head then pushed up from his seat and exited the small dining room without a word.

The night air swept over Grant when he stepped out the back door, and with it came relief. Anger and frustration seemed his constant companions, as they had for nearly all of the last six and a half years—for nearly all of his marriage to Emma. He shook his head and tried to hold back the thought that his marriage was a mistake. And he tried to hold back the sweet memories of another. Corinne. The name floated through his mind like a piece of silk on a gentle breeze. Corinne. Silky brown hair and soft brown eyes. He had loved her with all his heart. He still loved her—for all the good it did him. She had left him, obviously not returning his love. Though deep in his soul he could not bring himself to believe she had not. Not with the way she had given herself to him—so tentative but loving—so scared but giving.

The memory of her touch was seared on his mind. The day he first met her was carved in his heart. He had been in El Paso for a week when he saw her—in the distance—lovely beyond words. And he had known then and there that he wanted to spend the rest of his life with her. They had been so happy for six glorious months, and then seven years ago, she disappeared—fled—and no matter how he tried to find her, he was unsuccessful. It was as if she had vanished from the face of the earth.

And then came Emma—appearing at his side when he wanted nothing but to be left alone, persisting in her attention until he gave in and sought refuge in her arms, convincing him that marriage to her was the answer. And it had been for a few months. And then everything had begun to change. He still wasn't sure why. Was it that he could not banish Corinne from his mind? It was easy to blame himself, but he did not think it was that simple. Emma had known of his love for Corinne, and had wanted him anyway. Emma had changed, not him, as if once she had him, she no longer wanted him.

A sound snapped him out of his reverie, and he found he had walked to the edge of the river. The swirls and eddies mesmerized him. The dark depths seemed welcoming.

"What do you see?"

The voice startled him and he turned. She was a little thing with haphazardly braided hair, not much older than Adam.

"Did you lose something in the water?" she asked when he would have ignored her.

He looked back at the river, his thoughts far away. "In the water? No," he said, before suddenly remembering himself. He turned back to her sharply. "Go home, little girl. You shouldn't be out here at night. It's not safe."

"How kind you are to think of my safety," she said with a radiant smile into the moonlight. "And if you'd like, I will help you search for what you have lost."

Grant sighed. "I haven't lost anything, little girl."

"Oh, how very impolite of me. My name is Lou."

He turned slightly and shook his head. "All right, Lou. You need to get home."

With that Lou offered him a tremendous smile then skipped off into the dark, a haunting tune drifting back to him. Grant watched her go, staring into the darkness until the night gave way and suddenly Emma appeared.

"There you are!" she snapped.

Grant turned away.

"Don't you ignore me, Grant Weston. How dare you just get up from the table like that and leave. How are you ever going to please Father acting that way?"

"I'll never please your father, Emma. I'd think you would know that by now."

"Only because you don't try."

"You mean, only because I don't bow and scrape to his every whim."

"The least you could do is go to work for him."

"No, Emma! We've been over this."

"That's right! We have! And every time you fail to be reasonable. You're being selfish. You don't care how I feel. You only care about those damn horses of yours. You don't love me anymore."

His body tensed. "Emma, that's not true—"

"It is! And you know it. When was the last time you said I was beautiful?"

Grant was silent. She didn't ask him how long ago he had said he loved her or kissed her or hugged her. No, he thought bitterly, she only wanted to know about her beauty.

"See!" she hissed. "It's been so long ago you can't remember. And don't think I don't know why. You blame me because I haven't gotten . . . with child."

Pressing his eyes closed, he sighed. At length, he turned back to his wife and pulled her close. "It's not your fault, Emma. I don't blame you." He pressed a kiss to the top of her head. "And we'll have children yet."

Her stiff body melted against his. "Tell me I'm pretty, Grant," she whispered.

"Of course you are."

They stood under the stars, reminiscent of years long past.

"You do want children, don't you, Emma?"

Emma hesitated. "Well, certainly. Every woman wants children." She reached up and ran her finger down his chest, a smile curving on her rosebud lips. "Did I tell you I saw the most beautiful hat yesterday. Why not a soul in town has one so striking. And it looked absolutely stunning on me."

Grant tensed, but didn't step away. "We're saving to buy a house, Emma, you know that. We can't afford to buy you a new hat."

"I never get to have anything because of some dream of a new house," she spat.

Casting a quick glance over a dress he had never seen before, one her father undoubtedly had paid for, he didn't contradict her.

"And a dream it is," she continued. "I will not live in a hovel, Grant Weston. And with the kind of money you make shoeing horses it's only a hovel we can afford."

Grant finally stepped away, his anger and frustration quickly returning. "I think it's best if we return to the others."

When she resisted, he took her arm in a firm grip and led her back down the sandy path toward the boardinghouse.

The family was gathered on the front porch when Grant and Emma returned.

Emma forced a smile. "Such a lovely evening. We've just had the most delightful walk. Isn't that right, dear?"

Without answering, Grant tipped his hat to Abigail. "Thank you for the wonderful meal, Abigail. Now if ya'll will excuse me, I have work to finish up at the barn."

"Work!" Emma glanced quickly at her father, then smiled. "Don't work too hard, Grant. I'll wait up for you."

Grant didn't look back, he simply walked off into the darkness.

Sherwood grumbled, but it was Virginia who spoke. "Thank you again, Abigail, for a lovely evening."

The family started down the front steps, leaving Abigail and Noah at the door. Walter hung back.

"Such a beautiful night shouldn't go to waste," Walter said.

Noah scowled. But Abigail did not notice. She was exhilarated over her father's praise, lukewarm as it was. Nothing could dampen her mood.

"Why don't we go for a stroll," Walter added. His mood was tentative, he was not his usual authoritative, insensitive self.

Abigail studied him for a moment. "I think that's a lovely idea." She came to the top of the steps, then hesitated. She looked back at Noah and started to speak, to offer some type of thanks for his help, but before words came, he stood, then slammed through the front door. The abrupt departure darkened her mood, but only for a moment, before she and Walter walked out into the moonlit night.

Neither spoke as they made their way across the road and into the plaza. Cicadas called in the darkness.

"I see you're taking this boardinghouse business more seriously than I had realized."

Walter's stiff though quietly spoken words surprised Abigail. "It means a lot to me, Walter."

"Yes," he replied, clasping his hands behind his back as they traversed the hard-packed dirt path toward the thick vein of the Rio Grande. "I see it does. And I admit I didn't think you could do it. But after this night's meal, and from the looks of the house, you seemed to be doing better than I thought."

Thankfully, the semi-darkness hid her blush of guilt. The same part of her demanded she confess, that she not live such a lie. But the other part of her, obviously the insane part, convinced her to hold her tongue. The taste of success was too sweet to destroy—besides, she reasoned, she had every intention of learning to do everything that had been done for her this day.

"Your father told me of his plans to give the boardinghouse to . . . you . . . if you do a good job." Walter's voice took on a professorial tone of knowing. "And after seeing how you managed the property this evening," he hesitated as if searching for just the right words, "I'm inclined to reevaluate my original assessment of the situation."

Abigail tensed.

"I have come to the conclusion," he continued, "that indeed you should continue on at the boardinghouse. It could bring us significant dollars. That is if costs are kept to a minimum and repairs aren't needed, or at least aren't needed too frequently. I'll need to have a look at your books to be certain, but I can't imagine that there are a great many expenses associated with this place."

Common sense told her she should be happy. She was getting exactly what she wanted—to do something purposeful and to have a family and children of her own. Here it was. But the way Walter spoke made her angry.

"I think it's time I get home, Walter."

Walter stopped and studied her closely. "Is anything wrong?"

"No," she offered with a lame smile. "It's just that I have an awful lot of work still to do before I retire this evening."

"Yes. Yes, I suppose you do."

They turned back toward the house, Walter taking her elbow. When they reached the front porch, Noah was once again sitting in one of the wickerwork chairs, smoking his pipe. Walter suddenly grew gruff and uncomfortable.

"Good night, Walter," Abigail said, when he did not immediately leave.

"Well, goodnight then."

Abigail and Noah watched Walter retreat in the distance.

"What happened to your good cheer and confident smiles?" Noah asked quietly.

Her snort of self-deprecating laughter floated off on a gentle breeze. "My unwarranted good cheer and undeserved confidence, you mean?"

"What did old Walter say now?"

"Nothing."

"Why do I find that hard to believe?"

Abigail didn't respond.

Noah puffed on his pipe, the smoke drifting out to wrap around her. Moments ticked by until finally Abigail turned to him. "Please send Millie my thanks."

"What about my part in all this?" Noah teased softly.

"Your part?" She looked at him with a reluctant smile. "You mean the roast that was a little dry, and the mashed potatoes that could have been better? That part?"

Noah puffed up and became indignant all over again. "That was the best damned roast your father has ever tasted."

"Don't curse, Mr. Blake," she snapped. "And good or not, if it hadn't been for you I never would have been in this mess in the first place." No sooner did she speak the harsh words than she cringed. "I sound like an ungrateful shrew."

His own good humor revived. "Ungrateful, without a doubt," he said with a chuckle. "But a shrew . . . oh all right, that too."

Abigail gasped then huffed her laughter. "I guess I deserved that," she conceded.

The breeze caught one of the many wayward strands of Abigail's hair. Without thinking, Noah reached out and pushed the strand back behind her ear. "You don't deserve that at all, Abby."

Her breath caught in her throat and it took great effort to speak. "I really shouldn't let you call me that."

"What, a shrew?"

"No, Abby. And you know it."

"Yes, so you've told me, at least a dozen times." His strong fingers lingered on the very edge of her ear. His countenance darkened. "Damn, there is so much life you are missing out on . . . like laughter and . . . kisses." His eyes found her lips.

Her pulse fluttered in her throat. "Who's to say I've been missing out on . . . those."

Noah chuckled, casting a quick knowing glance over at the darkness through which Walter and her family had disappeared. "I am," he said as he looked back at her.

Red surged through her cheeks. "Well, you're wrong, Mr. Blake. I've had lots of laughter in my life."

"After spending an evening with your family I'm inclined not to believe you. And kisses? From Walter?" Noah shook his head. His forefinger trailed down her cheek to the very edge of her lips. "I don't believe that either."

Her blush intensified, but her chin came up. "Of course I've been kissed," she stated defiantly, her heart hammering in her chest. "And let me tell you it's not all it's cracked up to be."

Noah shook his head. "Then you need to be kissed by someone who knows how."

Before she could respond to his outrageous presumption, Noah drew her close. Abigail could only watch, torn between desperately wanting to feel his lips on hers, and knowing she should slap his face for such impertinence. He hesitated as if giving her a chance to perform the very task she knew she should, and when she didn't, he leaned over and pressed his lips to hers.

Her world swirled and collided. The touch was heaven—everything and more she had dreamed it would be. And, yes, she realized, she *had* dreamed of this, this very kiss, with this very man. Lord, and how she savored it. Firm yet gentle. And she only wanted more.

She leaned into him and her hands came up to his shoulders. At first he tensed, but then he pulled her to him so close that it nearly took her breath away. He groaned her name and the kiss grew heated, his mouth slanting over hers, their bodies molding together like two halves of a whole.

In some clouded depths of her mind, Abigail realized that she was on the path that could easily show her where his kisses would lead. Her body yearned to know. But then the murky depths began to clear and the image of Millie McAllister came to mind. Millie knew where kisses led. And she was a fallen woman. She was not allowed in decent homes. All because she knew a man's touch. Just as Abigail was longing to know—with this man of all people. Good heavens what was wrong with her?

With that, sanity filled her mind in a blinding rush. Abigail jerked free from his grasp. Mortification filled her. With the back of her hand she wiped her mouth with disgust. Her breath came short and quick and her eyes narrowed with anger. "And you expect me to believe you know how?"

Surprise washed over Noah's face before he threw back his head and laughed. "A challenge, Miss Ashleigh?" he asked, one slash of dark blond brow tilted. But when his hand shot out to pull her back, to meet her challenge, she stepped aside then dashed into the safety of the house.

He chuckled aloud and shook his head. "That woman needs to loosen up—break free from those damned imaginary chains of propriety." But then his chuckle trailed off and his lips faltered to a hard line as suddenly he wondered if that was all he wanted, if all he wanted was to steal a few kisses and show her how to live. Or did he want more? He scoffed at this. Of course he only wanted to set her free, to help her. But as the image of her came to mind, such a mixture of wildness and propriety, he told himself he should steer clear of Miss Abigail Ashleigh. Let someone else set her free.

9

THE FOLLOWING MORNING, ABIGAIL WOKE WITH ALL the excitement of a horsefly stuck in ointment. Heavens have mercy, how could she have let that man kiss her!

Staring up at the ceiling, she pressed her fisted hands over her ears as if she could block out the voice that repeated itself over and over again, the voice that whispered that she had done more than simply let the man kiss her— she had engaged willingly and had wanted more!

Good Lord, how many times did she have to remind herself that the man was a beast! An uncouth heathen! He in no way resembled anything safe and proper. Unlike Walter who was the picture of propriety, who didn't drink, who was safe and had stable employment. She could no more imagine what Noah Blake did during his days than she could imagine what went on behind the swinging doors of the Red Dog Saloon. Drinking, no doubt, she concluded, her brow wrinkled with disgust. Singing, probably. Without realizing it, her brow softened. And dancing. With Noah Blake. Holding her in his arms. The insidious thought of Noah's devastating good looks and abundant charm sliced their way right into her brain. But then she got a hold of herself, her brow furrowing once again, and she chastised herself for such insanity. Good looks and outrageous charm do not a good man make. The man was a nightmare. He was the first to notice a pretty face, and her initial encounter with the man had been when he was coming out of a saloon, a notorious saloon at that.

And that kiss. Mercy! No respectable woman would put up with a kiss like that! Granted, she had nothing to compare it to, the fact that she had lied about her experience, or lack thereof, didn't even cause her to flinch, but instinct told her that that was the kind of kiss that led really quickly to places a decent woman had no business going. Yes, indeed, the man was obviously a fiend!

But then the issue that had plagued her dreams even more than the kiss forced itself to the forefront of her mind. His words. She could hold them at bay no longer. *There's so much life you're missing out on.* Just as she had suspected for the last several weeks, there truly was more to life than she was living. If nothing else, Noah's kiss had convinced her of that.

With a jerk, she turned her head, pressing her cheek into the pillow. Why did Noah Blake have to come into her life? It was hard enough just dealing with the thought that she wanted more to *do* in her life. But now to have to face the kind of future that didn't hold kisses such as the one she received last evening was next to impossible to face. She cringed at the thought of what that said about her morals— that she was indecent, not respectable. But even that knowledge couldn't change the way she felt, because she knew like she knew her own name that the kiss had been filled with passion and desire—the kind of things Noah Blake was filled with—the kind of things that simmered beneath her surface, but married to someone like Walter, would have to stay buried as long as she lived.

The thought made her angry, not at Walter, rather at Noah for showing her her true nature, then showing her what she couldn't have. With a sudden burst of energy and a few choice curse words aimed at her nemesis, she threw back the covers and leaped out of bed. Work. That's what she needed. And lots of it.

"The eggs!" she cried, only just then remembering. With a quickness that would have made a racehorse proud, Abigail dressed and readied herself for the day. She snatched up her skirts and flew out the back door just as Lou and Gertrude came around the corner.

"Forgot, huh," Lou stated simply.

Abigail tilted her head. "Maybe just a little. But it won't take long."

Lou plopped down on the bottom of the ramp and made herself comfortable, making it clear how quick she thought Abigail would be.

As Abigail made her way into the confines of the hen-house, Lou started in on a description of all her friends, a whole assortment of people, some of whom Abigail knew, others whom she had never heard of.

"Maybe one day you can come with me to talk to the man who walks crooked," Lou called thoughtfully up the ramp. "He would like it very much. He does not get to go out much."

Lou rambled on without prompting. "And you must meet my dog. Happy Claudius. He didn't used to be my dog. But now he is. You would like him." She laughed and shook her head. "And of course you know the Widow Kent. I do so love the beautiful jars filled with jellied fruits." Lou shook her head. "She is so very unhappy. That is why she is so mean to little girls. I make sure I tell all the little girls hereabouts not to take it personal like. Otherwise I am so afraid they would have their feelings hurt."

Who is this child? Abigail suddenly wondered, much as she had the day of their first meeting. So smart yet sensitive to a world that forgets that children are smart and sensitive.

"Since the mama and I have moved here I have met Doc-tor Peters," she continued. "And Sheriff Dickens, and Mable Roddenheizer. Such a long name she has. I like it very much. Mable Roddenheizer," she repeated as if feeling the word roll around on her tongue. "And of course there is Miss Millie—the most beautiful woman hereabouts. Often-times she lets me sit in her parlor and look at all her pretty things. Feathers all tied up to wrap around her neck—so soft. She makes me feel so very happy. And all the men do love her so."

Abigail's eyes opened wide with astonishment. She still held the basket in her hand and looked on speechlessly at this itemization of the town citizenry.

At length, Abigail set the basket aside and sat down next

to Lou. "Sometime I would like to come along with you and meet your friends. They all sound very nice."

Swiveling around, Lou's eyes widened with delight. "Do you think you could?"

"Of course, Lou. And perhaps one day I could meet your mother as well."

Instantly, the child's face darkened. She seemed as though she had no idea what to say. And so she didn't say anything, simply jumped up from the ramp, grabbed the basket of eggs, called Gertrude, and started away.

The sun was up by this time and the day was well on its way for most inhabitants of the area, but not for someone like Emma Ashleigh Weston who just then appeared around the corner of the house when Lou was trying to make her exit. Both Lou and Emma stopped dead in their tracks at the sight of one another. Emma's flawless face grew angry and her rosebud mouth opened to speak. But Lou wasn't interested in finding out what was about to be said as she dashed around Emma's flowing skirts and hurried out to the rapidly filling streets.

"Why don't you like Lou?" Abigail demanded.

Emma's mouth hung open as if the words she was about to speak were left waiting to be spoken. With effort, she snapped her mouth shut, seemed to gather her composure, then said, "Never mind, dear sister. I just wondered what such a child was doing here at this hour, or any other hour for that matter."

"She takes the eggs for me."

"Takes eggs?" Emma asked. "Where in heaven's name does she take them?"

"Around town."

A slight grimace marred Emma's face as she suddenly noticed Abigail's attire. "You're a mess."

"Thank you."

Emma scowled. "I tell you only for your own good. I'd think you'd appreciate my sisterly concern. But alas, I am forever unappreciated."

It was all Abigail could do to keep from saying that Emma did nothing to be appreciated for. And of course, then she felt guilty for thinking such things about her sister. "Of course I appreciate the things you do for me."

"Well, anyway, I thought it would be nice to come have a cup of tea with you," Emma said.

"At this hour?" Abigail asked, surprise making her normally circumspect tongue lax.

Emma stiffened. "Why not at this hour?"

"Well," Abigail shrugged. "I have Alberta to deal with and the chickens to feed and beds to make . . ."

"Why you are doing this is beyond me, and if truth be known that is exactly the reason I came over this morning." Emma smoothed her skirt. "Really Abigail, you're making a fool of yourself, and as your devoted sister I cannot sit by and let it happen. People are beginning to talk."

"Let them," Abigail said, surprising herself as much as Emma.

"Abigail! Really! How can you say such a thing? It was bad enough when you insisted that you take over this boardinghouse, but then to make such a fool of yourself over that Noah Blake is too much. And a ruder man I have never met. He has barely offered me more than a simple hello. Both you and father are fawning over that man. It's enough to embarrass a person to the depths!"

"All I did was dance with him!"

"And you didn't want more?" she asked with a slyly raised eyebrow.

If Emma had walked into the yard stark naked she couldn't have shocked Abigail more than she did by uttering such a statement. "Emma!"

The raised eyebrow softened and Emma smiled. "Oh, admit it, Abigail. You're twenty-nine years old and have never . . . been with a man. And you find someone like that big brute, Noah Blake, well . . ." Emma shrugged her delicate shoulders. "While I wouldn't give the man the time of day, mind you, I can see how someone as ungainly as you might find such brute strength appealing."

With mouth agape Abigail couldn't imagine how she could possibly continue such an outrageous, and blatantly improper, conversation with her sister. Fortunately, or perhaps unfortunately, Abigail was inclined to think, Emma merely continued.

"Well, let me tell you, the more . . . carnal aspects of life are not all they are cracked up to be. It's certainly not worth embarrassing your family, and of course yourself, over such a messy and painful affair. I would avoid it at all costs."

Abigail suddenly felt she understood the tension that was more than evident in her sister's marriage, but that was none of her business—just as her life was none of Emma's business.

"So stop drooling over that man," Emma continued, "and snag Walter while you can. If you lose him the chances of finding another man, I don't need to tell you, are not very good."

Without warning, Abigail thought of Millie. She remembered the slender hand giving her a quick squeeze of comfort and she realized then that that was how she and Emma should be. Supportive and loving. But instead of the emotions coming from her sister, Abigail had received them from a woman whom other women crossed streets to avoid. How unfair life could be.

"Anyway," Emma continued, "a perfect opportunity to make amends with Walter for your outrageous and embarrassing behavior will present itself in the form of the Women's Auxiliary picnic this weekend. Decorate your basket and make sure Walter knows what it looks like so he can bid on it and put to rest any rumors that are beginning to float around that you have your eye on the very man who lives under your roof."

Emma left Abigail alone in the yard then, chickens squawking in the henhouse, young Pepe demanding instructions as to what he should do with the milk. Abigail ignored it all and sank down onto the bottom step of the porch, trying to assimilate all her sister had said.

Lou delivered the eggs in record time, nearly making up the time she lost because her mama had made her do extra chores that morning. Humming a tune, Lou made her way down the boardwalk, swinging the empty basket in circles around her arm. At the end of the buildings, instead of taking the steps as she normally did, she leaped off the end and landed on the hard-packed dirt road in a billow of ragged skirts. A patch of wild flowers had sprung up through a crack in the unrelenting earth. With delight, she reached down and carefully snapped the stems one by one until she held a small, scraggly bouquet.

In the distance she saw a barn she had never noticed before. She skipped down the way until she came to the slightly jarred door. Her breath caught with joy at the sight that met her eyes.

"Hello!" she cried out, squeezing through the space left between the door and jamb.

Grant turned with a start. At first he didn't seem to recognize her, but then he did. "What are you doing in here? This is no place for little girls," he stated, his voice gruff.

Lou simply smiled and walked from anvil to fire to horse with great care. She stopped in front of the horse. "He is so very beautiful."

"Careful," he said, "you're going to get hurt."

"One day I will learn to ride." Turning, she looked at Grant with serious eyes. "Do you know how to ride on a horse?"

"Listen, I don't know who you are, but . . ."

Lou turned back to the beast and ran her tiny hand across its chest. "I imagine you are the very best horse-rider there is. So handsome and strong. Yes, the very best horse-rider in all the land. Maybe one day you will show me how to ride. Do you think?"

Grant was clearly flustered. He pulled a handkerchief from the inside pocket of his brown vest to wipe his brow.

"Well, I best be going," she said. "Thank you for showing me your barn. I'll come back tomorrow."

Lou smiled, then skipped carefully to the door. Just before she slipped back through the entrance, she reached over and set her flowers on a small table. Grant stood quietly, staring, wondering. He glanced at the table, then turned back to his work, putting from his mind the strange little girl.

Hours passed. Heat grew and filled the wood and adobe walls. Setting his hammer aside Grant went to the door to push it wide. And there he noticed the scraggly wildflowers the little girl had left. Lou, he remembered she was called. Strangely his heart clenched in his chest. He started to throw the weeds out the door, but stopped. They wouldn't last long in the heat, but that didn't matter. He set them back on the table.

Later that day he left early for home. Passing the General Store he noticed the jellies in the window. He had the sudden childhood memory of times of happiness long past. Without thinking, he entered the store and, much to Myrtle Kent's surprise, purchased a piece of hard candy and nothing else. As he headed home, he whistled the whole way.

At supper that evening, he was quiet as usual, but without a trace of sullenness or anger. Virginia raised a questioning eyebrow across the table to her husband. Sherwood, however, seemed unaware of any change.

When Grant and Emma retired, Grant took Emma's hand in his.

"Why, Grant," Emma said, her normal confidence evaporating. "I just don't know what to make of your sudden good humor."

Pulling her hand into the crook of his arm, he smiled down at his wife. "Today I was thinking about the conversation we had last night."

"What conversation was that, Grant?" she asked nervously.

They stood in the long hall and he turned her around to face him. "About children."

Emma stilled.

Grant's smile hardened. "You do want children, don't you?"

"Well, as I already told you, of course I do, Grant," she said, pulling away, her hand coming to her chest. "Of course I want children."

He relaxed then and pulled her back to nuzzle her neck. "Then perhaps we should do something about it."

Kissing her gently, he pressed his body to hers. "Emma," he murmured into her hair. "It's been so long."

"Really, Grant." Each syllable vacillated between anger and cajoling. "Not here in the hallway."

He swept her up in his arms and carried her to their bedroom, then kicked the thick wooden door shut behind them. He felt her tension, but tried to ignore it. He wanted her. She was his wife. He had a right, he repeated to himself as he traversed the thick oriental carpet that covered the hardwood floor, and lowered her onto the bed.

He kissed her neck and eyelids, telling himself she would relax, that he would make it good for her—this time. But as her body lay stiff and unyielding, memories of all the other times forced their way into his mind. And he knew that no matter how hard he tried, no matter how much patience and loving he used, she would never give herself willingly to him, much less enjoy it—unlike the very first time he had made love to her when he was hurting and alone. She had wanted him then—or so she had said.

His body stilled. His kisses stopped. With a sigh, he rolled off Emma and lay on his back with his wrist over his eyes.

"Are you angry, Grant?" she whispered.

He didn't respond at first. His body was trying to make sense of what had put an end to the journey it had not been on in a great long while and desperately wanted to take. Grant held back a groan and wondered, not for the first time, why he didn't visit Millie as the rest of the men in town were rumored to do. But he had been brought up to believe in the sanctity of his vows.

"Grant?" Emma persisted, her voice growing stronger. "What's wrong?"

"Nothing, Emma," he finally said, rolling off the bed, straightening his clothes, then heading for the door.

"Where are you going?"

"Out."

"Where?"

"Just now, I don't know. But don't wait up."

~ 10 ~

Harmon Davis had extended his business trip, though Abigail had little hope it had anything to do with business. More than likely, she felt certain, he was staying away, fortifying himself with good meals and clean clothes before he ventured back to El Paso and the boardinghouse she was having such difficulty running.

But while her pride stung from Harmon's absence, she was also filled with relief. Noah was gone much of the time, and was never around for meals. All of which was giving her a chance to try and learn how things were done. Still she had to admit, things weren't going all that well. She had never found the list Penny had said she left. As a result, she had no idea what things had to be done—until they didn't get done and someone brought it to her attention. And she wasn't in a position to ask anyone for help.

She was certain Mr. Self-sufficient himself, Noah Blake, could have told her what she was doing wrong with the laundry or the bread, but she would dance the jig in the streets at high noon before she asked him for help. Telling her she was missing out on life—telling her she needed to be kissed by someone who knew how—the impertinence!

Red singed her cheeks at the thought of just how well indeed he knew how things were done. Cooking, cleaning, talking, laughing, eating—kissing. Her stance relaxed and her lips parted as her mind filled with the memory of his kiss. Sensation tingled down her spine before she realized what was happening. Instantly she stiffened, then marched into the front parlor, determined to keep Noah Blake from her mind.

The Women's Auxiliary picnic was the following day, and if she didn't start making her basket now, she knew she'd not have a box lunch to provide. No sooner had she started decorating a basket with ribbon, than she glanced out the window and saw her father—coming this way! In a swirl of skirts she raced around the house, straightening as best she could and praying that nothing was on the verge of exploding or falling apart. Deciding things were as good as they were going to get, she ran back to the front parlor to finish her basket, determining that it was best to look busy when her father entered.

But minutes ticked on and no one knocked or entered. It occurred to her that he was just passing by. A sudden burst of pain pierced her heart, mixing with the wave of relief that washed over her at the same time. The relief she understood, but the pain surprised her. And she knew it shouldn't. After all these years she was a fool to care that he would pass by her door without so much as a word. He had passed her door, her room, her chair, her life, without so much as a word for as long as she could remember. But even at twenty-nine years of age she wished it had been different.

Just when she turned back to her basket she caught sight of her father, coming up the front steps, with none other than Noah Blake. He was coming after all! Her hand automatically came to her hair, but it didn't matter what she looked like because the men stayed out on the porch, and Noah, she noticed, looked none too pleased.

"I'm certainly not trying to push, Mr. Blake," she heard her father say. "But these aren't the old days when a man could bury his money in the yard or stuff it in his mattress. From all accounts you've made a lot of money over the years, especially this year."

Noah sighed. "Who's to say I didn't waste away all my money on liquor and good times like most fellows."

Sherwood eyed him speculatively. "They also say that despite your freewheeling appearance, you don't put much store in wasting money on wine and women. Say you have an Indian partner. Say the two of you sell your pelts, then disappear into the countryside, never to be seen again until next year. And as a free trapper, beholden to no one, you make a considerable amount of money. It's not safe to be storing your money somewhere where it's not secure."

"Like a bank is secure, I suppose you want me to believe," Noah offered.

Sherwood smiled. "Of course. A bank would keep your money safe as a babe in its mother's arms."

Turning away toward the house, Noah simply said, "Like I said, I'll think about it." Then he pushed through the door, leaving Sherwood out on the porch.

Abigail was dumbfounded by the way Noah treated her father. No one treated Sherwood Ashleigh like that. But Noah did, and apparently he got away with it, because when she glanced out the window once again, her father was heading back to the bank. She felt a bit of new respect for the callous mountain man.

And then she wondered what her father meant when he said Noah didn't put much store in wine and women. Was it possible she had misread the man? She considered this possibility for a moment. No, she concluded after remembering all too well that he was never far from some den of iniquity, and never long without Millie McAllister on his arm. Her father must be wrong. He hadn't had the misfortune . . . misfortune? Yes, *misfortune* to have been around him as much as she had.

Regardless, she was still amazed that anyone could stand up to her father. Suddenly her mind wafted away on a breeze of daydream. In her mind's eye she saw herself standing before her father, her chin held high, telling him . . .

The daydream fizzled as quickly as it came. Telling him what? she wondered. She would no more tell her father anything but what he wanted to hear than she would throw a pie in his face, and she knew it. With a sigh, she turned away from the window.

"Mr. Blake!" The sight of him, standing in the doorway, watching her, unsettled her greatly.

They both stared at each other, she framed by the sun

from the window, he by the doorway that led to the hall. Abigail immediately realized he was angry. The oversized schoolboy was gone, replaced by a man that looked as hard and formidable as the ferocious mountain men about whom one heard such terrible tales.

"Eavesdropping, Miss Ashleigh?"

His voice was void of his usual good cheer. "Of course not," she lied, and blushed immediately.

Noah's brow tilted in disbelief.

"So all right," she admitted. "I might have overheard a thing or two. But who are you to raise an eyebrow over eavesdropping?" she said in a voice meant to embarrass him, which of course, she noted, did not. "Besides, goodness gracious, how could I not? The two of you certainly weren't trying to be quiet. Old Mrs. McCrady down the road could have heard you, and she's deaf!"

Noah scowled and shook his head. "That is surely the God's own truth. Your father says he's trying to keep my money safe. Hell, the way he keeps badgering me about his bank in front of anyone and everyone, my money is in more jeopardy now than ever. And how the hell does he know if I have any money or not?" he demanded. Noah leaned forward and looked directly into Abigail's startled brown eyes. "Your father is the most aggravating man I have ever had the bad luck to meet. And let me tell you, I've met a great many aggravating men."

He started to look away, and as he did he saw the picnic basket. His hard eyes hardened even further. "Don't tell me you're making a basket for that damned picnic everyone keeps telling me about?"

Abigail did not respond.

Noah shook his head. "I suppose you're making it for old lover boy himself," he added caustically.

"If you are referring to Walter," she stated, her lips tight, "most certainly I'm making it for him."

He responded with an unintelligible, ill-humored grunt. The animal, she thought with disdain.

"Lucky Walter," he added as if he didn't really mean it.

"And I suppose Millie will be the lucky woman to receive your bid."

He looked at her for a long time without answering, his countenance as unreadable as stone. At length he ran his large, strong hand through his hair. "At least she can cook," he said finally, before he turned on his heel, pounded up the narrow flight of stairs to his room, and slammed the door, leaving Abigail alone in the parlor, furious, jealous, and oddly disappointed.

The late October sun blazed down from the heavens. The Indian summer day was more typical of the area than not and the Women's Auxiliary picnic began as scheduled under a perfect blue sky with just enough of a breeze to keep bodies cool without ruffling bonnets or skirts.

Abigail had ended up buying fried chicken, cole slaw, potato salad, and cake from Mrs. Holloway, and swearing her to secrecy. She couldn't afford for Walter to suspect that she couldn't cook. She cringed at yet one more deception in her ill-laid plans. But what was she to do? Buy her picnic lunch from Holloway's Restaurant, that's what she was to do, she stated emphatically to herself as she placed her basket next to an already large assortment of baskets on the table.

The townsfolk gathered around the platform on which the mayor stood ready to start the auction. Abigail caught sight of Millie and she nearly raised her hand to wave, but stopped when a man she had never seen before put his arm around Millie's waist and led her away. Abigail wondered suddenly if Millie enjoyed the life she led, or did she feel trapped, much as Abigail felt trapped in her own life. But the warm fall day held no answers and she looked away from the retreating couple.

Abigail did not see Lou who stood in the crowd, her hair braided haphazardly, though obviously painstakingly, by her tiny hands. Lou looked around, glancing from face to face, until she turned and left the clearing. No one noticed the little girl who skipped down the street. And no one noticed when she stopped in front of two massive wooden doors, one as usual left slightly ajar. Ducking to miss the latch, Lou slipped inside.

For a second she did nothing more than take in the sweet smell of fresh hay. Then she searched her surroundings. Stepping further into the barn, her forehead knotted when she didn't see or hear anyone.

"Hello, there," she called, her voice echoing in the high-ceilinged space.

The normally blazing fire lay cold in the hearth and all was quiet. But her heart soared when she noticed a door that stood open on the opposite wall. With a smile, Lou skipped carefully around an anvil, tongs, and hammers lined up along one wall, then peered inside. Instantly, a smile lighted her tiny face.

"Hello, there," she called again.

Grant turned with a start. His hands stilled on the beautifully wrought bridle he held in his hand. Grease glistened on his fingers.

"What are you doing here?" Lou asked with a trace of exasperation in her voice. "You're supposed to be at the picnic. I looked for you everywhere."

"You shouldn't be here," he said, his voice gruff as his fingers returned to their task.

"What are you doing?" she asked, ignoring his statement as she slid closer.

Grant looked down at her with a hard glare. Lou only smiled in return.

"It looks messy," she observed.

"It is, and you'd do well to stay out of the way. This is no place for little girls."

Her buoyant face seemed to deflate. "For little boys?"

His fingers stilled once more and he seemed to consider her suddenly sad features. "No," he practically grunted. "Not for little boys either."

In a flash, her good cheer was restored. "Oh, I am so terribly pleased. I was afraid you just didn't like little girls."

Grant grew flustered. "Well, of course I don't . . . I mean . . . I do like little girls."

"Oh, wonderful!" she exclaimed, coming up right next to him on his stool. "I would hate it if you didn't."

"That's not the point. You shouldn't be in here. You could get hurt."

"Oh, don't worry yourself a bit over that. I will be ever so careful."

A groan rumbled deep in his chest. "Look . . ."

His words were cut short when Lou reached up with one tiny finger and carefully touched his own. "Your hands are so big. If I had a papa he would be big and strong just like you." Dropping her hand, she crossed in front of him until she came to a stool a few feet away from his which she dragged closer, climbed up on, then made herself comfortable, hooking her heels on the top rung.

Grant could only stare. When Lou had herself situated and looked up to find his eyes focused on her, she smiled, then looked back to the bridle with unwavering interest. The barn grew quiet, then without another word, Grant went back to working the bridle.

The auction was well underway, more than half the baskets already having been sold. Abigail fidgeted. Hers was next. Walter was standing at the front of the crowd talking to her father and Virginia when the mayor held up Abigail's basket.

"Who will start the bidding for the basket of our latest citizen to join the ranks of landladies?"

A few giggles rippled through the crowd along with a few grumbles. But no one bid. Abigail's cheeks grew hot.

"Come on folks," the mayor said a little louder. "Don't be shy."

Suddenly Virginia snapped to attention. She jabbed her husband in the arm. Sherwood looked up, irritated, before he took notice of the proceedings and motioned Walter toward the basket that hung forlornly in the mayor's hand.

"Ah, hum, fifty cents," Walter called.

Sherwood grunted. Virginia groaned. Every basket in the house had started at a dollar and had sold for close to five.

"You can do better than that, Jackson," the mayor ribbed good-naturedly.

Walter forced a chuckle. "One dollar."

"One dollar," the mayor announced. "Do I hear two?"

No one spoke. Abigail wanted to die.

"Surely I hear two dollars out there. It's for a good cause."

Still silence.

All the years of loneliness and hurt from her past surfaced and washed over her like a hot wave of shame and embarrassment. Every incident of the heartless and thoughtless things people had said to her over the years passed through her mind like reality. How she hated never fitting in. And now, just like always, she didn't understand what it was about her that made people shy away from her.

"Well then," the mayor's voice penetrated her thoughts. "I guess I've got one dollar going once, going twice . . ."

"Ten dollars."

Abigail sucked in her breath. She pressed her eyes closed. She was afraid to move. A murmur of surprise rippled through the crowd as everyone turned to the sound of the voice.

"What's that I heard?"

"Ten dollars," Noah repeated, his voice rumbling through the masses, clear and understandable.

"Well, that's more like it," the mayor declared. "Do I hear eleven dollars?"

Walter stood dumbfounded at the front, craning his neck to see from who and where the insult came. At the sight of Noah, his eyes narrowed.

"Do I hear eleven dollars?" the mayor repeated in Walter's direction.

Sherwood nudged the younger man who slowly turned back to the front. "Eleven dollars."

Someone cheered.

"Twenty."

A gasp reverberated through the air, and Abigail wasn't sure if she wanted to melt away into the cracks in the hard-packed earth or strut about like a peacock.

Walter fumed. "Twenty-one."

"Well, boys, this is grand," the mayor chirped with excitement. "The Women's Auxiliary won't be needing to have another fundraiser for months at this rate. How about thirty?"

"One hundred dollars," Noah announced.

Titters of excitement exploded. Sherwood stood back and took Walter's measure. Walter turned from red to blue as he stood silent.

"Well, then, a hundred going once . . . twice . . ."

Everyone glanced from Walter to Noah, then finally their eyes came to rest on Abigail.

"Gone, for one hundred dollars! And we thank you, Mr. Blake."

Abigail looked up and met Noah's stare.

"I'm sure," the mayor continued, "your meal will be well worth it."

With the mayor's words Abigail watched as Noah's determined countenance transformed, as if he only just then realized what he had paid one hundred dollars for. And suddenly the pain and betrayal of years long past melted away, much as she had considered doing. It was all she could do to hold back a smile.

"Serves you right," Abigail teased when the crowd broke up to enjoy the picnic.

Noah glared down at her as he snatched up the basket and took her arm. He pulled her along at a rapid pace. Every few steps she had to run to keep up. But instead of noticing the almost painful grip or the angry pace, all she could think about was how wonderful it felt to have someone put up a fight for her. She didn't dare think about what it meant, or that the victor didn't seem all that victorious just then, she only thought about the novel feeling of being desirable.

She felt free and alive, and every time she had to run to keep up, she felt as though her feet were dancing. Giddy excitement bubbled up inside her. And for the moment, strict propriety was forgotten altogether. The life she recognized was gone. Gone away, her mind whispered, and her heart soared.

They came to a towering cottonwood tree by the river. Noah stopped and stared down at her, his mind a churning cauldron. His face was hard and lined. Hers, he noticed, was more beautiful than ever, her happiness and gaiety almost contagious. Almost. He cursed. He had told himself to steer clear of Miss Abigail Ashleigh. No sooner had the words floated through his mind than he found himself bidding outrageously for her picnic basket. All because he had hated seeing that look in her eyes. So hurt and betrayed. And that damned Walter Jackson. The man should be horsewhipped and hogtied for treating Abigail as he did. Noah sighed. Miss Abigail Ashleigh. Whom he was trying to avoid. Abruptly he turned away.

Abigail took the basket from his hand and made short order of spreading the blanket and setting out the food. "I don't think you'll starve after all," she said, her voice filled with laughter.

Reluctantly, Noah looked down at the fare spread out before him. His scowl softened, but didn't disappear.

"Fried chicken," she said, holding up the plate for inspection.

No response.

"Well, then, how about potato salad?"

Nothing.

"Coleslaw? Mouth-watering flaky rolls? No? Hmmm," she seemed to consider. Inspiration lit her eyes. "Cake!" With something close to reverence, she carefully pulled out a huge slice of moist chocolate cake with thick, swirling chocolate icing. Teasing impudence danced in her eyes. "Now, don't try and pretend indifference to this slice of delicious decadence—you, the great defender of decadence and debauchery."

A reluctant grunt of laughter slipped through his lips. "Great defender of decadence and debauchery?" he repeated, one slash of dark blond brow raised as he lowered himself to the ground, leaning back against the craggy tree trunk. "And when did you come to this conclusion?"

"Good Lord, practically from the first moment I saw you."

"As I recall, the first time you saw me you were having difficulty with mere speech, much less complex personality assessments."

Abigail blushed as she recalled, but then she shrugged her shoulders. "Admittedly, I was a little taken with your . . . size," she offered, then laughed.

And then the world seemed to stop. Certainly, Noah felt as if his heart had. With that one uninhibited laugh, everything he had been feeling came crashing down around him. She was more beautiful than he ever dreamed possible. He only wished she could see it in herself. He stared at her, trying to understand what it was that he felt. But like always, he could come up with no explanation. He couldn't explain why, since the day he broadsided her with the door of Red Dog Saloon, she had plagued his mind until every time he saw her he felt the perverse need to punish her for plaguing him so. But as he looked at her he realized that perhaps he had known the answer all along. He wanted her. Physically. Not simply to set her free as he had told himself, though certainly that was a part of it. He wanted to press his body to hers and lose himself to her softness. He wanted to possess her, to know her intimately.

"Maybe we should start with the cake," she said, breaking into his thoughts. "Perhaps that would sweeten your mood."

Noah eyed her speculatively. He reached out and touched the strand of hair that had sprung loose to curl about her face. Abigail sucked in her breath, and her smile wavered. His fingers trailed down her cheek to the pulse in her throat, grown rapid from his touch. "You should smile more often," he said, his voice like gravel. "You were meant to smile, sweet Abigail. Sweet, sweet Abby," he whispered as he drew her close, disregarding both the better judgment that demanded he steer clear of her, and the sumptuous fare that lay out on the ground.

When his face was scant inches from hers, he stopped. He should let her go and return to the safety of town, to the safety of people milling around. But as he looked down into her brown eyes, partly frightened, partly intrigued, he could not let her go. With infinite care, he touched her lips with his—barely, softly. And with that touch all the desire he felt for her surged forward and he was lost.

He groaned and pulled her to him. He kissed her wildly, his breath coming fast. Her head fell back and he kissed her neck, her ear, her chin, unable to get enough. Licks of fire spread through his loins. He wanted her so badly that he ached—proof that he had wanted her for a very long time. From the moment he pulled her up from the boardwalk and looked into her startled brown eyes, he had wanted her. He wanted her innocence. He wanted to see life through eyes that hadn't seen. And he wanted to be the one to show her another kind of life—to show her how to live. He felt the need that she should know the precious gifts life had to offer.

Her eyes opened wide as he pushed her down to the ground, half on the blanket, half on the grass, her hair coming loose from its pins. As soon as his lips touched hers once again she groaned into his mouth and her arms came up tentatively to touch him.

"Yes, sweet Abby, touch me," he groaned into her mouth.

Carefully, slowly, her hands began to explore the hard planes of his back and neck, trembling as they came forward to trace his jaw.

His tongue sought entrance to the recesses of her mouth. The intimate caress surprised her, and she tensed. With infinite care, he soothed her body until she relaxed in his arms. His lips trailed down her neck, his fingers pushing away the material to reveal her silken flesh.

His body ached with yearning. He had never before wanted so badly to sink himself in a woman's warm flesh, over and over again. And he could tell she wanted him, too. He pressed against her at the thought. Running his hands up her arms, he held them above her head, clasped in his grip. "You want me as badly as I want you," he whispered, kissing her to prove his words.

She stiffened beneath him, but he barely noticed. His mind was filled with the feel of her and his own long-held desire. And it wasn't until long moments later when he realized she was trying to move away, hesitantly at first, then frantically—that he was forced to conclude she was desperate to escape. She tried to roll away, but his body held her captive. He looked down into her eyes. "What happened, Abby?" he asked, his voice ragged. "What changed the course?"

"Get off me," she said with steely determination, her hands which he held above her head fisting tightly.

Noah sighed and shook his head. "Are you afraid of what you feel, sweet Abby? Are you afraid of wanting to touch me—of wanting me to touch you?" His words made her gasp, but he wouldn't let up. "Are you afraid of the consequences of life? Is that why you're willing to forgo pleasures such as this? Is that why you're willing to settle for someone like Walter Jackson?"

She sucked in her breath and started to speak.

"That's right, Abby, get worked up in a lather of righteous indignation. But I'd like to hear you actually deny the charge. Deny that you don't love Walter."

He hesitated, waiting for her response. At length she turned her head away.

"You don't love him, sweetness, because he is not worthy of you. Walter Jackson doesn't know the first thing about you."

"And you do?" she said, her voice tight.

Noah chuckled and shifted his weight, though not enough to let her up. "Better than you think. Let's see," he said as he seemed to consider. "For starters, your favorite color is red, though you wouldn't dare tell a soul."

Abigail blushed. "How in the world did you ever come to such an absurd conclusion?"

"The only apron you wear out of a whole slew Penny had is the red one. And every time you set the table, you put red roses in the vase and red napkins under the fork. Though you wouldn't be caught dead in a red dress."

Crimson singed her cheeks. She hated that he was right.

She hated even more that she had been unaware of what she had been doing.

He let go of one wrist and ran the back of one long finger across her cheek. "You look good in red."

"Get off me!"

Noah only chuckled before his brow grew serious. "You dream of being free and alive, of experiencing life, of living on the edge. You are alternately drawn to, then repulsed by Millie McAllister, all because she turns her nose up at society." He leaned down and pressed his lips to her forehead. "You're much too young and beautiful to be sitting around like an old woman with no life left to live."

She pushed at his shoulder again, this time harder. He tightened his hold. "I saw the joy in your eyes when I twirled you around the night we danced. I heard your laughter. You want to have fun, Abby. You want to experience the passion inside of you. I can feel it, I can hear it. But for some reason that I can't fathom, you won't allow yourself to live, to have fun, or to feel passion. Why is that, Abigail?"

His words were filled with an urgency that left her confused. She stared at him as he stared at her. Why? he had asked. What could she answer?

"Damn your father! Damn Walter Jackson and that sister of yours, too! Don't let them kill your joy and excitement."

She met his gaze and pleaded with rounded eyes. "They are all I have," she whispered.

But he would not relent. "That's no excuse."

"Maybe not to you."

"You blame the way you are on your family. And maybe there's some truth to that. But that is no excuse for not stepping forward, for not moving beyond the past to make a better way for yourself. No, Abigail, your only excuse is that you're afraid—you're a coward."

He might as well have slapped her. "But I tried to do something with my life," she defended. "I went to the boardinghouse."

"True. But once you got there, you went back to your old ways and were afraid. Afraid of failing, but also afraid of succeeding, because you are uncertain where that success will take you."

"That's not true!"

"Isn't it? You're afraid to live, Abigail Ashleigh. You're afraid of life. You want excitement and adventure, but you're afraid. You'd rather play life safe than go out and live, and accept the risks involved in living. Why else would you consider marrying a boring man like Walter who only wants you because you're Sherwood Ashleigh's daughter."

His last words, spoken so confidently, seared her to the core, and brought up a surge of anger that she didn't know she possessed. With a spurt of energy and strength she wrenched free, surprise more than anything gaining her release. Like a wild woman she rolled to her knees. "How dare you! How dare you say those hateful things to me!"

"Face it, Abby, it's true," he pressed on relentlessly, not understanding why he pushed her. "You live vicariously through other people's lives instead of living your own."

"That's easy for you to say," she snapped, "because you have no ethics or morals. Sure you live—you don't let a little thing like morality or obligations kill your fun."

Noah stiffened and his blue eyes darkened.

"No, you bellow and back slap and dally with all the pretty ladies. You say things others wouldn't dream of saying. You don't conform and you live on the edge. But that is all fine and well for you because you're a man, but more importantly because you're a man who lives in the wild most of the year with only God and nature to answer to. You're not a twenty-nine-year-old, unmarried woman living in a small town that watches your every move. Trade places with me for one day, Noah Blake, one day, and then make judgments on my life and the way I choose to live it."

Abigail rolled back onto her feet and stood. Her hand came up to her hair that caught in the breeze and blew into a cloud around her head. With a frustrated sigh she jerked her hand to her side and tried to gather the fragments of her composure. Noah hadn't moved. He stared at her, looking dangerous and threatening and just like the man from the wilds that he truly was.

"I hope you enjoy the rest of your lunch," she said, her voice tight and angry.

Noah didn't move. He merely watched her hurry along the sandy path, not toward the clearing where the auction had been held, but toward the boardinghouse, along the backroads—the safe way. Finally he looked away. He glanced out at the flowing river without seeing.

He was the last of a dying breed and he knew it. Beaver had been hunted and trapped until there were hardly any left. Silk was cheaper and easier to make hats out of, and companies were doing just that. But he didn't like thinking about it. He didn't like thinking about the fact that life as he knew it was changing and he was being pressured from all sides to change with it.

He thought of his money and Sherwood Ashleigh's bank. Change and more change, and he didn't like it. But that was one area he could control. He might not be able to bring the beaver back, but he could damn well keep his money out of a newfangled bank.

His brow furrowed and his eyes filled with anger when he realized how obstinate and inflexible he sounded. But that was untrue. He could change, he knew it. He just didn't want to, he told himself forcefully. He thrived on the wilderness, the freedom, the hunt. Or so he told himself, as he looked back to the place in the river brush where branches leapt to close the path through which Abigail had disappeared.

He stood quietly on the river bank for a minute, or maybe it was an hour. He didn't know. The growing breeze rustled through his hair. His mind wandered. It wasn't until he heard the faint snap of a twig announcing someone's approach that he turned.

"Wanderer," he said when he saw the other man. A faint smile tilted on his lips.

"You've been expecting me," the man named Wanderer said.

He was a big man, though not nearly so large as Noah. He had long dark hair, braided, hanging down his chest. His eyes were dark as coal and his skin was lined with age and long years in the sun. He wore the costume of the trapper, a hunting shirt of dressed buckskin, ornamented with long fringes, and pantaloons of the same material, decorated with porcupine quills and long fringes down the outside of the leg. A soft felt hat covered his head and he had moccasins on his feet. Though he did not smile, it was clear he was glad to see his friend.

"Expecting you?" Noah repeated. With a short grunt he shook his head. "Trapping hasn't been much on my mind these days, I'm afraid."

Wanderer glanced toward the spot where Abigail had disappeared. "Is it the woman you think of?"

Noah followed his gaze. He didn't answer at first. He had no idea what to say. "It doesn't matter if it is or not." He turned back and looked at Wanderer. "I take it you're here about what you found?"

"Yes, and it is not good. As we suspected, the beaver is even harder to find. There are fewer and fewer to trap every year. Too many men hunting for too many years."

"It may not be so good for others, but you can find beaver. You always do. The others will find it more difficult and become discouraged. They'll move on to other things. This could end up being even better for us," Noah said, his voice determined.

Wanderer shrugged. "Perhaps. But my woman has had another child and she is not young. My oldest son is to become a warrior. Soon he will go on his vision quest."

Noah studied his Indian guide who had become a trusted friend. "What are you saying, Wanderer?"

"I was thinking that perhaps this year we forgo the hunt and I stay with my tribe."

"Not trap?" Noah asked, his voice void of emotion.

"We have made good white man's money for fourteen years, my friend. We need no more. And like my woman, I too am not so young anymore." Wanderer hesitated. "You are not getting any younger either, as you white men like to say. Perhaps it is time you think about a wife."

Noah jerked away as if burned. "I don't need a wife. Nor do I want one. We've been over this. I hunt—whether you go with me or not."

$$\sim 11 \sim$$

"KISS ME, WALTER."

Walter stared at Abigail across the smooth expanse of kitchen table as if she had spoken in a foreign tongue. His eyes grew incredulous and he shook his head from side to side so quickly that for a moment he seemed to blur right before her eyes.

"What?" he managed to say.

Leaning forward, her eyes intense, almost desperate, she reached out and grasped his wrist. "Kiss me."

"Kiss you! Good God, Abigail! That's what I thought you said." He sat back in his chair, pulling away, seeming uncertain and angry. "Why?"

Why? she wondered. A person asked *why* at a time like this? Shouldn't she be swept up into his embrace by now, her body alive with feeling, with desire? Should she have had to ask? Noah wouldn't have asked why, her mind said, and that made her angry. Noah was no gentleman. Of course he wouldn't ask.

"I want you to kiss me, Walter." She hesitated. "You never have."

"Well, really, Abigail. You should know it's because I respect your father and wouldn't dream of offending him by being forward with one of his daughters."

One of his daughters? Not simply her? For reasons she didn't understand, the kiss became all the more important. "Please," she practically begged and hated herself for it. But he had to kiss her. She had to prove to herself that after so many years of wondering, she simply longed to be kissed—that she would have reacted to any man's kiss as she had to Noah's.

Walter grew flustered. "This is neither the time nor the place to . . . do such things. Your father could walk in at any time. Good Lord, or a boarder for that matter."

Abigail pressed her eyes closed, but only for a minute. "Then tell me my favorite color," she said, her voice beginning to rise.

"Your favorite color?" Walter's eyes narrowed. "What's this all . . ."

"Yes, Walter!" she demanded. "What is my favorite color? My favorite food? My favorite flower? Tell me what I'm like, Walter. Tell me you know." She was nearly frantic now.

"Abigail!" he said sharply. "What's this all about? Kisses and colors. Have you lost your mind?"

His tone startled her, and she jerked in her seat. When she looked at him again, she was almost surprised to find herself in the kitchen with him. She sighed. "Perhaps I have lost my mind, but still, I want to know if you want to kiss me?"

"Well, I . . ."

"You've told me you want to marry me. Shouldn't that mean you want to kiss me as well?"

"Well, certainly, of course, but . . ." He eyed Abigail and considered. "Certainly I want to kiss you. Certainly," he repeated as if trying to convince not only Abigail, but himself of the truth of his statement. He took a deep breath, then stood and came around the table. Pulling a chair close, he cleared his throat, ran his hands down his jacket, then sat down and turned her head until they sat face to face. "Of course I want to kiss you." He leaned forward and pressed his lips to hers.

Abigail stiffened, then forced herself to relax. The kiss was cold and hard. No emotion, no feeling. But she had asked for this, she reminded herself, as she became aware of the smell of bay rum and talcum powder. No brandy or tobacco, or the sweet smell of wild winds.

But suddenly, without warning, as if Walter had read her

mind, he brought his hand up to the back of her head, slanting his mouth over hers and forced his tongue between her lips—to burn the other from her mind, she thought, to brand her as his own. Startled, she opened her mouth to protest, only to find herself in a nearly painful embrace. Walter's breath became ragged. His tongue searched, probing, and she thought she would be sick. Pressing her hands against his shoulders, she tried to free herself. This only seemed to spur him on. With effort, she twisted her head away, his lips trailing down to her neck, to her collarbone, as he murmured incoherent words.

"Walter!" she demanded, pushing from his grasp. "Walter, stop that this instant."

His hands groped. He felt her breasts, squeezing, painfully. He panted, heedless of her protestations.

"Walter!" she cried, finally wrenching free, nearly tumbling him from his seat.

They stared at each other, his eyes wild, hers leery and confused, until his eyes began to change. He took in her appearance, her hair messier than usual, her cheeks red where his late afternoon beard had chafed her skin. She would have sworn he looked guilty, even scared. But then it was gone and his eyes filled with accusation.

"What has gotten into you, Abigail?" he demanded. "First you ask to be kissed, then you push me away and act as if I've done something wrong."

"You . . . scared me."

At her words, he sneered and shook his head. "If you are going to act like Millie McAllister, you are going to be treated like Millie McAllister."

Her gasp echoed through the room. They sat, mere inches apart, their eyes locked, until Abigail looked away. The accusation stunned her. But how should she respond? Because deep down inside she suspected he was right. The thought had been there all along—since she had lain in Noah Blake's arms earlier and had wanted nothing more than to stay there forever. She didn't even like the man, but she loved his kisses. And just like in her daydream, she had longed to see where the kisses would lead. She *was* acting

just like Millie McAllister. And in truth, she had been acting that way since she had had that daydream in the General Store, then told her father she would run the
boardinghouse and moved in with three unknown male
boarders.

Heavens above, what had she been thinking. A life of her
own. A woman of means. Her world was crumbling, falling
apart. She was ruining the one life she knew, a life that
while void of laughter and adventure, was safe and secure.
The life she had been trying to achieve was failing miserably. She had been taught her whole life that her place in
this world was to provide a home for a husband and children. To do the bidding of that husband. To care for the
children. And here she was, going against everything she
had been taught. Running a boardinghouse, against Walter's wishes and her father's better judgment. She had been
foolishly longing for a few meaningless compliments and
kisses from a man of lesser reputation, being more than
slightly callous to the feelings of this man who was supposed to become her husband.

Walter's kiss loomed in her mind. A shiver of foreboding
raced down her spine. And that feeling, she realized, was
nothing like what she felt when she had kissed Noah Blake.
But that was only girlish foolishness, she told herself
quickly, and she needed to put it out of her mind once and
for all. Walter was to be her husband. He was well-re-
spected. He would provide her with a home and family.
They would be happy. Surely.

And before she lost her nerve, she said, "If you still want
to marry me, I think we should. The sooner the better."

If Walter had been surprised when she asked him to kiss
her, he was nonplussed by her request that they marry, as
quickly as possible at that. He gasped and sputtered and
couldn't string enough coherent words together to form a
sentence. This, Abigail thought ruefully, was not a man
overcome with joy—overwrought, perhaps, but not over-
joyed. But then he got a hold of himself, and smiled a smile
that didn't quite meet his eyes.

"Splendid," he said. "Yes, we'll marry with all haste. Your father will be pleased."

"What about you, Walter? Are you pleased?"

"Of course I'm pleased," he stated impatiently. He pushed up from his chair, his smile growing more real by the moment. "Let's go over to your father's house right now and share our glad tidings."

He walked over and pulled his hat off a peg on the wall. Abigail didn't move. Her chest was tight and her eyes burned. The memory of Noah's gentle touch made her ache. His concern and kindness—that would lead her nowhere she had any business going, she reminded herself sharply.

With that, she stood, took a deep breath and followed Walter out the door. They were going to be happy, she repeated silently to herself. Surely.

They had walked almost the entire quarter mile to her father's house when Abigail made another decision.

"After we make our announcement, I'm going to tell Father that he will need to get someone else to run the boardinghouse."

Walter stopped in the street. "Whatever for?"

For a moment she couldn't speak. "Whatever for?" she repeated. "I thought you didn't want me running the boardinghouse. I thought you'd be pleased."

"Well, as I told you, the boardinghouse has the potential of providing us with a tidy little income. We could even live there if we wanted." Walter smiled. "Though I'm sure we'd be much happier in your father's home."

Abigail clenched her fist at her side. "I don't want to live in my father's house. I want a house of my own."

Walter tisked and shook his head. "A house of your own is expensive, Abigail. We will have to save. One day perhaps."

"But . . ."

"No buts. I know best. Now let's hurry to tell your father the good news."

They arrived at the white clapboard house minutes later. The house smelled of flowers and home-cooked meals.

Abigail nearly wept at the reminder that she had been un-able to provide such a setting.

"Hello," she called, Walter close behind her.

When she received no answer, they walked toward the back of the house where Virginia had built a garden room of sorts to have a place to avoid the harsh desert sun. It was always cool and fragrant, and though Sherwood often complained about the expense, he spent as much time there as anyone.

"Hello," Abigail said, when they came to the garden room and found her father and Virginia.

Sherwood glanced up, but didn't rise. Virginia smiled her delight and came over to Abigail with outstretched arms.

"Don't you look lovely, Abigail. The sun has done you good," Virginia said.

Immediately, Abigail's hand came to her cheek, but she only managed a thank you before she turned to Walter. "We came to tell you—"

"Abigail. Walter," Emma stated as she sailed into the room in a fragrant cloud of rose water. "What brings the two of you all the way out here?" She ran her eyes over Abigail. "It would seem you survived your lunch with that mountain man. Though you resemble a redskin with all the sun you got. Good heavens, how many times do I have to remind you to wear a bonnet." She laughed then turned to Walter and swatted his wrist with her fan. "As for you, how naughty of you not to outbid that horrid man."

Sherwood eyed Walter.

"Well, umm . . . he bid outrageously. How was I to compete?"

"You saying I don't pay you enough, Walter?"

"Oh, no sir. Of course I'm not saying that. But one hundred dollars for a picnic lunch?"

Emma laughed. Sherwood shook his head.

"The point is not the money, Mr. Jackson," Virginia said, surprising everyone.

Abigail grimaced, hating that a scene was being made

over her. Sherwood leaned back in his chair and eyed his wife.

"The point," Virginia continued, "is to want Abigail's basket above all else."

Walter's lips thinned.

But before anything else could be said, Abigail quickly stepped forward. "Tell them our news, Walter."

After one last glance at Virginia, Walter turned to Sherwood. "We're going to be married."

"This is news?" Emma asked, her voice laced with sarcasm, before she dropped into a seat next to her father.

Sherwood raised an elegant silver brow. "Actually this is news. I had begun to believe it wouldn't happen."

Virginia's questioning glance met Abigail's. Their eyes locked. And Abigail knew her stepmother wondered at the course of events. But what could she say? That it was best this way? That she was afraid if she didn't marry Walter soon, she wouldn't marry him at all?

Saying nothing, she looked away.

"Well, I suppose this deserves some kind of a toast," Sherwood said. "Why don't you get us some lemonade, Virginia."

Virginia turned, and just as she did, the sound of tiny feet pounded through the house. Within seconds, Adam flew into the room, a friend right behind him.

"Damn, woman, how many times—"

"Miss Abigail!"

Everyone stopped. Lou stood next to Adam, her eyes grown wide with pleasure, before she ran forward and threw her tiny arms around Abigail and hugged her tight. A simple joy surged through Abigail until she noticed that all eyes were on her. Sherwood was startled and Virginia smiled fondly. But Walter looked on, clearly outraged, the look duplicated on Emma's face.

Lou turned back to Adam. "Miss Abigail is my very best friend. Just like Mr. Brown Vest at the barn."

Emma sucked in her breath and Abigail turned. She watched Emma stare at Lou. She remembered the morning they had met at her house. And she wondered what lay beneath the surface of her sister's obvious dislike. It was the same with Walter. Both adults clearly did not like this child. But why?

"Come along, children. Let's go make some lemonade," Virginia said, receiving a whoop of appreciation for her effort.

The room became painfully silent. In the distance, muffled laughter and clinking glassware could be heard as Virginia and the children prepared the treat.

"So," Sherwood said, "when's the date?"

"The date?" Walter asked, his eyes still locked on the long hallway that led to the kitchen.

"For the wedding, boy," Sherwood added impatiently.

Emma clutched her fan between her breasts before she turned away and walked to the window.

With effort, Walter dragged his attention back to his employer, soon to be his father-in-law. "Uh, well, Abigail and I haven't discussed the exact date, but we both agree it will be soon. Very soon."

"That's probably best," Sherwood said, thoughtful.

"Here we are," Virginia chimed, a tray of lemonade in her hands. "And next week we'll have a party to announce your engagement and celebrate."

"Oh, no, Virginia," Abigail said quickly. "That's too much trouble."

"Darned right it's trouble," Sherwood interjected. "But we're going to have a party to celebrate. I'll give no one reason to say I'm cheap."

"Of course, Father," Abigail said.

The glasses were handed around and toasts were made, though the joyous occasion seemed sadly lacking in good cheer.

Walter and Abigail left as soon as the lemonade was finished. They walked silently back to the boardinghouse. It wasn't until they came to the steps of the front porch that they noticed Noah in one of the chairs, his pipe clamped between his teeth.

"Evening, folks," he said, though he looked only at Abigail.

Red flooded her cheeks and she wanted nothing more
than to make it to the relative safety of her bedroom post
haste. She wasn't sure what she would do if her eyes met
his. Fall in his arms? Beg him not to let her marry Walter?

"Evening, Blake," Walter replied, his voice void of its
usual tightness when he was around the man. For this night
he could afford to be magnanimous. "Have you heard the
news?"

Abigail turned quickly at the question, but Walter didn't
return her gaze. He held tight to her arm, his eyes locked on
Noah.

"News?" Noah asked, his brow furrowed, the pipe held
in his hand.

"Abigail and I are to be married."

Noah turned and locked his gaze with Abigail's. She returned his bold glare for as long as she could, but it was so
cold and ruthless she was forced to look away. She stared
down at her shoes, but she could feel the heat of Noah's
angry and questioning glare as if he had placed his hand on
her head. The tension confused her. Why should he care if
she married Walter? she wondered. The silence stretched
out.

"Is that a fact?" Noah said finally. "No, I can't say as I
had heard that. Certainly hadn't heard it between now and
when I had lunch with Miss Abigail this afternoon."

Walter's grip tightened. But Abigail thought only about
the fact that she had been wrong to think Noah was angry.
From his comment, he was obviously disgusted because he
thought her morals lacking, and who could blame him. She
had lain in his arms only hours before, and now she was engaged to another man.

"I guess congratulations are in order here," Noah said
when he finally returned his attention to Walter.

Abigail glanced up in time to see a sly, triumphant smile
slice across Walter's face, and she had to tell herself once
again she was doing the right thing.

"Well, I've got a busy day at the bank ahead of me tomorrow, so I'll bid you goodnight, Abigail." Walter

dropped her arm and turned to leave. "Good night, Mr. Blake," he added before he disappeared into the night.

The moon hung in the sky, a slice of luminous light. The stars, Abigail noted, did not seem nearly as bright as usual. She seemed paralyzed, couldn't move. The front door seemed miles away with the major obstacle of Noah Blake in the way.

"Why?"

His voice startled her. She felt as if he had yelled the simple word for all the world to hear. Of course, he hadn't. It had barely been a whisper.

"Why what?"

"Why are you marrying Walter?"

She clasped her hands together and held on tight.

Noah took a step toward her. "You don't love him, Abby. And you deserve better." He hesitated. "Don't go doing something that you'll undoubtedly regret just because you hate me."

The words stunned her. "Of all the arrogant things I have heard in my life, this is the worst! Undoubtedly regret? Who are you to say what I will or will not regret?"

He took another step closer. Her body tensed like a cornered animal.

"I said before," she continued, trying to keep her voice calm, "that you think too highly of yourself. You have proved my sentiments correct once again. I don't hate you, Mr. Blake," though certainly she had told herself she did. "I don't care about you one way or the other."

He stepped closer until he stood scant inches in front of her. She could feel his heat. She longed to reach out. "You mean nothing to me," she repeated.

With the very tips of his work-calloused fingers, he touched her cheek. The feel was rough but gentle, hard but infinitely caring, so like this man who stood before her.

"Don't," she whispered.

"You don't love him, Abby." His fingers slipped down her cheek to the collarbone beneath her prim dress.

"You're wrong," she lied.

"I'm not and you know it." He leaned down and his lips grazed her cheek. "You deserve better."

His words came out on a wisp of shimmery breath and sent tingles of sensation coursing down her spine. Her body started to rule her mind, and without thinking better of it, she said, "Ha! You mean someone like you?"

She meant it sarcastically. She didn't for a second think he was trying to get her to marry him. But when he stiffened, his lips so close to hers that she felt the sharp intake of breath hiss through his teeth, she felt as though he had impaled her heart with an iron stake. The hurt she felt over her family's careless remarks was negligible compared to the pain she experienced over his obvious abhorrence to the idea of marrying her. She didn't want to marry him. She didn't even like him, she told herself. But the fact that he so clearly felt the same about her, even more so from the look on his face, hurt her in a way she didn't understand.

She grunted a short spurt of sarcastic laughter and pushed him away. "I was only fooling you, Mr. Blake." Her throat was tight and her eyes suddenly burned overbright. All she had to do was turn around and make it to her room without making a bigger fool of herself than she already had. Then she would be safe. Then she could cry, or scream, or kick, or whatever else she might feel like doing. For now, however, she refused to embarrass herself any further.

He started to reach for her once again, but she hurriedly stepped aside. "No, Mr. Blake. Please don't touch me ever again."

With that she slipped away, but not before she heard him whisper her name.

"Abby," he said again, his voice hoarse.

But she didn't stop. Her step didn't even falter. She walked with her spine straight, as regal as a queen. He listened until her footsteps receded into her room and he heard the door click shut. He had hurt her. He knew it. And he longed to follow her inside and make things right. But he couldn't. He couldn't follow her. He couldn't make things right. Because truly there was nothing he could do to change her life—or his own.

12

Harmon had returned, but had taken to eating all his meals over at Holloway's. Noah had not been around for days. And not a day went by that Walter didn't badger Abigail to set a date for the wedding. For someone who had seemed reluctant at her proposal, he was charging forward with a tenacity that gave her pause.

Slowly, Abigail was getting better at taking eggs, but the wash and milking Alberta still proved impossible. All she had to do was look at the cow or a basket of dirty laundry and frustration surged through her with a vengeance. She had given up on cooking altogether as there was no one to cook for except herself and she preferred Holloway's as well.

Just the other day she had had the fright of her life when she mentioned the possibility of having chicken for supper. Noah had grumbled about the poor chicken, and Harmon had shaken his head and said he hoped she could chop off the head in one clean swoop. Nothing worse, he had added, than maiming a hen before actually killing it. Her blood had run cold. Kill the chicken? she wondered in dismay. Kill Henna or Gerta or Jezebel? She had taken to naming the fowl and talking to them each morning as she tossed grain across the yard. Kill one of her exasperating but precious birds from which she gathered eggs? She couldn't imagine that was what he meant, but wasn't about to ask to find out for sure. So oatmeal was all she served, and only to Noah at breakfast since Harmon had yet to eat another meal under her roof.

She tried to tell herself she didn't care that she had

failed. Miserably. But she could no longer return home. She laughed out loud to the empty house. She had convinced her father and Walter so thoroughly of her abilities that she was forced to stay. One day, however, they were bound to find out the truth, and she was certain that hell would have to be paid when they did.

The sun was almost up, the basket of eggs sitting on the table, when Abigail finally realized Lou had not yet appeared.

A knock sounded at the back door. Standing, she gathered the eggs and smiled. But when she pulled open the door, it wasn't Lou who had knocked. A woman whom she had never seen before stood on the back porch. She might have been called pretty at some point, but years of obvious neglect had hardened her features. Her pale skin was heavily lined, though she couldn't have been much older than Emma. Her white-blond hair was dull and lusterless, and her much mended dress could have stood a good washing.

"Are you Miss Ashleigh?" the woman demanded, her tone harsh and accusatory.

"Well, yes," Abigail stated. "What can I do for you?"

"I'm looking for my kid."

"Your kid?"

"Yeah, Lou. I know she comes over here all the time. Every time I turn around that girl is goin' on about you. So where is she?" she asked, peering past Abigail suspiciously.

"I don't know. I had begun to wonder myself where Lou was this morning. Has she been missing long?"

"Missing? She ain't missing. I just need to . . . talk to her."

From the woman's tone, Abigail did not know what to make of the situation. It was almost as if she wasn't really looking for Lou at all, rather only wanted to see Abigail and her home. "So you're Lou's mother?"

The woman eyed Abigail's dress with disdain. "Of course I am."

"I've been meaning to talk to you about Lou."

"What about?" Her tone was belligerent.

"Well, I . . ." Abigail faltered. What could she say? I

think your daughter needs new clothes or more baths or more care. From the looks of the mother, clothes, baths, and care were not high on her priority list. "I am simply concerned about the child," she said finally.

The woman's eyes narrowed. "Save your concern for someone else, and keep your nose where it belongs. Lou is my business, not yours."

Abigail's mouth fell open, but even if she had managed to gather her scattered wits and respond, she was given no opportunity, as Lou's mother turned and fled down the steps.

The day passed and all the while thoughts of Lou were never far from Abigail's mind. The child never showed up for the eggs, and when she failed to bring the bread at the end of the day Abigail began to worry in earnest.

Tying her bonnet beneath her chin, Abigail went in search of Lou. She went to the General Store and through the streets, but saw nothing of the little girl. Remembering how fond Lou was of Millie, Abigail squared her shoulders and took the stairs that led to the woman's home. With her hand poised to knock, she hesitated. What if Noah was there, or any other man for that matter? Butterflies jumbled in her stomach. But the most important thing was Lou. Firmly, she knocked.

It took only seconds for the door to pull open. Surprise stretched across Millie's face.

"Miss Ashleigh, what are you doing here?"

Abigail was struck once again by how beautiful Millie was. If only . . . but that was absurd. She didn't look like Millie and never would, she thought, then forced her mind back to matters at hand.

"I'm looking for Lou. Have you by chance seen her?"

"Lou?"

"Yes, her mother came by this morning looking for her."

Millie's eyes widened. "Hester Smith came by your house?"

"Well, if that's Lou's mother, then yes," Abigail replied, somewhat startled by Millie's reaction. "You seem surprised."

Millie quickly erased all emotion from her face. "Surprised? No. It's simply that Hester rarely comes to town. As far as Lou is concerned," she said, quickly changing the subject, "I haven't seen her. But you could check your brother-in-law's barn. She might be there."

If Millie had said she was the Queen of England Abigail wouldn't have been more surprised. Lou at Grant's barn? It made no sense. He barely tolerated children. "You mean Grant Weston?"

Millie smiled. "Yes. They have become quite good friends."

Suddenly Abigail remembered Lou boasting to Adam that her two newest best friends were herself and Mr. Brown Vest. Grant always wore that brown vest. She also remembered Emma's look of shock, or was it fear that ran through her eyes at hearing the news. What, Abigail wondered, was going on?

"Thank you, Miss McAllister. Perhaps I'll just run over to his place and see." She turned to go, but stopped at the sight of the most beautiful partially made dress lying across a table. "Oh, Millie, it's beautiful."

Millie turned then smiled. "Thank you."

"Do you make all your clothes?"

"Most of them, yes. Have for years."

Abigail looked at Millie and before she could think better of it she asked, "Why do you . . . lead the life you do when you can cook and clean and sew such gorgeous garments?"

The smile on Millie's face melted and her countenance grew pained.

"Oh, I'm sorry," Abigail said quickly. "I had no right to ask such a thing."

"That's all right. It's only the truth. But it's also true that once you've set your life on a certain path it is very difficult to alter the course." Millie sighed. "Women don't want to buy their dresses from . . . a woman like me. And with my looks," she shrugged her shoulders, "no woman wants me in her house doing her chores."

Abigail realized there was no conceit in Millie's statement, only resignation.

"And," Millie continued, "while the world is a very large place, it's amazing how a reputation gets around."

"So you've tried to start over?"

"Many times. As I told you, I came to El Paso to start over. But an unmarried woman traveling alone is always suspect."

"That's so unfair!" Abigail knew she should leave, but found it difficult. If only circumstances were different, she thought. If only she could do something to help Millie. But then she sneered silently to herself. She had been miserably unsuccessful in helping herself, how could she possibly help someone else.

Millie smiled. "Don't you worry yourself over me, Miss Ashleigh. I'll be just fine."

Abigail left. With thoughts of the unfairness of the world swirling through her head, she arrived at Grant's barn. Uncertainly, she peered inside. It was empty. But from the back she could hear the faint sound of voices. Stepping through the doorway, she made her way to the tackroom.

The sight that met her eyes stopped her in her tracks. They sat side by side, Grant silent, working a bridle, Lou talking up a storm, helping him with his task. For a moment, Abigail couldn't speak. A glimmer of memory hovered at the edges of her mind. But it would not come clear, and when she blinked her eyes it disappeared altogether and was forgotten. After a moment, Abigail discerned that Grant was teaching Lou how to grease the bridle. The sight was sweet and touching, like a father teaching his daughter about his trade. And she realized then that it wasn't that Grant didn't like children, he obviously must want children of his own. No wonder there was so much tension between Grant and her sister. Emma had already told her how she felt about the act that brought children into this world.

"Hello," she said finally.

Grant started. Lou looked up and a smile spread across her face.

"Miss Abigail!" As quickly as it came, the delight fled.

"Oh, Miss Abigail, the eggs!" she cried, only just then remembering. "I forgot." She scrambled down from her stool.
"Can you ever forgive me."

Grant looked alternately guilty and concerned.

The days were growing shorter as winter was fast approaching. The days of Indian summer had fled without a
trace, bringing a welcome chill to the air in this desert
clime. And with the chill came shorter days and longer
nights. Dusk would be there at any time.

"I'll take the eggs now," Lou said.

"It's too late for the eggs today, dear. And I suspect it's
time for you to be getting home. Did your mama ever find
you?"

"The mama!" Lou was clearly alarmed. "The mama
came looking for me?"

"Yes, this morning."

"To your house?"

"Yes."

Lou pressed her eyes closed. "What did she say to you?"

Abigail tilted her head and frowned. "Why nothing, Lou.
Nothing more than that she wanted to know if I'd seen
you."

Lou's eyes popped open. "Well then, I'd best be getting
home."

"It's almost dark. I'll go with you." She turned to Grant.
"Perhaps you could drive us out."

Grant pushed forward from his stool.

"Oh no!" Lou said. "Don't you trouble yourselves, either
one of you." She headed for the door.

"Wait, Lou," Abigail called.

"No!" Lou repeated, insistent. "I can't wait for the
wagon. I've got to be going."

"Then we'll leave now and walk." Abigail intended to
take Lou home and see how she lived. She would not be
put off. Something with this child and her mother failed to
ring true. And she intended to find out just what it was.

With the authority of a schoolmarm, she reached out,
took Lou's hand, and headed for the door. Just when Abigail stepped across the threshold she noted that Lou turned

partly back and raised a hand in farewell. Abigail glanced at Grant. His hard, dark eyes were surprisingly soft, approachable. She never would have believed it had she not seen it herself.

Abigail ignored the despondent look on Lou's face as they walked to the outskirts of town then, upon Lou's reluctant instructions, continued on. They came to an area Abigail never would have guessed existed. Run-down mud huts were scattered haphazardly as if someone had tossed them out and let them lay were they landed. Chickens seemed to be running wild and dogs chased children around the compound.

"Here we are," Lou said, trying to pull free. "Thank you ever so much for walking me out here."

"Which one is your home?"

"There's really no need to take me any farther."

"I'd like to speak with your mother."

Lou's shoulders slumped. "I don't think that is such a good idea."

"Nonsense, Lou. What could possibly happen?" Then she gave the child a reassuring smile, trying to put her at ease, for she was obviously scared she was in trouble. "Show me the way."

With Lou dragging her feet and protesting the whole way, they came to a tiny shack set off from the rest. The sight broke her heart. Her darling little Lou actually lived in that house. And she knew then that she wanted to do something to make her life better. The thought loomed in her mind that she would love to have Lou as her own daughter—to love and cherish. The vision of Lou's excitement over seeing Noah surfaced. Lou and Noah—and her. A family and a home—filled with love and laughter.

Her heart ached at the thought, especially considering she knew it was nothing more than one of her many silly imaginings. Walter was to be her husband, and he had made it clear the few times he had seen Lou how he felt about her. And it made no sense. He didn't even know the child.

"Well, here we are," Lou said, trying yet again to make her escape.

They stood at the door and Abigail opened her mouth to protest. But the words didn't come. Her world seemed to stop. Confusion washed over her.

Laughter floated out through the makeshift door. Familiar laughter. But that was impossible. But then the laughter turned into words and suddenly it all came clear.

"I couldn't believe it when I saw her this morning," the woman's voice said. "You told me she was nothing to look at, but really, she was awful."

Lou tugged at Abigail's arm to no avail. "Please, Miss Abigail, let us go."

Then more laughter. Her confusion vanished, and her heart broke into a million tiny pieces.

"She's a cold fish, that's for certain, and if it weren't for her father's money, you can bet I wouldn't be around."

Abigail swayed on her feet. Lou reached out, frantically trying to steady her and pull her away. But Abigail shook her off then pulled back her shoulders and pushed open the door. She could hardly believe she did it. She didn't really know why she had. But she couldn't leave room for doubt, however minute.

The sight shocked and wounded her to the core. For there lay Walter, his bare back taunting her, stretched out beside the woman Lou called "the mama." Abigail's breath hissed through her teeth and only then did the illicit lovers become aware of her presence.

Walter nearly fell from the tattered and rumpled bed when the sight of his betrothed standing in the doorway registered in his mind. "Good God! Abigail! What are you doing here?"

For one insane second she almost answered, she almost explained that she had come to talk to the woman about her child, as if she was the one who was at fault for being there. Walter scrambled around in a tangle of sheets in a mad attempt to cover himself.

"Abigail!" he repeated.

Without answering, Abigail turned away. Her eye caught

sight of Lou who stood quietly, scared, miserable, with one tear trickling down her cheek. Abigail tried to smile to reassure the child, but the smile only quivered on her lips, then died before she walked away, fast, forcing herself not to run like she longed to do.

"Abigail!" She heard her name called in the distance from the little hut. But she didn't stop. She kept going, as fast as she could, tripping over tree roots grown into the path, scrambling over boulders and sidestepping tumbleweeds in her haste.

She walked without being aware of where she was going and she was half surprised when she found herself at the boardinghouse. She took the steps and no sooner did she push through the door than she came face to face with Harmon. He stood in the hallway, talking to Noah, a suitcase in his hand. The men stopped their conversation in mid-sentence when she appeared.

"Abby," Noah said, his tone questioning.

Harmon took a deep breath and stepped forward, seemingly unaware of her distress. And before Noah could stop him, Harmon cleared his throat and began. "I'm moving out, Miss Ashleigh. I'm sorry."

The only sign that indicated Abigail had heard was the tightening of her jaw.

"I'm sorry," Harmon apologized again. "If I could, I'd stay. I like you a lot, ma'am. But . . . I can't afford to eat at Holloway's every meal."

"I'll deduct the amount from your rent," she said simply, her voice tight.

Harmon shifted uncomfortably on his feet. "Well, there's the laundry, too."

"I'll . . ." Abigail began, but cut herself off. "I understand, Mr. Davis. You've been more than patient with my efforts. I'm the one who should be sorry to have put you in this sorry position in the first place. I wish you luck wherever you go." Then she stepped past the men, avoiding Noah's questioning gaze, and walked to her room, not stopping in the kitchen. She shut the door, carefully, softly, as if at any kind of noise at all, she would shatter.

She pressed her forehead against the smooth wood door and took a deep breath. In some distant recess of her mind she was aware of the finality of the front door shutting—shutting behind Harmon as he exited, no doubt. Soon, surely, behind Noah Blake, as well.

Turning slowly, she leaned back against the door, her breath coming out harshly. Where was the life she recognized? she wondered. The world had gone mad, she along with it. But she would not cry. For if she was truthful with herself, she was meant neither for the world she had inhabited only weeks before, nor this one as a woman of means. She belonged nowhere she could identify.

She felt now more than ever like a failure. She felt it in her bones as she never had when eggs broke in her fingers or Elden had stood in the doorway with his angry red rash and burned linen shirt. She was a failure. She could do nothing right. Not even keep a man. No wonder her father had no faith in her. He knew the truth—a truth that some part of her had wanted to deny. But no longer.

Her eyes burned and her throat ached unbearably. How easy it would be to give in and go home. The very place she had been trying to escape. She snorted her laughter, but it came out as a sob.

"Abby?"

She sucked in her breath and pushed away from the door.

"Abby," Noah repeated. "Are you all right?"

After a moment, "Certainly."

"Then open the door and talk to me."

"I'm busy, Mr. Blake."

"Abigail, come out here and talk to me or I'm going to come in there."

"You wouldn't dare!"

"Try me."

Silence.

Afraid he would follow through on his threat, she reached around to turn the key and lock the door. But her fingers had barely grazed the metal when Noah pushed through.

"Get out!"

"First tell me what's wrong," he demanded.

"Nothing's wrong. Now get out!"

"Something happened, Abigail. Tell me."

She wrapped her arms tightly around her waist, trying to hold on. "Harmon left," she offered.

"Before that. What happened, Abby?"

Abigail turned away, sharply.

"Abby," he whispered.

Her throat tightened. Her eyes burned. "Leave me alone," she cried, her voice hoarse and desperate.

Silence surrounded them in a quiet world all their own.

"I can't seem to do that, Abigail Ashleigh. No matter that I should." He stepped closer, until he was scant inches behind her. "What happened?"

Her anger and frustration began to dissolve into pain and misery.

"Is Walter bothering you again?" he asked.

"Bothering me! If he had his way he wouldn't bother with me at all!"

Noah grew very still. "What do you mean?"

"I walked Lou home this evening."

"And?"

Abigail pressed her eyes closed. "And much to my surprise, and Walter's," she said, trying for sarcasm, "I found my fiancé engaged in . . . the embrace of another woman. Lou's mother, to be exact."

With a long, angry sigh, Noah placed his strong, supportive hands on her shoulders and pulled her back into his embrace. And though she should not allow such behavior, though she knew she should pull free, she did nothing more than damn propriety and savor his warmth, his strength—his caring.

He pressed his lips to the top of her head, holding her tight. "I'm sorry."

"Oh, Noah, I've made such a fool of myself."

He turned her around with a force that startled her. "Abby," he said, the softness in his voice gone, replaced by firm resolve. "You're too hard on yourself. You are no fool. It's that damn family of yours and Walter who are the fools."

"No, I'm the fool. I was a fool to believe in Walter. I was a fool to believe I could run this boardinghouse. I just wanted to prove that I could do something with my life. If it hadn't been for you and Millie, I'd have failed long before now. The two of you gave me a reprieve by cooking and cleaning that day. I certainly couldn't have done it myself."

"Oh, hell, Abby," he said, pulling her close. "Maybe not that night. But soon. Soon you'll do it all by yourself. Perseverance and determination. That's what it takes. And you have shown great stores of both."

"Ha," she scoffed.

"You're still here, aren't you?"

"What were my choices?"

"You could have gone home long ago. If you'll recall, even I suggested it."

"Not much of a choice."

"But one many would have made."

Abigail couldn't be placated. "For twenty-nine years I've been called plain and mousy. I was a nobody who could do nothing. The only thing I had going for me was a rich father. This boardinghouse was my chance, my opportunity to show the world that I was somebody. Perhaps I even wanted to prove to myself that what I have been told all my life wasn't true." Abigail grunted. "All I succeeded in doing was proving the others correct."

He put her at arm's length. "How many times do I have to tell you, Abigail, that you *are* somebody. Somebody beautiful and smart and very capable of running the boardinghouse if only you would let someone help you learn. It doesn't matter what others say. It only matters what you believe. And you have to believe you can do anything you put your mind to. You have been so afraid of failing that you have ensured that you would. Let go, Abby. As I told you, don't let your fear of failure keep you from succeeding. Fight for what you want." His voice softened. "Don't

give up." He leaned down and pressed a kiss on her lips.
"Don't ever give up."

"Do you really think I'm beautiful?"

The question startled him, but then he said simply,
"Very."

She tried to turn away, embarrassed that she had asked,
and not believing his answer.

"Abby, listen to me." He forced her to look into his eyes.
"You are beautiful. I saw that the moment I plucked you up
off the ground in front of the Red Dog Saloon. You have
the most glorious hair I have ever seen."

Abigail snorted at this pronouncement.

Noah laughed. "It's true. And your eyes. Large and luminous. And your mouth." His hand came up to trace her
lower lip. "Full and wide. Sensual."

Red singed her cheeks but she didn't turn away.

"Over the weeks I came to see that you are also beautiful
inside. Your heart is good and true. And you have more
fight in you than most men I've met. It's just that you don't
give yourself any credit for your successes. Have you or
have you not learned to gather eggs?"

She scoffed at this. "But I can't milk a cow or clean a—"

"See that! You're making my point for me. You only see
what you think are failures." His fingers trailed back into
her hair. "You have had plenty of success while you have
been here. Hell, you're the best damned oatmeal cook I've
ever met."

She scowled and tried to turn away.

"No, Abby. I'm not making fun of you. I'm making a
point. You have learned things that you didn't know before.
But since there is so much to learn, your successes have
paled in comparison."

"Yes, there's so much I need to learn, things other
women do all the time, as easily as if they were breathing."

Noah gave her a frustrated shake. "Do you think for one
minute those women were born knowing how to do wash or
cook?"

Abigail looked away, her brow furrowed.

"Hell, no, they didn't. They learned. Just like you're

learning. Only they had the good fortune to learn early in life with someone teaching them how it's all done. That's what you need, Abby. Someone to show you the way." His voice softened. "That's all, darlin'. Just someone to show you the way. You've come too far to give up now."

13

Scenes from the day before played mercilessly in Abigail's mind. She saw Walter's naked back, hovering above one bare and dirty shoulder of Hester Smith. The woman had touched Walter as Abigail never dreamed of touching him. The memory made her want to retch. And she knew then that she would never touch Walter, in that way or any other way, ever. She pressed her eyes closed as if in doing so she could push the image away.

But oddly enough, mixed with all the wretchedness that she felt, there was relief. She was ashamed of herself to realize that the decision had been made for her, and for that she was relieved. She could no longer marry Walter after what she had learned, and she was relieved to have been provided with a clear-cut excuse not to have to do the very thing she didn't want to do.

And then she thought of Noah and all that he had told her. Realization dawned bright that indeed her fear of failure had made it impossible to succeed. She had been too worried about failing to give herself totally over to succeeding. But she hadn't wanted to believe him at the time. But now she could no longer deny that during the last several weeks she had moved boldly into new territory, but while doing so she had retained all her old fears and insecurities, making it impossible to deal successfully in her new world.

And suddenly she knew what to do. She was going to forget the importance of not failing. She wouldn't think about the consequences of failure. She was not going to give up. She was going to make things work if it killed her. At this point, what did she have to lose? She was going to

concentrate on learning, on succeeding. And her first step
was to go to her father, tell him that the engagement was
off, then find someone to teach her how the boardinghouse
business was properly done—just as soon as she dealt with
the eggs and Alberta and the rest of the things that had to
be dealt with before the sun rose.

She still couldn't get milk from Alberta but she gathered
an entire basket of eggs without breaking a single one. And
she was feeling remarkably good until she realized Lou
hadn't shown up. In her misery, she had forgotten Lou. It
all came back to her then. The obvious dislike between
Walter and Lou. Lou's insistence that Abigail not walk her
home. Lou had known all along. And had been afraid.
Anger at Walter and Hester Smith snaked down her spine.
That poor child.

Well, as soon as she finished with her father, she told
herself, she would go back to Lou's house and confront that
mother yet. The thought made her stomach turn. But that
didn't matter. What mattered was Lou.

Abigail arrived at her father's house while he sat at the
dining table, having just finished breakfast. Virginia was
there as well, but thankfully, no one else.

"Good morning," Abigail said to gain attention.

Virginia looked up, clearly surprised, but instantly
pleased. "Abigail!"

Sherwood lowered his paper and stared at her, hard.
"Morning, daughter," he said finally. "What brings you out
here this early?" Before she could answer, however, he
pushed up from his seat and continued. "No breakfast to
make? No chores to do? Could that be because you have
lost all but one boarder?"

Abigail tensed. "How did you know?"

"Nothing goes on in this town without me knowing
about it. I'd think you knew that."

Instantly, she wondered if he knew what she had witnessed last evening. But she doubted it. Surely, even her father wouldn't be angry with her because Walter was found
in bed with another woman. Though not necessarily, she re-

alized. "No doubt you have contacts in every crack and crevice in town. But that's not why I'm here."

Sherwood raised one silvered brow. "Then don't keep us waiting. What is it?"

Suddenly the words wouldn't come. Her bravado deserted her. Fear of repercussions overwhelmed her. Glancing back and forth between her father and Virginia, she turned her hand over and over again, squeezing it each time. Suddenly, she wondered why she had come here. Her father wouldn't understand. And she certainly wasn't about to tell him about what she had seen. If he found out, it most definitely wouldn't be from her.

"Come on, girl," he barked impatiently. "I don't have all day."

"The wedding is off." Just that, no preamble, simple as white icing on a white cake.

For a heartbeat Sherwood did not say a word. He stared at her, his eyes slightly widening. "Off!" he demanded finally. "How could it be off? You only just got engaged!"

Virginia lowered her paper altogether and studied Abigail. "What did he do?"

Her stepmother's voice was so kind and caring that it was almost her undoing. She had the sudden longing to confide in her like a mother and daughter. To ask her for advice. To spill her hopes and her dreams and her fears. Woman to woman. As she had never done before. But of course she would not. She had no interest in causing a scene. So she forced a smile, and said, "It's just better this way. It was a mistake to have become engaged in the first place."

Sherwood snorted. "I find it hard to believe Walter feels that way."

"Walter Jackson has made it quite clear that a marriage between us would be a mistake," she equivocated, certain the man would indeed feel that way when he realized his only other option was to be found out.

Sherwood tilted his head and eyed her dubiously. "Well, that's just about the shortest engagement I have ever heard of." His tone was derisive.

"Sherwood," Virginia said.

But he ignored his wife, simply continued to stare at his eldest, unmarried daughter.

Abigail fidgeted. "Actually, that is still not why I'm here."

"Now what?"

"I know things haven't been going as well as they should be over at the boardinghouse."

"Oh, really?" Sarcasm laced her father's words.

"But things will get better. And I'm here to ask you for an extension," Abigail said, standing up straighter.

"Extension! You can just forget that, missy. I'm tired of this farce. You are going to pack your bags and come home."

"Father! You can't do that."

"Just watch me. I can and I will. I only went along with the outlandish scheme because I knew you were going to be getting married soon. In fact, I thought it might hurry things along. And sure enough it did, that is until you went and ruined it! Engagement off!" he barked as if he couldn't believe his ears.

"But, Father," she said, trying to keep her voice steady. "You told me you'd give the boardinghouse to me if I succeeded."

"Only because I thought I'd be giving it to you *and* a husband. I want you married, Abigail. It's high time I was able to relinquish my responsibility of raising you over to a husband."

Abigail staggered and reached out to steady herself on the edge of the long mahogany table. Virginia rose from her seat.

"And since you've ruined the one chance you had at marriage, then you might as well come home so I can get rid of the boardinghouse once and for all. You've managed to get rid of two of the boarders. I'm sure I can talk Blake into staying at the hotel . . ."

Abigail did not wait to hear what else he said. She didn't wait for Virginia's comforting support. She turned and dashed from the house, filled with a sense of betrayal deeper than she had experienced at finding Walter in the arms of another woman. Betrayal mixed with anger and sadness and frustration. She wanted to be anywhere but in the house with her father—ever again.

Her heart was pounding and she was out of breath by the time she made it to the boardinghouse. Her mind raced, trying to come up with some kind of plan. What could she do to stay out of her father's house? Millie came to mind and she recoiled at the possibility. There had to be another way. But what could she do to change her father's mind?

She had thought she had nothing to lose. How wrong could she have been? To find that her father disliked her so much that he would use some sort of prize to dangle in front of a man's nose in hopes he would bite, shredded whatever vestiges of self-respect she ever had. She felt hopeless and worthless. She felt as though her back was against the wall. With that thought, however, she realized she couldn't give in, wouldn't give in—she had to fight. And no sooner did that thought rush through her brain than inspiration struck, just as Noah Blake sauntered through the kitchen door.

"Morning," he said, walking over to the stove to see if by chance there might be any coffee. "Looks like it's going to be a beautiful day." He cast a quick questioning glance back over his shoulder. "How you feeling today?" he asked as he came to the stove.

"Say you'll marry me!" she said without warning.

Noah's hand stopped in midair as he reached for the coffee pot on top of the stove. The kitchen filled with silence—ominous, oppressive silence. Somewhere in the distance a dog barked and a door slammed shut. But Noah made not a sound. He didn't turn back or drop his hand. He simply stood there, frozen, unable to move.

At length, he dropped his hand and turned to look at her. He closed his eyes, then opened them again as if trying to wake himself from a dream he didn't find particularly appealing. "A simple 'feeling fine, thank you,' would have done, Abigail. Even telling me you weren't feeling so fine would have done in a pinch. But asking me to marry you is a bit overdone, even for you, don't you think?"

Clasping her hands together, her eyes wide with inspiration, ignoring his less than enthusiastic response, she hurried to explain. "Oh, you have it all wrong!" She screwed up her lips in a silly smile. "I don't actually want you to marry me," she announced as if he were demented. "You just have to *say* you will. I mean, I simply want you to become engaged to me. Betrothed, you know. It's really very simple."

"Simple!" The word exploded from his lips as he came to life. "What are you talking about?"

"Mr. Blake," she said as if talking to an errant child. "It really *is* quite simple. You told me not to give up on my new life. I took your advice to heart and went to ask my father for an extension on my deadline to make the boarding-house work." Her smile faltered. "Well, he said I couldn't continue since I wasn't getting married. Had I known he had ulterior motives, I never would have told him my engagement to Walter was off." She shrugged her shoulders. "Alas, I wasn't privy to that information. So, I thought *we* could get engaged, thereby solving my dilemma. I get my extension. I learn how to run this place properly. And then once I've learned and I get everything turned over to me, we break our engagement and you go along on your merry way." She didn't mind in the least that her plans were manipulative. She had found that when she tried to play fair with her father she always lost. And this game she couldn't afford to lose.

Noah's eyes were slits of incredulity, and he looked at her as if she should be locked up for the safety of others. When she did nothing more than smile, he shook his head from side to side and grumbled. "Marriage," he said simply.

"No, Mr. Blake. Just an engagement."

"Oh," he scoffed, "*just* an engagement."

"Just so."

"You've made it more than clear you don't even like me. Why in the world would you choose me for your scheme?"

Red crept into her cheeks. "Well . . ." She didn't know how to answer. Tell him he was handy, that he was the only person that she could think of that was available? Or perhaps if she was truthful with herself, she would admit that she loved his kisses, thought perhaps she might enjoy one or two more before this deed was done. Of course, she wasn't about to admit any such thing, not in a million years.

As it happened, however, he didn't wait for an answer. "And how do you propose to learn how to run this place properly?"

Abigail smiled a smile that lit the room. This she could answer. "You seem to know an awful lot about lighting stoves and making meals. Good heavens, you prepared a roast that would give old Mrs. Holloway a run for her money."

"Just yesterday you said it was dry."

"Posh," she said, waving such an objection away. "I was simply repeating what my father had said, and you know it. You're just being difficult, Mr. Blake."

Noah cursed under his breath. "There's a hell of a lot more to running a boardinghouse than lighting stoves and cooking roasts."

"My point exactly, and who better to teach me than you, Mr. Blake, who has shown such a surprising aptitude for the job."

"Teach you! How am I supposed to teach you anything? You can hardly boil water!"

It was as if he had slapped her. He regretted the words before they were entirely out of his mouth. Her smile melted away. She stood there looking stunned. She started to turn away, but he reached out and took her arm.

"Damn it, Abby. I didn't mean that."

"No, you're right," she said, with a self-deprecating shake of her head. She had worked so hard to hold on to her sense of purpose and determination, had held on so tight that when it finally slipped away she felt defeated. Her enthusiasm suddenly evaporated. "What was I thinking? Who am I trying to fool? Obviously the only person being fooled over and over again around here is me." She hesitated. "It

was just that after last night I thought . . ." Her words
trailed off.

"I meant what I said last night, damn it. You *can* do it.
And I never should have said that about boiling water. It's
untrue."

This time Abigail scoffed and pulled away.

He grabbed her arm again, then turned her around until
they faced each other, her head tilting back to look him in
the eye. "I meant every word I said last night," he said.
"This morning you just surprised me, is all. Just talk of
marriage makes me do crazy things. I'm not the marrying
kind, Abigail. Or even the getting engaged kind. I'd like to
help, really, but . . ."

"There you are!" Sherwood's voice snapped like a whip
in the suddenly small confines of the kitchen.

Both Abigail and Noah turned with a start, neither having heard him come through the door.

"Father," Abigail gasped.

Sherwood stood before them, clearly in a rage. "How
dare you walk out on me! Pack your bags this instant.
You're going home. And after that I'm sending you to live
with your aunts in St. Louis."

Her head swam. St. Louis. Banished. So far from home.
Though why, she wondered suddenly, tired of fighting, she
cared where she lived when faced with so many who
clearly couldn't care less where she was, she could not
fathom. But still the thought of leaving the only place she
knew, and the budding friendship with Virginia, left her
bereft. And then there was Noah. *But what feel I?* she wondered. Cold, empty loss. But that was absurd. He was nothing more than a means to an end.

"Yes, daughter, St. Louis."

"You can't do this, Father," she whispered.

"I can and I will."

"That's unfair."

"I'll tell you what's unfair. Having a daughter who doesn't
have enough to recommend her to get herself a husband.
You couldn't even manage to stay engaged long enough to
have a celebration."

"Father, please . . ."

"Don't you 'Father, please' me, daughter. If you had managed to keep yourself engaged we wouldn't be having this discussion."

"She is engaged," Noah said, his voice rumbling ominously through the room.

The house grew silent.

Noah stepped forward and put his arm around Abigail's shoulders. Sherwood's eyes opened wide.

Noah's anger boiled and he nearly took Sherwood outside and beat him to a pulp when he felt Abigail's fragile weight sag against his arm in relief.

"To who?" Sherwood asked in disbelief, his face lined and angry.

"To me."

Sherwood stared at the younger man. Neither one spoke. For a second Noah thought that indeed the two of them just might end up outside having it out. But then Sherwood's anger magically evaporated and a slow, calculating smile spread across his face. "Well, well, well. It looks like we just might have something to celebrate after all."

14

"JUST ENGAGED!"

Noah stomped through the streets, his head down, his arms swinging with purpose, ignoring passersby who called their greetings.

"Just engaged," he muttered again and shook his head. He should have known better than to get himself into something like this. Any fool would know it could only lead to trouble. Yes, trouble. Abigail Ashleigh had been nothing but trouble since the day he opened that saloon door and met her—so to speak. If only he'd told another joke or even had another drink before he had gotten off that barstool and headed out the door, he would have missed her altogether.

But he knew he wasn't being truthful—or at least entirely truthful. Besides trouble, Abigail Ashleigh had brought a good deal of joy to his already, in his opinion, joyful life. He liked seeing her laugh and smile, then fume with frustration and anger. Hell, he just plain liked seeing her. But that didn't mean he wanted to marry her. As he had told her, marriage was not for him.

On top of everything, there was that damned father of hers. After the way he had treated Abigail, Noah knew he'd had no choice but to get involved. He wasn't a man who could sit by and let a lady get treated so poorly. Or so he told himself since he didn't like thinking about the feelings that ran through him when Abby had asked him to marry her. Elation. Joy. Followed rapidly by fear and desperation. Hell no, he didn't like to think about it one bit. Plain and simple he was a man out to protect a lady.

"Damn!" he cursed under his breath.

He took the steps to the front porch of the boardinghouse in one leap, then slammed through the door. "Abigail!" he bellowed.

When he received no reply he headed for the kitchen, though God knew she didn't know the first thing about what to do in that particular room. How in the world could he have told her not to give up? Abigail had about as much domestic sense as a gnat. And that was being unkind to the gnat. But no, he had to go and tell her to stick it out—perseverance and hard work. If ever his theory had been disproved it was by Abigail Ashleigh. Again and again and again. And now he was going to suffer for it.

He was worked up into a lather, and was just waiting to vent his spleen on the head of the household. But she was nowhere to be found.

"Abigail!" he hollered out the back door.

Nothing.

He noticed that the door to Abigail's room was shut. Without regard for propriety, he threw the door wide. "Abigail!"

His bellow trailed off to a near choke at the sight that met his eyes. There she was, startled like a deer, her pantaloons hastily pulled on, her camisole doing little to hide her body.

They stared at each other without moving. Noah forgot why he was there as his eyes slowly traveled the length of her. As if suddenly released from some invisible grip, Abigail finally reached out and snatched up her dress that lay on the bed, waiting to be pulled on.

Another man would have apologized profusely and hurried out the door. Noah never gave either possibility a thought. He simply stared at her. Even now, with her gown clutched to her breast like a shield, he could still make out the gently rounded curve of her hip and beautifully turned curve of her ankle.

He had been drawn to her from the beginning, he had come to acknowledge that, albeit reluctantly. He had wanted her with a physical ache that had left him mad with desire for days after the picnic. And that was without ever having any idea that she had the body of a nymph. He never would have guessed that under those drab and shapeless clothes he would find . . . this.

Desire snaked through his loins, leaving him hard. Not since he was a boy had he experienced such intensity. All he could think about was tossing her on the bed and burying himself deeply in the warmth of her body, moving within her, slowly, until she wanted him as much as he wanted her.

But that was absurd, he quickly berated himself. It didn't matter what he wanted. What mattered was that he was in a mess that was impossible to extricate himself from. And it was all her fault.

With herculean strength, he forced himself to turn away. And the motion had nothing to do with propriety—rather self-preservation.

He located an armoire against the wall. Pounding across the room, Abigail apparently frozen to the spot, Noah whipped open the cabinet doors to find a row of dresses.

"Get out," she finally managed.

"I'd like to, darlin', but unfortunately you've put me in a position where I can't do that."

"What are you talking about?"

Noah only grumbled as he took one dress after another out of the armoire and threw them on the bed. "Don't you have anything besides black or brown or some shade of the same?"

"Mr. Blake!"

"Look at this wardrobe," Noah demanded. "No wonder you don't laugh or smile very often. Dressed like this, who would?"

But then his wild hunt stopped abruptly when he came to the very last dress at the very back of the armoire. "Now this is more like it."

He pulled out a gown of white silk lace. Abigail made to step forward as if to protect her secret gown, but stopped when she suddenly became aware, once again, of her attire, or lack thereof.

"Mr. Blake," she said, her voice querulous. "Get out of my room this instant. And put that dress away."

"Sorry, darlin'. Can't do it. We've got to hurry."

"Hurry? What are you talking about?"

Noah tossed the silk lace dress on top of the heap. "Put this on."

"Whatever for?"

He didn't answer, but he grew very still. Taking a deep breath he turned back and sauntered over to Abigail. When he stood no more than a few inches in front of her, he tilted her chin and stared down into her eyes. Her heart hammered in her chest. He looked angry and sad and strangely resigned, but why, she had no idea. "Hurry for what?" she repeated softly.

A chuckle that held little mirth rumbled in his chest. "A wedding."

"A wedding?" she asked, sickening dread beginning to rise. "Whose?"

His blue eyes softened and his lips tilted with the hint of a smile. "Yours, sweet Abby," he said simply.

Abigail sucked in her breath and nearly dropped her dress. "Mine?"

"Yes, yours."

"What are you talking about, Mr. Blake?"

They stared at each other, and for a moment Abigail thought he was going to lower his head to hers and kiss her. For that moment, she forgot about his absurd proclamations and the fact that she stood before him so indecently clad, or unclad really, that she wasn't sure she would ever recover. But that, she'd think about later. Right then, she only wanted to feel his lips on hers—feel the warmth of his body.

Noah scoffed and stepped away, leaving Abigail dizzy and disoriented.

"That father of yours is a scourge, I tell you. Worse. He's like the black plague."

Once her mind cleared and her heart fell back into a normal cadence, she asked, "What are you talking about?"

"You know how he's been pestering me about putting

my money in that precious bank of his. Well, this morning I'd just about had enough of Sherwood Ashleigh and I told him I didn't want anything to do with his damned bank. He looked at me with those arctic cold eyes of his and said he wondered if I wasn't more like Walter Jackson than he thought. Then he asked me if I was taking advantage of his daughter. Taking advantage of his daughter!" Noah had to bite back the fact that it was all he had been able to do not to say, like he cared one whit for his daughter.

"Oh, dear," she said, her brow worried. "I should have anticipated this."

"I should have told him it was his daughter who was taking advantage of me!"

Abigail cringed. "Why didn't you tell him?"

Noah glanced back at her, his eyes grown dark with emotion, before he grunted and turned away. "Because I wasn't going to betray you like all the rest of those worthless men in your life."

Tears threatened. Her throat ached. How was it that this virtual stranger could be so kind and caring, when her own family was not? And how bittersweet was the feeling. The one person who seemed to care about her, really care about her despite his words that would imply otherwise, would be out of her life in a matter of months, if not weeks. "I'm sure you must be mistaken about the wedding," she said, trying to cover her emotions. "I've never heard of such an absurd demand—even from my father."

Noah only glowered, then began pacing the room.

"Well," she continued, "even if my father *has* done this, you really don't have to go through with it. It's more than anyone has a right to ask. We will simply go over to the bank right now and tell him the truth, that's all."

Noah sighed. "We're not going anywhere, except to a wedding."

"But—"

"I don't want to hear another word about it, Abby. You said you wanted this blasted boardinghouse, and I'm going to see that you get it if it's the last thing I do."

He turned away and Abigail felt as if her heart had been pierced. He cared for her yes, but in some nonsensical sisterly way. Nothing more. But of course her disappointment was absurd. She had known all along he thought of her as a nuisance. She took a deep breath. "If you're willing to go along with my scheme for now, it should be easy enough to accomplish without too much imposition on your life. We will stay in separate rooms. Without any boarders here, who's going to know the difference. Once things are running smoothly and we get everything settled with my father, we'll get the marriage annulled, then you'll be free of me and this absurd entanglement I've gotten you mixed up in. It's the only solution."

Noah stiffened, or so she thought. Maybe, maybe there was something more there. She remembered their kisses. Surely there was something more there. And when he looked into her eyes so deep as if he could see into her soul, she thought he was going to say something. Instead he merely nodded his head then headed for the door. "You better hurry. Your father's gone to get the preacher and they should be here any time."

Suddenly, something occurred to Abigail. "Noah, you know why he's doing this, don't you?"

With his hand on the doorknob, he stopped.

"I'm certain he wants to make sure that we do marry in order to get at your money. Oh, Noah, I'm so sorry."

Noah turned back and came to stand before her. "Here you are, being browbeaten by your father and even by me, and all you can think about is my well-being. I can take care of myself, darlin'." He leaned down and pressed a kiss to her forehead. "Though it's really nice of you to care." Too nice, he thought suddenly, and pulled back. "You need to start worrying about yourself. Your father won't lay a finger on my money."

A frantic knock sounded at the front door. Abigail jumped and glanced down at her partially clad form.

"I'm going," Noah said without having to be asked.

Just when he reached the door, she called out. "Noah."

He stopped and looked back.

She had the crazy urge to tell him so much, about how much she appreciated his kindness, that he was like no man she had ever met, and that his kisses truly were something to remember. But then the knock sounded again and she only shrugged her shoulders and said, "Thank you."

He stared at her for a long uncomfortable moment until he smiled. "You're welcome."

Then he was gone and she heard him talking in the front parlor. She barely had time to pull on a wrapper before Virginia burst through the door.

"Your father told me!"

"What? That I'm getting married today?"

"Yes. I tried to talk him out of it, but he's adamant."

"Of course he is. It's his chance at Noah's money and I handed it to him on a silver platter. And I could kick myself for that."

Virginia sighed. "I know, I know. That man can be as stubborn as any mule I've had the misfortune to meet."

"Noah or Father?"

Virginia and Abigail looked at each other. "Both," they said in unison, then burst out laughing.

"What's going on in here?" Noah demanded as he came back through the door with a huge trunk in his hands.

Abigail gasped, and wondered what Virginia must think of the fact that he just walked in the room with her only half dressed. "Noah!"

"Over there, Mr. Blake," Virginia instructed, seemingly unaware or unconcerned that any impropriety was taking place. "Now run along. We have things to do."

"What's going on?" Abigail asked.

"We're getting ready for a wedding."

"What do you mean?"

"I might not have been able to talk your father out of the wedding altogether, but I managed to get him to give us some time. Every woman desires a wedding to remember, and that is just what you are going to have."

"Oh, Virginia," Abigail said, when her stepmother pulled open the trunk filled with wedding finery. "Where did you get all this?"

"It's mine. I hope you don't mind. But on such short notice . . ."

"Mind? I'm honored."

"Good. We are going to do you up. Adam has gone to find Lou to be a flower girl, and Myrtle Kent is making the arrangements for some flowers and a small reception afterwards."

"Mrs. Kent is helping?"

"Yes, and she was more than happy to do so. She's rather fond of you I've noticed."

"But she's the one who's been telling Father about all . . . my failures."

"No, dear, Emma has."

"*Emma?*"

"Yes, Emma."

"How has she known?"

"She has been coming to town early every morning. And of course word travels quickly."

"Even quicker when Emma's bringing it straight home."

"I'm afraid so," Virginia said with a slight shake of her head.

"And all this time I blamed Mrs. Kent."

"Well, it's easy to see why. She's unhappy here in El Paso, and she can be an unpleasant person at times. But truly she cares for you a great deal."

After Virginia had stepped out to check on the other arrangements Lou arrived. At first the little girl held back, obviously not certain how she would be received after the fiasco at her house. Abigail opened her arms to the young child who immediately hurtled herself into them.

"Oh, Miss Abigail," she whispered. "I was feeling so scared that you would hate me so forever."

"What happened at your house has nothing to do with you. It's not your fault. Do you understand?"

Lou seemed to consider. "Yes," she said finally, then hugged her even tighter. "I wish you were my mama."

The words were spoken so quietly, and muffled, that it took a moment for the statement to register. Abigail's heart burgeoned with joy. Noah cared for her in some inexplicable way. Mrs. Kent was rather fond of her. Virginia had truly become a cherished friend. Even Millie, whether right or wrong, had shown she cared. Never had she been so surrounded by such caring. And it felt wonderful—awkward, yes, but wonderful as well, and she knew she could get used to it rather quickly.

And Lou. Precious Lou who wanted exactly what she wanted. For them to be a family. But how could she respond to such sentiments? She had no idea. She wasn't Lou's mother, though how desperately she wished it were so. If only she could tell her that. But as was usual in her life, caution prevailed, and instead of saying something she might regret, Abigail simply held Lou tight, and wished, like Lou, that she was her mother.

There was not a shotgun to be found that evening when the wedding was set to begin, though a shotgun wedding it seemed to be, if the scowl on Noah's face was any indication. The boardinghouse was filled with greenery and roses and dozens of candles burning bright. Abigail could hardly believe her eyes when she peeked into the parlor.

"Thank you, Mrs. Kent," she whispered when the proprietress came back to see if all was ready.

"It was nothing, Abigail. I was only happy I could help." Myrtle stood back. "And aren't you just the prettiest bride I have ever seen."

Abigail reached over and squeezed Virginia's hand. "I have Virginia to thank for that."

"Nonsense," Virginia replied, though her smile was radiant. "I loved every minute of it."

And it had taken more than a few minutes to accomplish. Abigail had had her hair washed and body soaked in sweet smelling water. Then she had been dried and coiffed within an inch of her life. Her scalp still tingled from the effort. But even Abigail had to admit it had all been worthwhile. She had never felt anything remotely close to beautiful, but this day she came pretty close.

And then it was time to get married.

She came to stand in the doorway of the parlor. Everyone turned. She wore the full white lace dress that she had secretly made, a replica of the wedding dress in her dreams. She never thought she would have an opportunity to wear it. Certainly never with Walter. She also wore Virginia's white netted mitts and carried her lace-trimmed handkerchief. Her hair had been pulled up loosely with tendrils falling around her face and neck. And when she saw Noah's face she knew in her heart that she had never been more beautiful.

The ceremony passed in a dream. She was aware of nothing more than Noah's strong hand clasped around hers, and the scent of woodspice and wild prairies that she loved so much. She longed for the end so she could feel his kiss. And she knew that even after their marriage was over, she would cherish this memory forever.

It wasn't until they stood amid the townspeople, as husband and wife, that her dream snapped in two.

"Isn't this quaint."

Abigail was barely aware of Noah's arm tightening around her. She turned and focused on her sister. "Emma."

"I should have known this would be the only way you could manage to get yourself married."

Myrtle gasped. The others who were near grumbled under their breath, shifting uncomfortably.

Grant stepped forward. "Emma!"

"That's all right, Grant," Noah interjected.

Noah's voice was smooth and jovial as it always was. But Abigail had come to know him over the last weeks, and knew the joviality was only surface deep. Noah Blake was angry, very angry.

"Your wife," Noah continued, "simply has it all wrong. I've been trying to convince Abby to marry me since the day I met her."

"Abby," Emma mimicked derisively. "You call her Abby?"

"Emma," Grant demanded once again.

Emma glanced at her husband, but no sooner had her eyes taken in his form than she noticed Lou standing next to him, holding his hand, leaning up against him as if he was her father. Her malice toward Abigail shifted to the little girl. Lou noticed and seemed to press even closer to Grant.

Emma's face twisted and contorted. "What is she doing . . ."

"Well, well, well," Sherwood called as he sauntered up to the group, unaware of the tension he walked into. "Here's my happy family now." He slapped Noah on the back. "Son," he said and smiled. "I like that." He seemed to have no regard for his other son-in-law who stood there as well, and whom he had rarely called anything, much less son. Then he looked at Abigail. "Well, daughter. I have to admit I never thought I'd see the day when I'd be impressed by something you did."

"Mr. Ashleigh—" Noah began, anger simmering.

"Dad, call me dad, son."

"You don't—"

"Noah, please," Abigail interjected. "Not now."

Noah grumbled, but held his tongue. "If you'll excuse me, I think I'll get some fresh air."

Stepping out onto the back porch, a burst of crisp air announcing the rapid approach of winter wrapped around him.

"So you have married after all."

Noah spun around to the sound. "Wanderer. You're back."

"Yes, and in time to witness your marriage. I am happy for you. Am I to believe that now you will think differently about the hunt?"

"No!"

The vehemence startled both of them.

"Sorry," Noah offered. "I'm edgy is all."

"And the hunt?"

"Nothing changes." Noah pulled his pipe from his coat pocket. He was silent as he filled the bowl with tobacco, tapped it down, then struck a match. "I'm going," he said finally, a tendril of smoke curling in the air.

"But what about your wife?"

"She's a wife in name only."

Wanderer raised an eyebrow.

"It's true," Noah replied gruffly.

"In name only? I don't understand."

"Hell, Wanderer. She needed help, and how could I refuse. A pack of wolves are kinder to their kin than that father and sister of hers are to her. I don't know how she's made it this far."

"Then you simply feel sorry for her?"

Noah thought about this. He wanted to say yes, but he had never lied to his friend and he didn't want to start now. "No, that's not all. But for as much as I like her, she drives me crazy. A more uptight female I have never met."

"So you want to set her free. Like the birds and animals you heal then free in the woods."

"I don't see how that is relevant."

"I've often noticed the disparity between your nature and the life you lead," Wanderer said.

"What are you talking about?"

"You support yourself by trapping beaver. But you work to free and heal every other animal you run across. Now, it seems, you are trying to free women as well."

"I don't know what you're talking about, Wanderer. But I'm just going to help Abigail out is all. Then I'm going to get on with my life. We're getting the marriage annulled once she's figured out how to run this boardinghouse. Like I said, this is a marriage in name only."

"I see."

"No you don't see, I can tell from your voice. She is in need and I'm helping her out. Nothing more. I'm married to her for now, and I'll teach her all I can about survival. Then I'm gettin' the hell out. This will be no marriage in the real sense of the word. Once things are worked out she'll go her way and I'll go mine."

"Who are you trying to convince? Me? Or you?"

Noah grumbled. "Yeah, that's just like you, Wanderer. Get all philosophical on me. Save it for someone who's interested."

Wanderer nodded his head with all the solemnity of a priest, but Noah suspected he was being sarcastic nonetheless. "And none of this means you need to be going on the hunt anymore just because I am."

"We've been over this. If you go, I go."

"That's the craziest damn thing I ever heard."

Wanderer tilted his head. "It is nothing more than the truth. But enough." He glanced through the window of the house. "It looks like you are being sought, my friend."

"Damn," he cursed. "Probably getting ready to do some other ceremonial foolishness. For all I like that stepmother of Abby's, the woman is filled with all kinds of notions about making this an event to remember."

"I will go then."

"All right, but be back in a month."

"So early?"

Noah didn't answer at first. "Yeah, the earlier I get out of here the better." And a month should be enough time, even for Abigail, to learn how to run a boardinghouse."

Wanderer said nothing more, simply nodded his head then disappeared as quietly and as mysteriously as he had come. Noah stared after him until he heard his name called from the house.

Sure enough, when Noah entered, the small crowd was waiting for him. Abigail stood amongst the group, her cheeks stained painfully with red. Noah could only wonder what had happened now.

"There you are, son." Sherwood slapped him on the back and grinned. "Time for the grand finale, so to speak."

A titter of laughter shimmered across the room.

Noah looked from Sherwood to Abigail, confusion etching his face.

The men started making ribald remarks and the women giggled and smiled. Then, with blinding clarity, he understood. It was time to take his wife to the marriage bed. The very place he needed to do his best to avoid.

Jesse ... of this house came to ... to .of the morning that must be ...

We are ... that this ...

∼ 15 ∼

"SO, WIFE, WHAT DO YOU PROPOSE WE DO NOW?"

They stood in her bedroom, having been prodded and taunted there by the reveling crowd. The house still clamored with voices, singing, laughing and merry-making, while Noah stood in all his wedding finery with his back against the closed bedroom door.

He looked devastatingly handsome. And Abigail longed to go to him. After a moment's hesitation, she turned away and shrugged. "Wait for everyone to leave, I suppose."

"All right," he said easily, convincing Abigail that she was the only one who felt the tension of this absurd situation.

Pushing away, Noah took the few steps between the door and the bed, removing his frock coat as he went. As he stepped past her, he offered her no more than a smile. But her inner lament was forgotten when he tossed his coat aside and he stretched out on her mattress.

"What are you doing?" Abigail demanded.

"Waiting. Just like you said." He crossed his booted feet at the ankles and his arms underneath his head.

"On the bed?"

Noah made an ordeal of glancing around the room. "As I see it, it's the bed or the floor." His teeth flashed his devilish smile. "In the short time I've been here I've grown accustomed to the comforts of a bed. The hard floor, even with your lovely rug, has lost its appeal."

Following his glance she noted that indeed there was nowhere else to sit other than the bed—not a chair or footstool to be found. And unless she was willing to hike her-

self up onto the top of the bureau in her wedding gown, her
choices were to remain standing, sit on the floor, or lie
down next to Noah. Her heart quickly sped up at the
thought. What would it be like to lie next to him? Shoulder
pressed against shoulder. Like husband and wife. To have
and to hold. Forever.

Quickly she looked away. No question, she would remain standing. Surely the guests couldn't stay much longer.

No sooner had the thought passed through her head than
someone pulled out a fiddle and the music and dancing
grew louder in the parlor. Abigail groaned. Noah laughed.

"Set yourself down, darlin'. From the sounds of things I
could be here a good long while."

Abigail glanced at the bed as if what he suggested was a
cross between punishment and reward.

"I won't touch you."

At this she snorted, but more at the fact that she knew
she longed for him to do nothing more than break his word.

"I promise," he added with a chuckle and moved over a
bit farther.

Eyeing Noah as he patted the place beside him, she
weighed her options. Finally, she approached the bed cau-
tiously. "You promise?" she said, feeling obligated to ask.

"Yes, Abigail, I promise."

Noah watched as she attempted to hike herself up on the
thick feather mattress. The layers of her dress didn't allow
her much movement, and as a result her efforts at gaining a
seat went without much success.

"This is ridiculous," Noah said finally in a sudden burst
as he rolled off the other side of the bed. He came around to
stand in front of her, and without asking permission he
began undoing her dress.

Abigail puffed up with indignation. "What are you
doing?"

"What does it look like, Abby? I'm undressing you,"
he said. The glint in his eye was half teasing, half
wicked.

"You promised!" she exclaimed, slapping at his hands.

"Good Lord, woman. I'm not trying to seduce you, I'm

simply trying to make it possible for you to get up onto the
bed."

"But—"

"No, buts. Just hold still."

He worked the tiny buttons with ease despite the size of
his fingers.

Abigail stiffened. "From the deftness with which you
handle those fastenings, I'd be inclined to surmise that
you've done this a time or two."

"Me?" he asked with a smile. "Nah."

"Why do I find that hard to believe?"

Noah threw back his head and laughed. "Do I detect a
note of jealousy in your voice, dear wife?"

"Jealous! Hardly, Mr. Blake," she said, her cheeks crimson as her dress fell in a pool of white silk around her ankles. "In fact," she added, her chin coming up a notch, "this
whole situation is absurd. Good heavens! We are adults—
hopefully mature adults, and we will deal with the situation
accordingly." She cocked her head toward the door. "I have
to agree with you that from the sounds of things out there,
this could be a long night."

"Agree with me? You?" He chuckled at his bit of humor.
"And what do you propose we do then, my ever practical
little wife?"

"Get ready for bed, go to sleep, then determine how best
to go about working things out in the morning. I'm exhausted." Abigail walked over to the bureau and pulled a
thick flannel nightgown from the drawer.

"Fine." Noah shucked his vest, shirt, shoes, and socks,
tossed them over the end of the bed with his coat, then
stretched out in his pants and watched with something close
to amazement as Abigail pulled the gown over her head,
then proceeded to remove her undergarments. All he could
see was a jumble of elbows and knees poking about underneath until finally she succeeded, turned triumphantly, and
started toward the bed.

She stopped with mouth agape when she became aware
of Noah's only partially clad state. But then without utter-

ing a word, or at least a coherent word, she pulled back her
shoulders and inched onto her side of the bed.

They lay next to one another, Noah on his back, Abigail
on her side, a good foot between them despite the fact that
he took up a large portion of the narrow bed. With a precarious hold on the edge, she lay stiff as a board, the covers
pulled up to her ear.

Neither one of them spoke. The only sounds came from
the ruckus going on in nether regions of the house. Minutes
ticked by.

After a while Abigail sighed and rolled over onto her
back, still on the very edge of the bed, and stared up at the
ceiling. "Everything was beautiful, wasn't it?"

Noah grinned into the semi-darkness. "I thought you said
you were exhausted?"

"I am, but . . . I don't know." She hooked her elbows
over the edge of the blanket. "I've never had a wedding before."

They lay side by side, strangely at ease for two people
who had done nothing more together than share a few
stolen kisses and fight like cats and dogs.

Noah crossed his arms behind his head. "I'm sorry."

"Sorry? Why are you sorry? Certainly none of this is
your fault."

"I know, but you deserve a big beautiful wedding that
you've planned for ages, with flowers all over and candles
burning, and a wedding cake and invitations and all those
other things women dream about." His words trailed off.

"Really, Noah, it was perfect," she said, her voice faint.
"Truly perfect." And it had been. She could not imagine
anything better.

"Then I'm glad." Noah rolled over and pressed a kiss to
her temple.

Abigail rolled away in surprise and would have tumbled
from the bed altogether had Noah not quickly reached out
and gathered her in his arms, pulling her close until her
back pressed against his chest.

"Mr. Blake—"

"Go to sleep, Abigail."

"But—"

"Go to sleep."

His arm was like a band of steel around her waist, locking her to him, though surprisingly gentle. And with an ease that surprised her, she settled down and drifted off to sleep.

Pain mixed with pleasure, mingling in the hazy depths of her mind. She tried to focus on the pleasure. But the pain won out, bringing Abigail up from her dream-filled sleep. Her eyes opened with a start as she tried to make sense of what was going on.

Gertrude! With Lou! She was late! Again! But then she became aware that she was wrapped in Noah's arms, his hand pressed intimately to her hip, his eyes closed softly in sleep. He was beautiful really, she thought, if such a man could be termed beautiful. She started to reach out to touch him, to trace his chiseled jaw with her finger.

Bang!

And with that Noah awakened and flew out of the bed, naked as the day he was born, ready to do battle. He stood before her, slightly crouched, his face fierce, all beauty gone, his arms slightly extended, hands clenched. It came over her with a startling certainty that this man was primitive at the core with a thin facade of civility, easily peeled away at the slightest provocation. He was every bit as dangerous as she had thought that first day, only more so.

She watched, mesmerized, as he became aware of his surroundings. The sight of Noah left her breathless. He could have been chiseled from stone, his body taut with readiness, muscles rippling. The noise that reverberated through the house had stopped and Abigail forgot about Lou and Gertrude and the eggs that waited for her outside.

"What happened?" Noah asked finally, running a hand through his tousled hair, totally oblivious to the fact that he stood there without a stitch of clothing to cover his loins.

And with that Gertrude rammed the door once again, bringing Abigail out of her reverie. "Oh my word!" For the first time since she awoke, she noticed the hint of sunlight that peeked around the edge of the window shade. "They're going to be ruined if I don't hurry." And she couldn't let that happen, not again.

Without bothering with shoes or clothes, Abigail fled the room in her flannel nightgown, images of Noah's body mixing with images of smashed up eggs in her head, as she raced across the kitchen to the back door. And it was because of her haste and wayward thoughts that she flew out the door and hit the dew covered stairs at a run.

Time hung suspended. Her feet flew out from underneath her. She groped hopelessly for the banister. But the banister was not to be had, and she tumbled down the stairs to land in a heap on the ground.

"Miss Abigail!" Lou squealed from the porch. "Oh my word! Are you dead?"

Abigail lay on the ground, her breath knocked clean from her chest. Her lungs ached, her head swam, and her body screamed in pain.

Lou panicked when Abigail failed to answer. "Oh, Mr. Blake!" she cried in relief when Noah appeared at the top of the steps, his pants hastily pulled on. His face was lined with fear and he leaped down the steps in one fell swoop. Falling to his knees he hovered over Abigail.

"Abby!" he demanded, his voice hoarse.

He stared down at her, nearly paralyzed as Abigail lay on the ground, her eyes closed, her body limp. His mind shifted and swayed. Memories of another time, another woman, laying on the ground, eyes closed, body limp, came to him. The smell of charred wood and blood filled his nose. His body racked with fear and impotent anger.

"No!" he cried, pulling her to him.

Lou stood off to the side, her fingers intertwined in Gertrude's wiry fur, her brow furrowed with worry. "Is she dead?"

Abigail's breath came back in a rush. "I am most certainly not dead!" she gasped on a ragged breath into Noah's massive chest. "Though I'm going to be in a matter of minutes if you don't loosen the death grip you have me ensconced in, Mr. Blake."

Noah loosened his hold so quickly he almost dropped her to the ground. With effort he steadied her, then rolled back onto his heels. His eyes stared at her but held no focus and Abigail had the eerie sensation that he was seeing something else, someone else, some other scene that played in his head.

She forgot her pain and predicament. "Noah?" she questioned softly.

Myriad emotions drifted across his face like storm clouds drifting across a winter sky.

"Noah?" she called again.

With effort his eyes focused. He ran his hand over his face, almost surprised to find her there. "Are you all right?"

"A better question is, Are *you* all right?"

Minutes ticked by and eventually the dark shadows that had crossed his eyes faded and a shaky smile surfaced. "You gave me a fright is all."

"Something certainly did," she conceded, then started to get up, and instantly regretted the movement. "Ah," she groaned.

"You're hurt."

She pushed his hands away when he started to pick her up. "No, I am not hurt! Sore, maybe. But the only thing hurt is my pride." She tried to get up once again, only to bite back another groan.

"Enough," Noah stated, then swept her up into his arms with ease. He turned to Lou. "Lou, sweetling. Go on over to Mr. Roberts's and get eggs from him."

She eyed Abigail dubiously.

"I'm fine, Lou, really," Abigail said.

"Truly?"

Abigail forced a smile. "Truly."

"The eggs, Lou," Noah interjected.

"Oh, all right," she grumbled.

"And don't you kick him in the shins this time either," he added.

Lou's eyes opened wide. "How'd you know?"

"He told me."

"Well, he deserved it. I told you I was going to if he was

mean. And he was—mean, mean, mean. I wouldn't go except for Miss Abigail almost dying and all." With that, Lou
led Gertrude from the yard, her nose tilted in the air.

"Yet again I'm not off to such a good start, I suppose,"
Abigail offered as Noah took her into the house.

He set her down on the bed. As soon as her leg touched
the mattress she flinched.

"You *are* hurt," Noah accused.

Abigail started to deny the charge when his hands ran
over her, assessing the damage, and he came to her knees.
Her denial died on her lips when he pressed the tender spot.

He started to pull her nightgown up.

"What are you doing?" she demanded, pressing her arms
tight along her sides, holding the fabric tightly to her body.

"Good Lord, Abby. I'm just going to see what you've
done to yourself."

"You can't. It's not proper."

"Quit acting like a child."

"A child!"

But when he tried to move the gown away once again,
she didn't resist.

Her calf was scraped raw from her tumble down the
stair, but bones didn't appear to be broken or cuts too deep.

"Where do you keep alcohol around here?" he asked.

"It's six o'clock in the morning!"

"Not to drink, Abigail," he said in exasperation. "To
clean the wound."

"Oh," she said simply, her mind wandering through the
cabinets in its mental search for such an item. "I don't
know. I haven't seen any, or if I have I didn't recognize it."

Noah's mood got no better. "What the hell have you
been doing all your life, Abigail?"

The only answer she could come up with was, nothing.
That, in fact, was what had propelled her to this precarious
position she was in now.

"Ah, never mind," he grumbled as he stomped out of the
room.

The next thing she heard was cabinets opening then

banging shut all through the house, until she heard his grunt of triumph waft back to her.

"See this, Abby," he said once he had returned, holding a bottle of spirits in his hand. "Lesson number one. Use this to clean wounds."

"Why not soap and water?"

He considered this. "Can't say that I know, offhand. But every camp I've been in, the doc uses alcohol to clean wounds."

"Oh. Why thank you." She started to roll out of bed, but was stopped more by Noah's bark than the dull throb in her calf.

"Stay there, woman!"

"I need something to write on."

"What for?"

"To take notes."

"Good God Almighty," he swore.

"Really, Mr. Blake, you shouldn't use the Lord's name in vain."

"Quit calling me Mr. Blake for God's sake. We're married. And I'll use the Lord's name any goddamned way I please. And I'm sure he would be the first to forgive me besides, as there is no doubt that at the pearly gates he will agree with me that you would try the patience of a saint."

"That's unfair! I'm just trying to learn, and how can I learn and remember everything if I don't write it all down?"

Without answering, Noah whisked up her gown once again and dabbed a cloth wet with whiskey on the wound.

"Ouch!" she cried, her voice shrill.

"It wasn't that bad," he replied as he set the cloth and bottle aside.

"That's easy for you to say. You're not the one with your leg burning off."

"No, I'm not. But I'm also not the one with all the grace of a flatfooted oaf who tumbled down the stairs."

She gasped her outrage and squirmed about, trying to escape. Her efforts only managed to hike up her nightdress in a tangle around her legs.

His smile vanished at the sight of creamy flesh. She was beautiful. Fragile as a doll. He remembered the way she had looked when he had burst into her bedroom. And then he cursed when his body leaped to life.

"Why do you hate me so?" she demanded, hurt at his belligerent tone, unaware of the change in him.

His eyes snapped up from her limbs and he glared at her. "I don't hate you, Abigail. Quit acting like a child."

Biting her lower lip she looked out the window, forcing back the tears.

"Ah, damn it, Abby. Don't do that to me."

"I hate it when you're angry."

"I'm not angry," he demanded, his face fierce.

"Yes, you are."

With a sigh, he softened his tone. "It's just that you're so damn beautiful . . . and it makes me mad."

Well, she certainly hadn't expected that. "Beautiful? Me? And it makes you mad?" she asked, confused.

"Yeah, mad. Mad as a dog. Your life is a waste, Abigail."

She looked away, biting her lip in hopes of keeping everything she felt inside. "I'm sorry," she whispered.

"Sorry!" Pressing his eyes closed he cursed. "Damn it." Then with a groan of defeat he gave in and leaned forward until he hovered over her. Sliding his fingers under her chin he turned her head back. "You shouldn't be sorry, you should be as mad as me, even madder."

She lay in the tangle of sheets, her brown hair a turbulent cascade across the plump, feather-filled pillows. "Why?"

"Why?" he demanded, his voice a low angry growl. "Because you haven't tasted life. You've been kept in a secluded little world of books and little else, no doubt intentionally by that father of yours. It's as if you don't feel you deserve all the wonders life has to offer."

Then, with infinite care, he leaned down, his muscles rippling, the faint dusting of blond chest hair catching a strand of light, and pressed his lips to hers.

"Noah," she said, turning her head.

His lips trailed back along her jaw.

"Noah, really. I don't think this is such a good idea."

"It's the best idea I've had all morning," he responded on a faint breath as he nibbled on her ear.

Shivers of desire coursed down her spine. "Noah, please don't," she whispered as her hands came up of their own volition and gently touched the sides of his arms.

"Yes," he murmured, "touch me." He lowered himself even further until his chest barely brushed against the flannel that covered her breasts. "Oh, sweet Abby."

Her hands crept up his arms until they came to his shoulders and his body brushed back and forth, gently, and truly she began to wonder if she wouldn't go mad—mad with wanting—though she shouldn't.

He turned slightly until one leg ran the length of hers and the other crossed on top. She lay passively, trying not to feel, trying not to want. This was no way to start this marriage. Then she nearly laughed. This was exactly how a marriage should start. But the laughter died in her throat. Not this marriage, she reminded herself, for in a matter of days or maybe weeks, it would be over. He would go back to his way of life and she to hers. And where, she wondered suddenly, was that life? Here at the boardinghouse? Could she stand to live in the same house with him once they were no longer married? Could he? Would he move out, leaving her alone? Alone. The word reverberated in her mind. Alone, without this man bellowing out her name? No more teasing smiles and laughing taunts? She felt bereft and empty. And she started to push him away.

"No," he whispered. "Let me love you."

His hand found the hem of her nightgown. Slowly, maddeningly, his hand ran up the length of her calf to her knee, then further, inching up her thigh, the flannel gathering against his wrist, until she felt the heat of his palm against her hip. His woolen-clad thigh followed his hand, his lips biting and sucking her neck, until she felt the hardness of his desire against her thigh. He pressed her tighter to his arousal.

"I want you," he groaned into her neck.

She knew he did. And her heart soared.

He pulled her gown up further until he revealed her breasts. He stared at her for an eternity, at the rose-tipped peaks, something close to reverence in his eye. And then he leaned forward, his thigh pressing rhythmically against her hip, the wool brushing back and forth against the triangle of curls at the juncture of her legs. Her body quivered.

He brushed her skin with his lips, kissing and licking, her neck, her shoulders, above her breasts, beside them, beneath them, teasing and taunting, never kissing her where her body demanded she be kissed. And when she could take it no longer, and still his lips failed to meet her throbbing need, she wound her fingers in his hair and guided his head to her breast.

Her back arched when he drew the nipple deep into his mouth with a groan. His hand slid beneath her to her hips. He pressed her to his desire that strained beneath the wool. His mouth traversed the valley, his tongue laving the nipple, his hand coming up to take hers, to press it against the wetness he had left behind. "You're beautiful," he whispered, pressing her hand against her breast. "So full and taut." His hand flattened over hers, his palm to the back of hers, moving in slow circles. "So worthy of love. You, sweet Abby, are so worthy of love."

His hand never relinquishing hers, he guided her hand down over her ribs, over the gentle curve of her stomach until they reached that place between her thighs. Her body tensed. She tried to jerk her hand free.

"No, love," he urged, pressing kisses to her temple and forehead. "Free yourself. You are beautiful. Your love and desire is beautiful, never shameful."

"No, Noah. This is—"

He kissed her lips, cutting off her words. "This is beautiful," he whispered and lowered their hands still further until her fingers touched the wetness between her thighs.

Her hips stiffened and she groaned against his cheek. "No."

"Yes, Abigail, let go."

He circled their hands at the juncture between her thighs,

until her hips began to move, slowly. "No, Noah," she repeated breathlessly. "We shouldn't do this. It's not right."

He relinquished her hand and spread her legs. His finger slipped inside her and she gasped. "It is right," he panted into her hair. "So very right."

She groaned and writhed, wanting, needing, but in the end she couldn't. With an effort that amazed her, she pushed him away, nearly toppling him from the bed.

"No! This can't happen," she cried, coming to her knees amidst the tangle of sheets and bedcovers.

"Why?"

"Because . . ." She looked away.

He reached out and forced her to meet his eyes. "Why, Abigail? We're married."

"In name only. As soon as I learn how to run this place this marriage will be over." She hesitated as if waiting for him to respond, desperately wishing he would disagree. "We agreed," she added finally when he said nothing.

His face grew fierce. He crouched at the foot of the bed, she at the head. The room was filled with light, the sun full up, the window shade doing little to keep it out. The soft and hazy edges of early morning had been burned away to the harsh reality of the day. There was work to be done. Supplies to be gathered. Skills to be taught. He pressed his eyes closed. He would be leaving soon. And everything she said to him was true. The marriage would be over. The thought made him angry.

She moved slightly and he caught sight of the raw scrape on her leg. The vision of her lying on the ground, lifeless, came to mind. And with that, memory washed over him once again as it had earlier. But this time he could not push it away.

He saw her there, on the ground, lifeless. But instead of Abigail's cascade of brown tresses, he saw white blond hair stained with blood, spread out across hard dirt floor. And next to her, a child. Sweet, innocent, her eyes closed in eternal sleep.

His chest tightened and his eyes burned. If only he had been there. But he hadn't been, he reminded himself harshly, and not for the first time. He had been far away, as usual.

"Noah?"

It was a moment before his name penetrated his dark thoughts, and a moment longer before he recognized Abigail. Sweet Abby who deserved better and more than he could ever offer.

"Please tell me what's wrong," she whispered. "What is it that you see?"

His eyes locked with hers and for one insane moment he almost told her. But the moment passed and anger filled him. "I see that you're right. And it's a good damn thing you put a stop to things before they went too far."

He saw her flinch at his harsh tone, as if he had struck her. That hurt him as much as anything. He hurt people without even trying. Without a word, he went to the pile of clothes that had fallen to the floor. He gathered his things then headed for the door. Just as he reached for the knob, she called his name.

"Talk to me, please. Tell me what just happened."

His fingers wrapped around the brass knob, clutching so tightly that his knuckles turned white.

"Noah," she whispered once again.

"No, Abigail," he growled, then opened the door, slamming it behind him, before he pounded up the stairs to his temporarily rented room.

~ 16 ~

"WHAT ARE YOU DOING?!"

Abigail nearly jumped through the ceiling. She twirled around, flour covering a good portion of her torso, to find Noah standing in the doorway.

"I'm cooking," she replied, with a regal tilt of her chin.

"Cooking?" He eyed the mess on the counter with a dubiously arched brow. "What are you cooking?"

Abigail scoffed. "Even a dimwit could tell that I'm cooking bread."

Shifting his weight, Noah scowled. "There's a dimwit around here all right, though you'd be hard pressed to make anyone believe it was me."

Abigail gasped, but Noah didn't care. He hadn't slept a wink last night and it was all her fault. Engagements and weddings and a damned near bedding had left him alternately cursing the woman and willing her back into his arms. He was tired and miserable and none too pleased to walk into the kitchen to find her whistling some unrecognizable tune as if all was right in the world. *She* obviously had slept like a babe. *She* obviously had pushed out of his embrace last night, then never given him a second thought. Just the idea made him bristle. He'd had a long stream of women fighting for his attentions over the years. But not Miss Abigail Ashleigh. He grumbled under his breath.

"You don't cook bread, Abigail, you bake it. And why the hell do I know that and you don't?"

Abigail merely pursed her lips.

"Hell, it doesn't matter. What matters is that we made a

deal. I'm going to teach you the essentials of running this place. And I'm in charge now."

"But—"

"No buts, Abigail. I'm the teacher, you're the student and I don't want any back-talking, you understand?"

Abigail's mouth fell open, her eyes opening wide.

"When I say jump, you say—"

"This is absurd!"

He moved closer then leaned down until he looked directly into her eyes. "—how high."

"In your dreams!"

"No, Abigail, in reality. You asked me to teach you how to run this place, now you're going to get exactly what you asked for." He stood back and cast her a slow, cold smile. "Any objections?"

With narrowed eyes and fisted hands, she thought of the hundreds of objections she had, not the least of which was to his boorish, ill-bred attitude. But she had to concede that she needed him—or at least she needed his help, she quickly amended. "No, Mr. Blake, no objections."

His smile hardened still further. "Good, *Mrs. Blake*, I'm glad we understand each other."

What Abigail came to understand over the next few weeks was that Noah Blake had a dictatorial streak as long as the Rio Grande—maybe longer. He bossed her around and pushed her relentlessly until she began to dream not of kisses and desire, but of ways to bring her persecutor to his knees. Groveling, begging for mercy. She imagined him in a thousand different scenes, she as master, he as servant. But then she would wake, generally to Noah pounding on her door well before a chicken even considered laying an egg, and demanded they start the day. She began to chant all the different ways she would like to do him in just to keep herself going.

It was the third Saturday of the month, winter well embedded in the river valley, and Abigail curled beneath the covers, fast asleep.

"Abigail! Wake up!"

"Go away," she grumbled into the pillow, burrowing deeper within the soft folds of the bed.

Noah reached out and took hold of the covers and yanked. Frigid, early morning winter air washed over her, bringing her fully awake as effectively as if he had thrown a bucket of water over her head. She gasped and jerked and came up from the bed like a drowning cat.

"Give those back to me, you . . . you churl!"

"Churl?" he questioned, holding the blanket and sheets just beyond her reach. "Where did that come from? Don't tell me you've had time to read any of those novels you love to stick your nose in. Is that why you're so tired? Staying up late reading?"

"You know darned well I was doing no such thing. As usual you are just dying to make me angry. As you know, I was up late pounding the life out of those stupid rugs." She didn't add that her arms felt weak and her back ached and all she wanted to do was go back to sleep. Hoping to catch him off guard, she grabbed at the covers, only to have Noah pull them farther out of reach.

"Get up, Abigail. We have a lot to do today, and less time than usual."

"What are you talking about?" she grumbled and pulled her knees up into her flannel nightgown.

"Tonight is the Saturday Social."

She tipped over and fell sideways into bed. "Go without me," she mumbled into the mattress.

"Not on your life. We've been putting on a show for this town for a good two weeks now. We're not going to quit before the final act." Noah looked pleased with his analogy.

Abigail groaned. "I think you're the one who's been reading my novels."

"One or two. Now get up," he said, practically dragging her from the bed.

Abigail stood, her hair swirling around her head, her arms hanging down at her sides, and scowled. She had long given up on decency. Noah came and went about the house as he pleased. He had seen her in unmentionables as well as her nightgown so often she had lost track. Thank goodness she had managed to bathe when he wasn't around or she wouldn't have had a bath since they married. Seeing her in dishabille was one thing, seeing her stark naked was another thing altogether. She still had a bit of pride left—if only a bit.

"Come on, Abby. We've got work to do."

"I've worked enough," she grumbled.

"Oh, really?" he asked, towering over her. "When did you come to this determination?"

Abigail looked up through her cloud of unbraided hair and glared at the man.

Noah seemed to consider. "Could it have been when you swung the stick at the rug, missed, and got tangled up in the line? Hmmmm? Or maybe it was when—"

"I hate you, you know that, don't you?" she muttered without much conviction.

He smiled then. "Yes, so you have told me, at least a hundred times—daily."

"Arggh!" she cried, then turned and stomped over to the bureau. She pulled out clothes with a vengeance until she came to a clean set of the "work clothes" Noah insisted she wear while she worked.

"Good," Noah said. "I'll just go start the coffee."

Noah closed the door just as what sounded like a shoe hit the door. Probably those damned egg-taking shoes, he chuckled silently.

But then he leaned back against the frame and sighed. When would it ever end? he wondered. It seemed every day that went by brought about more of a change in Abigail. Her cheeks began to glow. She was more relaxed than he had ever seen her. And though she made him madder than hell most of the time, he was impressed more than ever with her unflagging perseverance and determination. She might bellyache the whole time she was doing something, but she didn't quit. Right before his very eyes she was blossoming into a full-blown beauty and a respectable woman of means. And driving him to distraction in the process. Jesus, how he wanted her, whether she was scrubbing floors, cleaning the fireplace, or freshly dressed and coiffed to run errands about town. Plain and simple, he wanted her.

He had coffee on to boil when Abigail came out of her room. A surge of pure, unadulterated lust rushed through his loins at the sight. Her hair was brushed and loosely pulled back, soft brown tendrils curling about her face. His fingers itched to reach out and pull the ribbon free along with her skirt and blouse and whatever else she had on underneath. And that was impossible.

"What the hell do you think you're doing now?" he demanded.

Abigail jumped. "I'm getting ready to start the day. What do you think I'm doing?" she snapped right back.

Noah glared at her. "Nothing," he ground out. "Let's get started."

"What about the coffee?" She had grown to love a cup before she started her day. And Noah knew it.

"Forget it," he said cantankerously. "Come on."

For a second Abigail considered deserting rank and file, telling him to boss someone else around, or to go soak his head. The thought brought a smile of pleasure to her lips. But the smile quickly faded when she conceded that she needed the beast, at least for a while longer. With her eyes shooting daggers at his back, Abigail followed him out into the early morning darkness.

Once outside, she forgot her irritation with the man. She was improving in her abilities, and this fact as nothing else in her life had filled her with pride. She took the eggs in record time, though admittedly this improvement was due in great measure to Noah teaching her to simply let the hens out of the henhouse to go eat, leaving her with nothing more to do than fill her basket with the eggs left behind. When she had grumbled that he could have shared that tidbit of information weeks before, he had laughed and told her he had no idea she hadn't been attempting to do just that.

"Ta da," she chimed, holding out the basket, waiting for praise.

Noah only grumbled and headed for the barn.

"I'll be here all day if I wait for praise from him," she huffed.

Setting the eggs aside, she followed in Noah's wake. Trepidation mixed with excitement. She felt certain she was going to get milk today. She had had a long talk with Alberta the night before. While raking the cow's stall and filling the water trough, Abigail had pleaded with the bovine to be more cooperative. Today she planned to enjoy the results.

When Abigail entered the barn, Noah stood waiting impatiently, the stool already in place, his forearm resting against the wall. "Let's see what you can do today."

Praying up to the high heavens, Abigail lowered herself to the stool. "All right, Alberta," she said quietly, her voice calm and soothing. "You can do it, honey. I know you can."

She started to reach out.

"Warm your hands," Noah whispered.

Abigail rubbed her hands vigorously against her thighs until her skin tingled.

"You don't want to burn her, for Christ's sake," he hissed.

"Never satisfied, Mr. Blake."

"That's right. Not until you do it right."

Abigail cast a quick, superior glance over her shoulder before she turned back to the matter at hand. It was time. She could put it off no longer. Pretending as though she had all the confidence in the world, she reached out and took hold of Alberta's udder. And then she began to work each teat, just as Noah had shown her again and again and again until she dreamed about it. At first, nothing happened. Dismay started to swell. "Come on, Alberta," she whispered. "You can do it."

And then it happened. Milk hit the pail with a triumphant hiss that nearly caused Abigail to fall off the stool. Noah steadied her and willed her to keep going. Not until the pail was full did he shout, "You did it!" his scowl gone, replaced with a huge smile of pride.

They danced about the barn, Alberta eyeing them with a skeptical eye.

"I told you you could do it," he stated.

"As I recall, you also told me I had no business being in a kitchen."

"I was angry."

"Mad, I believe you told me. Madder—"

"—than a dog," he finished for her. "And as I recall, that wasn't the first time you had driven me to distraction."

"Nor the last."

They stood close together, washed by amber lantern light.

"No, certainly not the last," he murmured, his eyes locked with hers.

"Miss Abigail! Mr. Blake!"

They both turned with a start. Lou stood in the doorway.

"Don't the two of you look as pretty as a picture." Lou marched into the barn. "Just like two love birds, kissing and carrying on."

Red seared Abigail's cheeks. Noah's scowl returned with a vengeance. Lou seemed oblivious to any tension at all.

"I suspect I should go and start breakfast," Abigail said finally.

Her heart pounded the whole way across the yard. When would she ever stop feeling that way whenever the man came near? she wondered. It was a darned nuisance, yes it was. And embarrassing most of all. She was swooning over the man like she was no better than a schoolgirl.

Once Abigail had learned the fundamentals of cooking, she took to the chore like a duck to water. She still couldn't deal with chicken unless she was taking eggs or the chicken was already dead, plucked, gutted, and cut up so she could pretend it wasn't a chicken at all. But she hadn't served oatmeal in two weeks.

This morning she whipped up a feast of fluffy eggs mixed with cheese, fresh baked bread dripping with butter, and slices of ham grilled to perfection. She placed a plate in front of Noah and still he did nothing more than grumble. His one lapse of enthusiasm in the barn was gone without a trace, making Abigail wonder if she had only wished it were so.

They ate in silence. After he had finished, he threw down his napkin and headed for the door.

"Where are you going?"

"Out!"

"Out?"

"Yes, out, Abigail."

"But what about the rest of the chores?"

"You have shown you are perfectly capable of doing everything here all by yourself. You don't need me anymore." He did not turn back, but the edge melted from his voice. "As far as I can see, I have done my job." And with that he pulled open the door and was gone.

Abigail sat silently at the table, her hands clasped in her lap. She really had learned all there was to learn about running the boardinghouse. Noah's job was done. They could go to her father, have the boardinghouse turned over to her, then annulment proceedings could begin.

Her heart plummeted. Her chest tightened and her throat burned. But that was as it should be. A deal was a deal. He followed through with his end. Now she had to follow through with hers. She had to give him his freedom.

Abigail and Noah walked toward the church for the Saturday Social, stiff and quiet. Abigail pulled a heavy paisley shawl tightly around her shoulders, as much to ward off the chill she felt in her heart as to ward off the winter winds.

The minute they stepped through the door, people began calling out their names. Not only Noah's name, but Abigail's as well. She felt more a part of this town than ever before. A bittersweet smile tugged at her lips. How her life had changed since Noah Blake came into it.

She glanced up and met his gaze. She offered him a tentative smile. He stared at her for long moments before his scowl deepened still further. Without a word, he turned away and strode stiffly to a group of men who circled around a bowl of punch.

Watching him go, her heart plummeted. She wanted to go after him, and had to force herself to stay put.

"Abigail," Virginia called. "Don't you look lovely."

"Thank you, Virginia," she answered as she drew near.

"Marriage seems to agree with you. Your cheeks are glowing, and your eyes are shining."

"The color is from the hot desert sun I have been out in for hours at a time, and my eyes are shining because I am delirious from lack of sleep," she said with a shake of her head.

"Whatever for?"

Her eyes opening wide, Abigail suddenly realized her mistake. "Uh," she stammered. What could she say? She couldn't admit what she really had been doing.

"You've been learning how to run the boardinghouse, haven't you?"

Abigail's mouth fell open. "How did you know?"

"Just a guess." Virginia reached across to Abigail. "Don't worry. Your secret is safe with me. I think it's a brilliant idea." She glanced around until her eyes lighted upon Noah. "And I think you've found a wonderful man to . . . teach you."

Abigail followed her gaze. Her countenance grew troubled. But what did she feel? she wondered, uncertain and confused.

"Now don't look so troubled. Everything is going to work out."

Again Abigail could only hope.

The citizenry of El Paso were shocked, though pleasantly so, over the new Mrs. Noah Blake. Everyone commented on it. Mrs. Kent and Mrs. Holloway stood back and observed their new neighbor with pride, telling all who cared to listen about how their dear Abigail was blossoming before their very eyes. And while Noah steered clear of Abigail, dancing with every woman there except old Mrs. Bailey—and she was crippled—his eyes were never far from his wife.

Abigail became the belle of the ball. And even if Noah

had attempted to dance with her he would have had to wait in line. She laughed and smiled like a debutante, and ignored Emma's less than complimentary remarks. Noah only watched, becoming angrier by the second as Abigail twirled around the room, time and time again.

Not until an unmarried young buck who had a reputation for being something of a lady's man approached her did Noah finally escort his own current dancing partner back to her seat and pursue his wife. He came up to the couple just as Abigail laughed at something the other man whispered in her ear. Despite himself, Noah's blood boiled.

"Excuse me, old man," Noah said, grabbing the young buck by the shoulder. "But she promised this dance to me."

The young man turned around, his face belligerent until he saw that it was Noah. Reluctantly, he handed Abigail over.

"I don't recall promising you anything, Mr. Blake," she said, her smile coquettish.

Noah glared. "In case you forgot, you promised me a great deal, Mrs. Blake, with a preacher standing on listening to every word."

His words flustered her. It was almost as if he wanted their vows to be real. Her breath caught in her throat. Was it possible?

But then he shook his head and a sudden smile parted his lips. "But I guess you're just doing what I told you to do."

"Which is?"

"Having fun. So come on, show me what you've learned during the last hour while you were dancing with everyone in here wearing pants."

They danced and laughed and played the part of happy newlyweds so well, even Abigail began to wonder if perhaps it wasn't true. And when the night drew to a close, ending the only Saturday Social she had ever enjoyed, they walked toward home, side by side, their hands grazing each other every now and again.

They came to the plaza, empty of merchants hawking their wares. The moon was full, casting them in silver light.

He turned and gazed at her, that deep troubled look stirring in the depths of his blue eyes.

"Why is it, Mrs. Blake, that you make me forget all that I should do?"

Abigail's heart stopped in her chest. What did he mean? she wondered.

But then his mood changed with lightning quickness. "You were beautiful tonight," he said with a soft smile. "The most beautiful woman there."

Her head swam. One minute he was serious, the next playful and teasing. And his mood was contagious. "More beautiful than Miss Wilcox?" she began, then continued with the long list of other women he had danced with.

"You forgot Miss Jamison," he said, drawing her close.

"You cad," she quipped, while her heart hammered at the nearness.

"Always," he whispered as he dipped his head to kiss her.

She ducked out from beneath his embrace. "Noah! Someone might see!"

"Good," he stated, following her.

"Good! How can you say that? What will people think?" Trying her best to stay beyond his reach, she hurried down the path toward the boardinghouse, glancing back over her shoulder every now and again.

Noah stalked her, seemingly in no hurry, a sly, nerve-racking smile spread on his lips. "They'll think that Mr. and Mrs. Blake were having fun on the way home from the dance."

"They'll think we were drunk!"

He reached out and caught her arm. "Too bad you're not. We might actually have some fun," he murmured, dipping his head to her neck.

Abigail groaned, partly from the exquisite feel of his lips on her skin, partly from the fact that she knew this was no way for two people to act when they were on the verge of ending their marriage. With willpower she didn't realize she possessed, she slipped away once again.

He caught her at the top of the steps to the front porch.

"Are you afraid of what you feel?" he asked as he ran his fingers down her arm, the tips grazing the side of her breast.

"No!" she blurted as sensation washed over her. "I'm not afraid."

"I don't believe you," he said, his arm coming around her waist, his hand coming to her hips and pulling her to him.

She jerked in surprise at the evidence of his desire pressed so intimately against her.

"I want you, Abby," he whispered, staring deep into her eyes.

It was all she could do to force her lips to move to speak. "I want to go inside," she managed to say.

She escaped one last time, though she only made it through the front door of the house before he caught her again. His chuckle rumbled through the darkness. He trapped her against the wall, his arms on either side of her head. He pressed a soft, fleeting kiss to her brow.

"I want you," he repeated, "though I shouldn't."

"Then let me go." She tried to free herself, her heart pounding against her ribs, but his arms came around her like bands of steel, locking her to his massive chest.

"I can't seem to do that."

Her body stilled. Their eyes locked. She wanted to give in. She wanted him as badly as he seemed to want her. But she knew that the minute she gave in she would never be able to forgive herself. Still her body yearned for his. Logic, reason, and better judgment paled in the face of such longing. Her body burned with feelings she didn't understand. Yes, she wanted to give in. But as always, that was impossible.

"Let me love you," he murmured against her skin.

His breath washed over her like velvet. Her will began to disintegrate, the hard packed dam giving way against the flood. Her body trembled from his touch. She longed to touch him in return. She longed to find out where his kisses would lead.

Oh, how she wanted to give in. Her heart battled with

reason, and in the end her hand came up to caress his cheek as she had longed to do so often.

He turned his head until his lips pressed against the palm of her hand. Inhaling sharply, sensation tingled down her spine. She murmured his name and when he slipped his arm behind her knees, easily lifting her, she didn't resist.

He carried her into the bedroom, kicking the thick wooden door shut in their wake. With great care he relinquished his hold on her legs and lowered her to the ground, her body sliding against his. Her back pressed against the wall. Long rays of silver moonlight flooded the room. For a second she started to panic. What was she doing here with this man? But then he looked at her, and she knew, just as she knew weeks before, that he would never hurt her. Her heart swelled with emotions she didn't understand.

"You are so beautiful," he told her. He grazed her skin with infinite care, watching his fingers glide down her arm. "So beautiful."

"So are you," she replied, her voice barely heard.

His glance lifted to hers as he chuckled, and she would have sworn he blushed.

"Men aren't supposed to be beautiful, Abby."

"Why ever not?" Her voice turned oddly playful and breathless.

His grin turned boyish. "Well, for starters, men are supposed to be handsome, rugged . . . you know . . . manly."

"Oh, I see," she replied, her eyes sparkling with mischief. "You would have preferred I had said something like, You are so . . ." she hesitated in thought. "You are so powerfully virile."

Noah lifted a brow. "For starters," he agreed, then dipped his head and brushed her neck with his lips.

Abigail sucked in her breath. Suddenly she felt off balance, her head swimming. "You're shameless, Noah Blake."

"I try, sweetness, I try." His tongue slid up to her ear. He took the lobe gently between his teeth. His breath grew short when she groaned and her hands came up and clasped his forearms.

He slipped his arms through her grasp until their hands met. Clasping her fingers in his, he pulled her toward the bed. She bit her lip, her eyes narrowing with concern.

"It's all right, Abby. Don't be afraid. Let me make love to you."

She took a deep breath, frantically trying to decide. But there was no decision to make, she realized. It had been predetermined the day he had run her down. From that moment their lives had been intertwined, and it came to her then that she loved him.

Loved him? The thought surprised Abigail. But in that instant she knew it was true. She did love Noah Blake. And she realized she had since the day he knocked her down and swept her up in his arms with no more thought for propriety than Gertrude the goat had. She loved his disregard for what should be done, how he simply did what he wanted. Certainly such an attitude could be taken too far, but Noah Blake never used it to hurt anyone. He simply used it to live. In fact, he seemed only to make people happy wherever he went. And now by some quirky twist of fate she was being offered this man that she loved. At least for this night. If only she could make it last—make him stay. And she realized with a heartfelt certainty that indeed she did want him to stay—forever.

A young giddy feeling skipped through her. Excitement laced her every thought. She was married—to the man she loved. Her dreams had come true. Laughter and love. And she would make Noah love her. She would make sure he didn't think of her as a sister or a nuisance.

Children and a home. All with Noah Blake. Just as she was making the boardinghouse work, she would make a life with Noah Blake work as well.

Purpose coursed through her veins. She would make him love her. But how? How could she show him that she did not hate him as she had told him hundreds of times? And how could she show him that she did not think of him simply as a means to an end?

A glimpse of red satin flashed through her head. And with that sudden memory came her answer.

and... ...through, her hands in the...pulled thereover...
in his...

~ 17 ~

HER HEART RACED.

Noah stood so tall before her, his grip like velvet steel. But she had to show him.

She pulled free of his grasp. His brow furrowed and he turned his head away slightly as if confused. When he reached for her again, she quickly shook her head. "No," she whispered.

She stepped back, her eyes locked with his, the confusion turning to something she could only call a look of betrayal, before she took a deep breath then reached up and carefully pulled the pins from her hair. Her unruly tresses fell about her shoulders and down her back like a turbulent waterfall.

Noah looked on. His eyes grew deep and fathomless, washing all emotion from his face, providing her with no clue to his feelings. He didn't move or smile, he simply stood before her, seeming formidable, seeming suddenly unapproachable as never before. Was he displeased? she wondered. Did he think her overbold? She did not know. But she would not turn back.

And then suddenly she remembered not only the daydream that had come upon her in the middle of the General Store with a disagreeable Myrtle Kent looking on and the illusive rainbows wrapping around her, but the man in the daydream as well. She realized, with something close to shock, that despite all her beliefs otherwise, this man who stood before her, this man who had taunted and teased her, this man who had shown her that Myrtle Kent was not so disagreeable and that rainbows could be had, was the man from her dreams. How had she not seen it before? How had she not known?

She took a deep breath then released it slowly. The night was filled with silver moonlight, and long-held desires. But when she met Noah's glance once again, her resolve began to waver. Only moments earlier she had been certain he had not wanted to let her go. Now, however, as she stood before him, her offer unmistakable, he stood there, still as stone and as unreadable, staring at her, his expression both dark and turbulent. Uncertain. And she in turn grew uncertain. Her wavering determination began to evaporate entirely into the dimly lit room. Her old self began to surge forth. She had been wrong to offer herself. She was shameless, that old voice told her.

Mortification swept through her and she started to turn away.

"No," he said, his voice like gravel.

Pressing her eyes closed, she wondered what he meant. No, he couldn't. Or no, don't turn away. Which? But he said no more. Then, after what seemed like an eternity, he reached out and took her hand.

"You honor me," he said, his voice ragged.

She opened her eyes and looked deep into his. She knew then with a thrill that raced down her spine that he sincerely meant his words. He knew she was giving herself to him, the only gift she had to give, and he was pleased.

Her breath caught in her throat when the tips of his fingers grazed her cheek, barely, softly. His hands trembled. Reverently, he traced the outline of her body. "So beautiful," he whispered.

With utmost care, he undid the buttons until her dress finally fell free. She pressed her eyes closed when the old voice loomed in her mind. This was reality, not some silly harmless imagining. But she pushed it away. There was no place for the old here.

Meeting his glance, her shoulders coming back ever so slightly, she stepped free of the folds that gathered around her ankles. But when he started to push away her chemise, red scorched her cheeks.

"No, don't," he commanded as he pulled the rest of her garments free.

She stood before him, her hands trying to cover herself.

"Let me see you, Abby. Let me see all of you."

She stood in a slice of silver moonlight, her hair shimmering, her skin like pearls. He gently pushed her hands away. "You are more than beautiful," he whispered as he came close, pushing her hair aside and pressing his lips just behind her ear.

Tremors raced down her body. Elation filled her and she boldly reached out to work the fastenings of his shirt. The fabric fell away, leaving the smooth, hard planes of his chest and back free for her to explore.

His hands trailed down her body, his lips following in their wake. Lower across her chest to the side of her breast, the palm of his hand just grazing her nipples, before moving on, playing her body like an instrument.

When his lips grazed her stomach, her resolve began to waver yet again. Silently she cursed. Would the old always haunt her? she wondered. Would she always question anything different? Would she never be able to embrace the new without inhibition? And if she couldn't, would she live in a space that was neither in the old world nor the new, straddling some miserable fence that she was afraid to jump down from? Or could she climb down slowly, her feet tentatively touching the soil of the new? She had no idea how to answer such questions, didn't know if there were answers.

She started to move out of his reach, but he held her captive. "Don't turn away now. Nothing has changed. Don't be afraid of the unknown."

He spoke to her as if he could read her mind, and as she thought of their shared past, she wondered if perhaps he could. Since they had met he always seemed to know her mind.

He kissed her then and murmured sweet things, gently caressing her, until she would have sworn she felt damp, fertile earth between her toes. She forgot her nakedness and only wanted more of his touch, more of what he made her feel.

His kisses traveled lower and lower once again until he was on one knee before her, his arm around her hips. Her body was on fire, but when he forced her legs apart, her eyes flew open.

"Noah!" she gasped when he pressed his lips against the tight curls between her legs. She tried to break free of his hold but his hands kept her still.

His breath was ragged. "Let me love you, Abigail. Let me show you the pleasure and joy of love."

She hesitated, her body rigid with desire, unable to move, but unable to give in either. But when he pressed the inside of her knee, she widened her stance despite herself.

"Yes, sweet love, open for me," he murmured against the gentle curve of her belly.

His fingers scorched a path up from her ankle, along the inside of her thigh until they grazed the silken folds of her womanhood. He groaned when he felt her wetness. With infinite slowness, he circled his fingers, teasing, but never entering, just grazing her sensitive nub. Her body began to tremble. Her hips began to move of their own volition. She felt a need, an overwhelming intense need. She felt as if she was reaching, but for what she had no idea. She only knew she would die if she didn't get that illusive something. And then he slipped his fingers inside. Her body reeled from the sensation and she cried out his name.

Slowly Noah began to stroke, in and out, though barely in, barely out. Gasping for breath, she wound her fingers in his hair. She cried out his name and her last tenuous hold on restraint fell away when he eased his fingers deep inside her, his thumb grazing gently across the terribly sensitive nub.

Her body trembled. She was being propelled forward, her body taut with yearning for that elusive goal.

"Reach, Abigail," he whispered, his voice hoarse.

"This isn't proper, Noah," she gasped. "I can't."

But when his fingers slipped free, she cried out in frustration. Noah chuckled. "Yes you can," he replied, then dipped his head and pressed his lips to that most intimate spot.

Emotion churned within her. Her mind bade her move away—but that other part of herself she was becoming more and more familiar with pressed his head closer, wanting more.

His tongue circled then dipped and she cried out, her body on fire and she widened her stance. His hands cupped her buttock, spreading her gently, his tongue dipping one last time before her body exploded like a million shards of glass.

"Noah," she cried out, her body stiff, her fingers fisting in his hair.

He felt her quiver and stiffen with her release and he held her tight. "Sweet, sweet Abigail." He swept her up in his arms and walked over to the bed. He laid her down and stretched out beside her, his head propped up on one hand.

Her eyes were shut, but her breath was still ragged. He watched her as she gradually began to relax. At length she opened her eyes and shyly met his glance. "I didn't know," she said finally.

He smiled. "I know you didn't. Just like you didn't know about laughter and kisses." But then his brow furrowed slightly. "And I am infinitely pleased to have been the one to show you, all of it." Leaning over, he groaned as he pressed a kiss to the side of her breast.

"Noah!" She tried to push away, as propriety reared its irritating head. "Really, it's late and surely we are . . . done."

His hand slipped across her breasts and over her arm like a whisper until he took her hand in his. Her eyes widened as he guided her hand to that place she had been desperately trying to avoid looking at, though shamelessly wanting to see.

"Abigail," he murmured against her neck, his hand loosening his grip. "It's early and there is so much more." His palm slid down over the back of her hand, his fingers intertwining with hers, guiding. "I want you," he said, the words strained as he pressed her hand against his hardness.

She stiffened in his arms, though only for a moment before she wrapped her fingers around him. She could feel his body leap at her touch and she felt a rush of breath against her neck as he groaned. He was not immune. A strange sense of relief and a strong sense of satisfaction swept through her. And she grew bold.

She stroked him with maddening slowness, her fingers tight until he groaned into her hair and grabbed her hand.

"I can't wait," he said, coming over her, parting her thighs with his knees.

He guided himself to her sweet opening, but then he hesitated. "This is going to hurt."

Her only answer was to pull him closer.

"Sweet Jesus," he murmured, pressing into her. His body went still when he came to the barrier that marked her virginity. He nearly cursed his frustration, but cut himself short with the unadulterated awe over the fact that she was giving him such a gift. So he simply said he was sorry, then broke through until he was buried deep within her.

They clung together, motionless, until Noah began to move again, slowly, long and deep, easing her pain until she knew nothing but that same desperate longing she had know only a short time before.

Morning dawned, and with it came the all too familiar embarrassment and uncertainty about her life and relationship with Noah Blake. As a suddenly mortifying afterthought, Abigail realized there had been no mention of love or commitment. But surely—

"Uh hum."

Both Noah and Abigail had just entered the kitchen after finishing the morning chores, and were startled by the sound. Abigail's eyes opened wide and she screamed. Noah shook his head then smiled.

"Wanderer," he said. "Good morning."

A hint of a smile curved on Wanderer's face. "Yes, good morning."

Abigail looked on with disbelief, and not a little fear. A person couldn't live in Texas without having heard horrid tales of Indian massacres. Granted she also knew that for every tale of deplorable Indian acts, there was one of the white man's acts. No one, it would seem, was blameless— though recently, through some of her readings, she had begun to wonder if the Indian wasn't justified.

Either way, however, she had no interest in finding out the answer in her very own kitchen.

"Abigail, let me introduce my good friend, Wanderer. Wanderer, my wife, Abigail."

"A pleasure," Wanderer offered.

Abigail had to force her gaping mouth shut. The man stood there as if he were dressed in silks and velvet, not buckskins and bear teeth. "It's nice to meet you, too," she managed.

"I suspect," Wanderer said, "that right this second you are exaggerating. But rest assured that your scalp is safe from me."

Red surged through Abigail's face. "Oh, I never . . . well, perhaps for just a second I thought . . ."

Noah leaned back against the counter, arms crossed on his chest, eyebrows raised, and glanced between his friend and his wife.

"Good Lord, what must you think of me?" Abigail said with a sigh. "No manners, no manners at all. Could I offer you a cup of coffee?"

Noah laughed. "First you scream for your life, then you offer the man coffee." He glanced at Wanderer. "Only Abigail. But coffee's a good idea. Sit down, my friend."

They sipped coffee and talked, though whenever Wanderer ventured into talk of why he had come Noah deftly steered him away. Once Abigail got over the fact that she was face to face with an Indian, she became intrigued with her new guest. They talked and laughed for hours, Wanderer regaling Abigail with tales of her husband's heroism as well as his exploits in the wild. When the fire began to burn low, Noah went outside to get more wood.

"Well, I'd best be going," Wanderer said as he pushed up from his seat, intent on following Noah.

"But you only just got here."

"I was only passing through."

"Can't you stay?" She glanced at her hands. "I would love to hear more about Noah. Listening to your stories I realize there is so much I don't know about him."

Wanderer looked down at Abigail. "In time you will learn. And it is not for me to tell his tales."

"Yes, I suppose that's true." She met his gaze. "Does he have many?"

"Everyone has many tales to tell. It would be a shame if they did not."

They were quiet then, each lost to their own thoughts.

"I am happy that he found you," he offered quietly.

Abigail blushed. "I'm not sure that he had a choice in the matter."

"Don't let him fool you. A person always has a choice. And you are good for him. Deep down inside himself he knows that. He is happy." He looked at her then as if willing her to some truth. "But I'm afraid you are going to have to fight for him—you are going to have to fight to learn his tales."

With that, before Abigail could respond, he turned quietly and left the house. She watched the door close, the ruffled curtains rippling in its wake, and wondered what he had meant.

∽ 18 ∽

"MISS ABIGAIL! MR. BLAKE! COME QUICK, PLEASE!"

Abigail stood at the kitchen table, thinking of Wanderer's words, trying her best not to think about what had gone on in her bedroom last night—heavens above, all night. Red stained her cheeks at the memory.

"Miss Abigail!"

Abigail turned just as the back door was thrown open, bringing Lou in with a flurry of cold air.

"What's wrong, dear?" Abigail asked, forgetting her own concerns.

"It's the mama!" she panted.

Abigail's concern froze in her mind. Her spine stiffened. Just the name evoked the vision of naked shoulders and tangled hair. Her stomach roiled.

"She's sick bad," Lou continued, clearly frantic.

Seconds passed before Abigail could push unsavory visions from her mind enough to concentrate on what Lou was telling her. "She's ill?" she asked, trying to understand.

Lou reached out and grabbed her hand. "Yes, bad! You've gotta come help! Please!"

Help—that woman? Instinctively, Abigail pulled away. "You need Doctor Peters, Lou, not me."

"But Doc Peters isn't home. He's gone out to Iselta for a birthin'," she cried. "And no one who lives around us will help. You've gotta come!" Her voice grew tiny and quiet. "Please come. There's no one else."

Abigail pressed her hand to her chest. "Oh, dear Lord, I don't know the first thing about sickness."

"Please, Miss Abigail. I think she's dying." Lou's eyes narrowed with desperation. "And it's all my fault."

At this, Abigail finally cleared her mind. "Your fault! How could it be your fault?"

Lou hesitated, her brown eyes shimmering with unshed tears. "I hate her, and I wished she was dead," she whispered, squeezing her eyes closed. "Now she's dying and it's all my fault."

"Oh, Lou, that's untrue." Abigail's brow furrowed before she dropped to her knees in front of the child. "If everything everyone wished for came true this world would be a crazier place than it already is. You can't blame yourself."

Lou was not convinced, and Abigail sensed the child's distress as if it were her own. With a sigh, she pushed up from the ground. "All right then," she stated, pulling back her shoulders. "I'll go and see what I can do. And I can't imagine she's dying. I just saw her in town yesterday."

With all the feeling of a doomed woman approaching the noose Abigail gathered her bonnet and reticule. Her hand was stayed, however, when Noah came through the back door. His glance found Abigail and he studied her, perhaps remembering their shared night, she thought. He had stayed outside talking to Wanderer for some time, and she still had not had a chance to talk to him since she fell asleep in his arms.

He did not smile, simply looked at her as if trying to look into her soul. Abigail grew uncomfortable. Did he think her wanton, or did he relish their lovemaking? she wondered. Or had Wanderer said something that didn't sit well? She didn't know. Nor did she know how she expected him to react when first they saw each other. He had been gone from her bed when she woke that morning. But that soulful stare she had seen when first they met was not what she expected. She had told herself they had a future together. She had told herself she would make him love her. But this morning, all she had felt last night, all that had driven her on, seemed to have fled along with the slivers of silver moonlight.

Suddenly it seemed that an impassable chasm yawned

between them. Years, lifetimes, worlds of differences separated them, and Abigail wondered if indeed they could stay together. She wondered if indeed, given the huge differences that delineated them, she could make him love her.

He was a man of the wilds, with Indians for friends. She was a woman of society, strict propriety her only companion. How could they come together in harmony? Where would they meet? Wanderer had said her love was good for Noah, though Noah didn't know it. How good could something be for a person if it stared him in the face and he did nothing but rebel? And if indeed her love was like strong medicine that must be taken, was that the kind of relationship she wanted? Would the bitter taste of her love be left in his mouth forever?

Uncertain and uneasy she tore her glance away from his.

"Lou's mother is ill," she stated, tying on her bonnet. "I'm going with Lou to see if I can help."

It took a second for Noah to comprehend Abigail's words. At length he looked down and seemed to notice Lou for the first time. "I'll take you, I have a wagon outside."

Abigail wrapped her heavy shawl around her shoulders then followed Noah and Lou out the door. She was surprised to find that indeed he had a wagon outside. "Where did you get that?"

Noah glanced back at her as he lifted Lou up onto the seat. "I got it this morning from the livery."

Taking Noah's proffered hand, Abigail stepped up onto the bench. "What's all this stuff?"

Glancing back into the wagon bed, he simply said, "Supplies," then slapped the reins and they rolled out of the yard.

El Paso was firmly wrapped in the cold. Spirals of smoke curled up out of chimneys as the wagon passed through the quiet streets. Lou hovered on the bench between Noah and Abigail, and had circumstances been different, Abigail would have felt happy and content. But circumstances were not different and the scene only made her think of all she was afraid she couldn't have, and of the night she found

Walter in the arms of the very woman she was going out to help. But just then, Abigail realized as she wrapped her arm around the child, none of that mattered any longer. What mattered was Lou.

They pulled up in front of the dilapidated old house. Instantly Lou scrambled down and ran inside. Abigail hesitated, but when Noah took her hand in his she took a deep breath and followed.

The house was dank and cold. Hester Smith moaned and writhed on the only bed in the filthy house. Her eyes focused on Abigail. Hatred distorted her features until her lips screwed up with a hideous smile and she laughed. "If it ain't the ungainly priss who couldn't keep her man."

Abigail sucked in her breath. Lou moaned her distress.

Noah stepped closer to the filthy bed. "Careful what you say, woman. My wife has come to help you when we all know others wouldn't."

The fire of hatred seemed to die in her eyes and she fell back into the mattress with a groan.

Noah quickly checked the woman over. "She's burning up with fever."

Lou whimpered. "She's going to die, and it's all my fault."

"She's not going to die," Noah stated as he went over to the cold makeshift fireplace.

"What should I do to help?" Abigail asked.

Noah stopped in his task and looked back. "You don't have to do this. No one would blame you for leaving."

Their eyes locked.

"I'm staying," she said simply.

They stared at each other until he nodded his head and said, "You're an amazing woman, Abigail Blake."

And with his words a fierce pride surged through her.

They worked side by side, cleaning the tiny abode in order to rid the place of germs, bathing the woman's body, coaxing water down her swollen throat, working in a silent accord while Lou curled up in a blanket by the fire.

Hours passed. Finally, Hester Smith drifted into an exhausted slumber. Lou had fallen asleep as well. Noah and Abigail sat back.

"It's getting colder," Abigail stated.

"We've done all we can for now. Maybe you can find some more blankets while I ride into town to see if Doc Peters has returned."

When Noah left, Abigail hated to see him go. She did not want to be there without him. But there was no help for it, and knowing it was best to keep busy, she began to search for more blankets.

An old trunk sat in a corner. Lifting the lid, she found it filled with an odd assortment of items—trinkets, baubles, finely crocheted cloth. And at the very bottom, she found a delicate baby blanket, a finely sewn set of baby clothes, and underneath, a small packet of paper, badly yellowed with age.

She knew she should simply leave the papers where they lay. Her conscience told her to shut the trunk and look somewhere else for blankets. Instead, she unfolded the letters and started to read.

The world grew quiet. Time had no meaning as she read, then reread the five-page letter that took her breath away. How could this be? she wondered. How could anyone do this to a child? Her heart twisted violently in her chest. And the bile she felt for this woman at finding her in Walter's arms dimmed in comparison to what she now felt. But there was more hatred now, after the letter, for more than just Hester Smith.

Her hand fell to her side, the letter drifting to the floor, seesawing back and forth until it came to rest against the trunk. Abigail sank down, her skirts billowing around her. She glanced over at Lou. Was it possible? Could the letter really be true?

Sound asleep, Lou looked so tiny and fragile—and so familiar, just as she had that first day she saw her in the mercantile, proving as much as anything could the veracity of the letter.

How had the child survived? Abigail wondered. And more importantly, how could the wrong done her be righted? Suddenly so much that had transpired over the last several months began to make sense.

She sat on the ground, unaware of the passage of time. It wasn't until the sound of wheels crunching on gravel outside that she came out of her reverie. Noah must be back, she thought. Hester Smith still slept, as did Lou. And then she knew what she had to do.

Grabbing the letter up off the floor and her wrap from a peg on the wall, she flew out the door just as Noah jumped down from the wagon, the doctor in tow.

"Abigail—" Noah started to speak, but stopped when she ran past him.

"I'll be back," she called as she scurried into the wagon.

"Where are you going?" he demanded, the doctor looking on in confusion.

"To my father's house," she replied as she took up the reins with determination.

"What for? And you don't know how to drive!"

She glanced down at him, her eyes burning. "I'll learn. Just as I've learned all the rest. Please don't stop me now."

When he made no move to step closer she slapped the reins and urged the mount forward.

She left Doctor Peters and Noah standing out front of the tiny shack. The edge of town and her father's house loomed within minutes. It was late afternoon and soon the house would be alive with preparations for the evening meal. She had to get there before that happened.

The house was quiet when she entered, and she thought everyone was gone. For a moment she felt relief. The momentum that had carried her this far seemed to fade. She could hardly believe she had come at all. What would she say? Suddenly, standing there in the huge foyer that had instilled fear in her her whole life, she wondered how she could possibly think of confrontation. But then she saw her, standing in her father's study, gazing out the window.

"Emma," Abigail said simply, forgetting all the years of intimidation, remembering only Lou.

Her sister turned, her eyes strangely unfocused, strangely

sad for a moment before they cleared and the violet depths looked the same as they always had.

"Abigail, what brings you out here?" With the grace befitting a queen, she smoothed her skirt then her hair.

"I came to ask you about this?"

Emma glanced up and her eyes grew wary as she eyed the sheets of paper that rippled in Abigail's outstretched hand. But then the wariness fled. "What is that?" she asked, her tone nonchalant.

"A letter that I found in Hester Smith's house."

It was as if Abigail had struck her sister, dealt her a physical blow. If there had been any doubt left, it was gone. "You know about the letter then, I take it."

"I don't know what you're talking about. I don't know anything about any letter."

"Then perhaps you should read this to refresh your memory."

Emma's violet eyes sparked to life. She glanced between the pages and Abigail. She seemed to consider. At length she took the pages and glanced through them. "This is absurd." She started to turn away, the letter still in hand.

Before Emma could leave the room Abigail quickly retrieved the pages, her patience drawing to a sudden, frustrated close. "No," she snapped. "You certainly aren't going to walk away with a letter that says Lou is Grant's child."

The spark of bravado vanished and Emma wavered on her feet. "No," she whispered. "It's not true. It can't be."

"Yes, Emma. It is true. And you know it. How long have you known?"

Every ounce of weakness in Emma vanished and she turned on Abigail. "I will tell you nothing, Miss Perfect!"

Abigail was thrown by the tag, "Miss Perfect." It made no sense. Was it possible Emma didn't disdain her, but rather resented her for some unknown reason? "Miss Perfect?" she questioned.

Emma sneered. "Save the theatrics for someone like Noah Blake who can be fooled. I'm not. Never have been. Miss Perfect who reads and writes and does sums. Who acts so sweet and selfless. Who continually tries to make me look like a selfish imbecile." Emma reached across and snatched the letter away. "I'll not let you make me look the fool again."

The spew of venomous words left Abigail speechless.

"You have nothing to say, dear sister?" Emma stepped closer. "Of course not. You always thought I didn't know what you were up to. But I did. Always. And you proved it the day you asked Daddy if you could run the boarding-house—just the kind of thing that would impress him."

"I never—"

"Don't bother denying it. No one will believe you. Just like they won't believe you about this nonsense that the ratty-haired daughter of Hester Smith is my husband's child. So stay out of it, Abigail. This is no business of yours."

"I'm afraid I've made it my business," she responded, "because there is a sweet little girl out there who deserves the love of her father."

"Deserves the love of her father?!" Emma demanded. "She deserves! What about what *I* deserve? Virginia gets Father and a son. You get that heathen mountain man and the boardinghouse. Father gets his bank. And what do I get? I get nothing! And if you think for one second I'm going to let my husband know that Lou is his daughter, you can think again." Emma took a step closer, her eyes boring into Abigail. "And you had better not tell a soul or I will deal with you just as I dealt with Lou's mother." Her hand fisted at her side. "If only I had known Corinne was with child," she muttered, then started to turn away only to come face to face with her husband and her father who stood in the doorway.

It took a moment for understanding to come clear, but when it did Emma's hand flew to her mouth. "Oh my God."

Sherwood stepped into the room. Grant stood on the threshold as if he couldn't move, pain and disbelief etching his hard chiseled features.

"What is going on here?" Sherwood demanded.

"Oh, Daddy, what are you doing here?"

"I live here, damnit. And I'll give you five seconds to explain what I just had the misfortune to overhear."

Instantly, tears sprang to her eyes, and she ran to her father. Sherwood only held her at arm's length.

"Explain yourself, Emma," Sherwood demanded.

Grant still stood at the door, staring at his wife. Abigail felt certain he was holding himself together with tremendous willpower.

"Is it true? Is Lou my daughter?" Grant asked finally.

Emma glanced at her father, but when he did nothing more than stare at her, his eyes cold and unyielding, she broke down crying, and said, "Yes, curse you, it's true."

Grant's eyes burned with rage. "How long have you known?"

She started to look away.

"Tell me, damn it," he roared.

Emma flinched and turned to her father. But still Sherwood offered no help. "Tell him."

"Just for a while," she whispered.

"How long?"

"About five months."

"Five months!"

Sherwood sighed and turned away. "Explain yourself, daughter. From the beginning."

Emma sank down onto her father's high-back leather chair. "Hester Smith showed up in town and came to see me."

"When?" her husband demanded.

"Five months ago. She brought the letter."

Pain raced across Grant's features. "It was a letter for me, wasn't it? From Corinne." He staggered on the import. "Where is she? Where did she go?"

And then Emma snapped. Her husband's concern for his long gone mistress sent a spurt of unbridled fury riddling through her body. She felt the need to lash out, to wound. "That's right!" she snapped. "Lament all you like. But Corrine Mayhew is gone. Long gone. And I sent her away."

Grant flinched, his eyes boring into his wife.

"Yes, I sent her away, though certainly she didn't put up much of a fight."

Fury flashed through his eyes, and he took a menacing step forward, vanquishing Emma's bravado. Emma shifted uncomfortably in her seat then looked away.

With his hands fisted at his sides, he said, "Tell me the rest."

Her only response was to cry harder when he took another step closer, his stance forbidding.

"Apparently she went to San Antonio," Abigail offered, when it was clear her sister would say no more. "According to the letter, Emma threatened her with disgrace and worse if she didn't leave town. Corrine appears to have believed the threats and left," Abigail cleared her throat, "unaware that she was . . . with child."

"Lou," he breathed.

"Yes, though her given name is Maybelle."

"My mother's name." Grant turned to stare out the window. "And what happened to Corrine? Why is Lou with Hester Smith?"

"Corrine is dead."

Grant sucked in his breath.

"She wrote you this letter," Abigail continued, offering him the missive, "telling you of your child and explaining everything. When she realized she was dying, she put Lou in Hester Smith's care, with the instructions to bring the child to you."

"She died only five months ago?"

"No," Abigail responded, looking down at her hands. "Four years ago."

Grant groaned. "Corrine," he murmured. "And Lou. Lou has been with that horrible woman all this time. Why did she wait until now to find me?"

"My guess is that she was desperate and needed money. Otherwise she wouldn't have."

They looked toward Emma who sniffed into her handkerchief.

"Yes, damn you! She came looking for money!"

"Damn!" Grant roared, pounding his fist against the

hardwood window frame, then whirling around to face his wife. "How could you?"

Emma sank back further into the folds of the chair. But she was saved from answering when someone pounded on the front door, then burst in.

"Abigail!" Noah shouted from the foyer.

The house seemed to shake as he raced into the study. He didn't bother looking at anyone else, he looked directly at Abigail. "It's Lou."

"What's wrong?" Grant demanded.

Noah glanced at the other man as if noticing him for the first time. "She's fallen ill. The doc says it doesn't look good."

Without wasting another second Noah reached out and took Abigail's hand.

"I'm going with you," Grant stated.

Then Abigail, Noah, and Grant raced out of the house and headed out of town.

They found Lou on a makeshift bed on the floor, Doctor Peters bathing her brow with cool water. Hester Smith lay sleeping on the bed.

Grant took in the surroundings, and Abigail thought this dark, forbidding man would break down and cry. She didn't dare tell him that she had spent the better part of the day cleaning the place.

The doctor stood when they entered. "Grant," he acknowledged with a nod of his head, his glance questioning. "Miss Abigail."

"How is she?" Grant asked, his eyes straying to the child on the floor.

Jim Peters studied Grant.

"She's . . . she's my daughter." Grant said the words as if he had trouble believing them.

Jim merely nodded his understanding, needing no other explanation. "I'm afraid to say she's not as lucky as her . . . mother."

"Not her mother," Grant interjected, his eyes wild, his tone fierce. He took the few steps that separated him from Lou and knelt down beside her.

"Lou," he whispered, reaching out to smooth her brow. "She's burning up."

Jim came up behind him. "She's got the fever. It's hardest on the old and the young."

Pressing his palm lightly against Lou's forehead, Grant willed her his strength. "Get well, baby. Get well so I can make your life right."

Abigail stood back and watched, unable to move, unwilling to intrude.

Noah reached out and took her hand. "Why don't we take her back to the boardinghouse?"

"Hester is out of danger," Jim added. "And I'll check back on her. Lou stands a better chance where we can keep her warm and clean."

Grant had her up in his arms and wrapped tightly with blankets before Jim had finished speaking. They took Lou back to the boardinghouse and had her tucked into Elden's old bed within a quarter of an hour.

Evening turned to night and night to morning, and Grant stayed by Lou's side every minute. The stove in the corner kept the room warm, while they kept her tiny body cooled with damp cloths. But as the hours passed the fever merely grew dangerously higher. Night turned to morning, and for one brief moment Lou woke.

Her eyes fluttered open, their brown depths glazed by fever. When she saw Grant hovering over her, a smile fluttered on her lips. "Hello, Mr. Grant," she whispered, trying to reach out to him.

Grant took her hand and brought it to his lips. "Hello, sweetheart."

"I feel so happy when you call me that."

"I know you do," he said, his voice tight.

"Yes, I suppose you do. I've told you many many times." Her smile faltered. "Am I going to see the Angel Mama?"

Abigail watched Grant's shoulders stiffen as if he was forcing himself to be strong. She leaned back against Noah's massive chest. Her throat tightened and her eyes burned. She realized now what Lou had been talking about all these weeks before when she had mentioned the Angel Mama. Corrine, the Angel Mama, who had died so many years ago and left her daughter with Hester Smith in hopes the woman would bring the child to her father.

Then Lou saw Abigail. "Miss Abigail," she said, her voice growing faint. "Mr. Blake," she added when she noticed Noah. She offered them a smile before she turned back to Grant. With her free hand she reached up, her fingers shaking, and touched his cheek. "You love me, don't you."

The words were spoken as a statement more than a question. Shivers ran down Grant's body and it was all he could manage not to do physical violence to anything or anyone who was near. But his grip on Lou remained gentle and he looked into her eyes. "I love you very much, very very much."

Tears welled in her eyes as she smiled at him. "I love you, too." And then her hand fell to her side and her eyes fluttered closed.

"Lou?" he whispered.

She lay still in his arms.

"Lou!"

Still nothing.

"Oh, God, Lou," he cried, the words torn from his chest as he pulled her tight into his embrace.

Her head fell back, her body limp. Abigail started forward, but Noah held her back. When she questioned him with her eyes, he simply shook his head and guided her out the door. Glancing back over her shoulder as she was reluctantly led from the room, she saw Grant's body racked with sorrow as he held his daughter tight for the first and last time.

19

THE DAY PASSED IN A BLUR. THE DOCTOR CAME AND
went. Virginia, Myrtle Kent, and Mrs. Holloway came and
helped Abigail prepare Lou for burial. Sherwood walked
slowly around the boardinghouse, from room to room,
every now and again sinking down into a chair. Grant sat in
the front parlor staring out the window. Neither Hester
Smith nor Emma were anywhere to be seen. Noah built a
tiny coffin. And by the end of the day, before the winter
storm that threatened could hit, the town of El Paso buried
young Maybelle Weston, the little girl who had been
known as Lou Smith.

The kitchen was oddly quiet when Noah and Abigail returned home later that day. Abigail fell back against the
wall, her head connecting with a thick wooden beam, hard.
She had the crazy urge to hit herself again and again, as if
she could distract her mind from the pain she felt in her
heart.

"It won't do any good," Noah said.

She glanced over at him. "What won't?"

"Hitting your head against the wall."

Her head fell back again and she pressed her eyes closed.
"Why?" she whispered into the room. "Why Lou?" she demanded quietly.

Then silence fell, except for the frustrated rap of Noah's
knuckles against the table.

The pressure behind her eyes built and she felt her throat
burn. Suddenly she jerked forward. "Why?" This time the
simple word came out in a burst of anger. She pounded the
wall with her fist. Her brow furrowed with her effort to

keep from crying. "Why!" she demanded again, her face ravaged.

Noah came forward, and when he tried to comfort her she yanked free of his grip.

"Abby," he said, his voice soothing.

"No!" She went to the table and gripped the edge.

"Abby," he repeated, coming up behind her.

She flinched when he touched her but he persevered. "Abby." His grip tightened and he pulled her back to him, her spin rigid. "It's okay. Let yourself cry."

"No!" The word crackled with emotion. "I can't."

He turned her in his arms. "Why not?"

She looked not at Noah, but at the dark woolen shirt he wore, concentrating on the muted pattern. At length she leaned her forehead against him, the hardwood fastenings biting into her skin. "I'm afraid if I start," she murmured against his chest as her tears began to roll down her cheeks, "I'll never be able to stop." And then, when she could hold on no longer, she sank into his chest. "Oh, Noah," she wailed. "How could this have happened? How could God take an innocent little girl and leave that woman who kept Lou away from her father?" Her hands fisted in his shirt. "And how could Emma, my sister, my flesh and blood, have been so hateful as not to have told a father about his daughter? If only she had told him when Hester came to her, Lou would be alive! Oh, God, it's all so unfair!"

Noah let her cry. Not until her sobs began to taper off did he tilt her chin and force her to look him in the eye. "Life isn't fair. That's a lesson best learned as soon as possible. Death strikes when and where it chooses, without regard for who may or may not deserve to die."

Abigail tried to break free but he held firm, his grip tight on her arm.

"Look at me, Abigail. I should have been dead many times over by now. But here I am—alive when others should be instead."

His eyes grew stormy and his grip loosened. Abigail realized through her own blur of pain that Noah spoke from that dark place in his soul that surfaced only rarely. He spoke from pain. And like always, his eyes lost their focus and she knew he saw not her, but those distant places in his mind.

"Oh, Noah," she whispered. "What is it that you see?"

He stared down at her, but didn't answer.

She pressed her fingers to his lips. "Tell me, Noah. Tell me about that dark place in your soul."

His eyes narrowed.

"Tell me," she pleaded. "Tell me who should be alive in your place? Lou?"

He looked away.

"No, not Lou," she answered for him. "The look was there before Lou's death. What put it there?"

He stepped away from her but she followed. "You wouldn't let *me* pull away," she said, her voice gentle but firm. "Now I won't let *you* pull away either."

She wrapped her arms around his waist, her cheek pressed against the hard muscled plane of his back. "You're safe. You can tell me." She placed her hand over his heart. "I love you, Noah Blake."

His groan reverberated against the thick adobe walls as he turned in her arms and pulled her into a fierce embrace. He ran his hands along the contours of her body, then buried his face in her hair. "Sweet Jesus, you shouldn't love me."

Despite his words, however, he held on to her as if he held on to dear life. He knew he should stop now, set her at arm's length, leave the room and never look back. But the heat of his anger at the unfairness of life, in spite of what he had told Abigail, and the fierceness of his sorrow at what he couldn't have, melded into raging passion that licked at his loins.

Never had he reacted this strongly to a woman. Not even when he had met . . . Shadows clouded his mind. Darkness. Pain. Guilt.

For a moment uncertainty threatened to overwhelm him. He wanted to escape—run as fast as he could—as far away as possible. Scenes from his life flashed before his mind's eye. Trapping in the mountains. The frigid cold. The harsh life. Even death. But freedom. Though loneliness. Stark, biting loneliness. But how could he change? he wondered. He realized then that his uncertainty and rage was mixed up with a tremendous desire to do just that—change. But he didn't know if he could. A bitter cold washed over him—though a fire burned in the stove. Truly he didn't know if it was possible to change.

He pulled back slightly and loosened his hold. His eyes focused and he found Abigail, waiting, as if daring him to continue. He realized then that there was more to his feelings for her than simply the physical. The pounding desire was there, certainly, but there was something else as well.

When he remained quiet, she brought her hands up and touched his face. The fierceness in her countenance melted away and her lips began to tremble. "I love you," she repeated. "So very much."

His heart clenched in his chest. Love. From this wonderful woman. And suddenly he didn't care about what he should or shouldn't do. He didn't care to look more closely at what he felt for her. He simply wanted her.

He pulled her close, kissing her over and over again as if at any moment she would be taken away and he had to get as much of her as possible, and quickly. He stroked her cheeks, her skin smooth beneath his calloused fingers.

His hands ran down either side of her spine until he reached her hips. He pressed her against his harness, losing himself to the feel of her, the feel of sweet goodness and life. "Hold me," he murmured against her hair. "Hold me, sweet Abigail."

She did as he wished. She held tight and when he began to kiss her again, on her cheeks and eyelids and lips and ears, she returned his kisses, matching his intensity, matching his desire.

Their love turned frantic then. Her hands ripped at his belt, and at the fastening of his trousers. A soft cry of frustration came from her lips at her unsuccessful attempts. Another time he would have chuckled, this time he was moved to near tears by her desire, for him—so far had she come on her journey into life.

He kissed her again then smoothed her hair back from her face and met her eyes. There was so much he wanted to say. His throat burned with the words he held back.

"Love me," she whispered when he did nothing more than look deep into her eyes.

And then he was lost. Her lips parted as he kissed her. He traced the line of her mouth with his tongue, savoring her sweetness. He kissed her again, hard and deep, his mouth slanting over hers. Pulling at his clothes, she groaned until he freed himself from his trousers. He groped with her skirts until he felt the soft silken folds of her womanhood. Raging desire tore through him when he felt that she was wet—her desire was as great as his own.

"Yes," he groaned into her neck as he lifted her up, resting her against the counter.

"Hurry," she panted. "I want you, Noah. I need you."

He came into her in one driving thrust. She cried out his name and he stilled, afraid he had hurt her. But she'd have none of that. She moved on him, sending shivers of desire through his body the likes of which he had never experienced. He held her fragile form, carefully, moving slowly, until she urged him faster. Their hips came together, again and again, and he no longer thought about hurting her.

She flung her head back, wild with passion, free of inhibition. Instinctively, she wrapped her legs around him, taking more of him inside her. Their lovemaking was primal, harkening back to times long past, each trying to lose themselves in the other, each seeking—each trying to make themselves whole. And just when he thought he would explode into her sweet body, he remembered that day long ago when he told her she had a wildfire burning within her and if she wasn't careful she was going to get burned. He realized then that he had been the one in danger all along. For surely at this point no matter which direction he chose to take he wouldn't survive. With her or without.

The remainder of the night passed all too quickly. Noah lay awake, holding Abigail tight, unwilling to let her go— at least for a while. He looked down on her sleeping countenance. Sweet and beautiful and innocent—though capable of a wildness and unrestrained passion that left him in awe. And he knew then with a sinking certainty that he loved her—was not simply fascinated by her, not simply enamored of the way she made him smile. He loved her.

How long had he known? he wondered. Probably since that very first day. Why else would he have not been able to put her from his mind? Why else would he have stayed around her when everything he knew told him to leave? He was a fool to have stayed. Because now he *had* to leave her.

He was a trapper. A man of the mountains. A man of the wild. Unable to be restrained by the confines of society. She had been right in her assessment of him. He hadn't wanted to admit it then, but he had to face the truth now. He couldn't survive in the civilized world, not for any length of time. He had proved that years ago. He would always end up deserting the people who depended on him, leaving them alone and unprotected.

Sounds of the approaching dawn penetrated his thoughts. The sweet, warm curves of Abigail's body felt so right in his arms. Oh, how he loved her. She had said she loved him. And he believed her. How he wanted to tell her he loved her, too. To sit on the front porch, on white wickerwork chairs, sipping coffee, laughing, teasing . . . loving until they were old. Children running, playing, then grandchildren who had Abigail's loving brown eyes and her glorious wild hair.

But that, he conceded with a sigh, was nothing more than a fantasy. He couldn't remain her husband, then leave her over and over again, watching her grow more wary of him every year, the pain and hurt etching her face as years never could. He had to leave now, for good. Because he couldn't trust himself to stay. And he had to leave now to save her— to save her from eventually and inevitably growing to hate him.

His heart felt as if it might burst in his chest. The darkness that was always just below the surface overwhelmed him. He wanted to stay. But couldn't. He wanted her to know that he loved her. But knew that would only make things worse.

He pulled away gently. Without making a sound he dressed, then quickly wrote her a note. When all was done and still she lay sleeping, he leaned down and pressed a kiss to her forehead.

"I love you, Abby," he whispered.

Then he was gone, leaving the boardinghouse on the corner of El Paso and San Francisco streets, promising himself he would never return.

∽ 20 ∽

ABIGAIL WOKE WITH A START. HER CHEST FELT TIGHT and her mind was clouded with dread. Lou. Dear, precious Lou was dead. But then she remembered the night she had just passed with Noah, and she knew she wouldn't have to bear the pain alone.

She rolled over and reached out to him, to the man she loved, and now felt certain loved her. But when she turned her hand tangled in cold and empty sheets. Noah was gone.

Her heart shot to her throat. "Noah," she called.

The only sound that greeted her in the early morning darkness was silence. Trying to ignore the uneasiness that grew steadily within her, she forced a chuckle and swung her legs over the side of the bed. He was probably out in the kitchen right that minute, preparing a feast with which to surprise her.

She imagined him singing some unrecognizable tune, dancing every now and again, slicing ham, flinging flapjacks in the air, dropping them on the floor, dusting them off then throwing them right back into the pan. Her dear, sweet Noah who was afraid of nothing. How she longed to see him, to touch him—to convince herself that indeed he was hers. She ignored the fact that not a single sound came from the kitchen.

Pulling on a heavy robe and slippers against the winter cold, forcing herself not to contemplate the reason the house held no heat if indeed Noah was there, Abigail went in search. She took a steadying breath when she found the kitchen cold and empty, no sizzling ham or dirt-filled flapjacks on the stove.

It had been so difficult to come to the conclusion that Noah wanted her, even loved her. He had never told her, but she knew deep in her soul as if he had spoken the words aloud. The realization had been had, but only barely, and she held on to it now by the very thinnest of threads, its strands rapidly fraying. It had been so difficult for her to believe that someone as wonderful and happy and sought-after as Noah Blake could want her, and for no other reason than for herself. He disliked her father, couldn't stand Emma, and hated Walter. He had no designs on the boarding-house. It seemed he couldn't have it signed over to her fast enough. At the time it had been proof that indeed he wanted nothing to do with her father's money. Now she wondered what it meant. Had it meant that he wanted their deal said and done, finished? So he could get on with his life? Without her?

Her heart constricted painfully. Her breath came short. But then she chastised herself. Her mind was running wild without a lick of sense. The fact that he had not been in bed with her when she woke could mean a million different things, all but one of which had nothing to do with him leaving her. He was probably upstairs getting dressed, or outside doing . . . something.

Hurriedly, she went back to her room. With amazing quickness she dashed through her toilet, and within minutes she was dressed and ready, half expecting Noah to barge through the door at any second to tease her about God only knows what.

Noah, however, failed to appear.

With nothing to do but wait . . . and hope, Abigail took the eggs and milked Alberta. Minutes ticked by and the sun began to rise. And not only was there no sight of Noah, but it pressed in on her for the first time that Lou would never show up to take eggs again. She sank down onto a kitchen chair, tears scalding her eyes. And then through the blur of misery, she saw it. A single sheet of paper with her name scrawled across the top, a deed underneath. And she knew without reading a line that he was gone. Forever, never to return.

Without moving she stared down the table at the letter. Minutes turned into hours and still she simply sat at the kitchen table. The sun traveled up the horizon, the shadows cast across the kitchen shortening as they progressed.

At length, she took the sheet of paper and read. As she suspected he had left. Never to return. He was a mountain man. First. Last. And always. Short and to the point, businesslike, just as their arrangement was meant to be. Abigail had been fool enough to forget that.

She picked up what she knew was the deed to the boardinghouse. It was hers, all hers, only hers—just as she wanted. But her victory was hollow.

The pages fell through her fingers to lay forgotten on the table. The sounds of the thriving town barely penetrated her consciousness. She didn't know how she could bear the losses that weighed so heavily upon her. Noah had been her strength to deal with Lou's death. Now Noah was gone. Just then she did not know how she would make it through another day.

The sound of the front door shutting gained her attention. Was it possible he had come back? she wondered, hope rushing through her like a tidal wave.

"Noah?" she called.

"No, it's just me."

Abigail pressed her eyes closed. Her father. Please, God, not on top of everything else, she prayed silently.

But her prayers were left unanswered, and Sherwood came to stand in the doorway. For a moment, Abigail forgot all else. Her father, ever so handsome and powerful, stood before her, looking for all the world like a beaten man.

A faint smile spread on his lips. "Mind if I come in?"

Abigail almost didn't answer, so surprised was she that he had asked. "Please, have a seat."

He took a seat, but didn't speak. Seemingly lost in a world of his own, he furrowed his brow then eased it, only to furrow it once again. "I had a note from Noah Blake waiting for me when I got to the bank," he said without preamble.

This surprised her even more. What could Noah Blake possibly have to say to her father.

"It said he was leaving."

Abigail looked away. Out of habit she waited for her father's biting remarks. But for some reason it no longer mattered to her, she realized. She didn't care that she could never live up to her father's expectations. She didn't care that she could never be as beautiful as Emma. She was herself, and she was infinitely tired of trying to be something she was not.

But the biting remarks never came. Tentatively, she looked back.

"Furthermore, he informed me that if I even thought of taking the boardinghouse away from you, he would personally come back to El Paso and wring my neck." He chuckled, but the sound was vacuous and quickly trailed off into a sigh. "I suppose I deserve that, and perhaps worse." He shook his head and met his daughter's glance. "I don't know how everything went so wrong."

"Things went wrong, Father," she began, wanting everything out on the table, tired of the lies, "because I bargained with Noah. Plain and simple, I made a deal with him to become my husband. Once I had the boardinghouse, we agreed we would get an annulment." She looked away, realizing an annulment was no longer possible. "Or a divorce."

Sherwood's eyes widened, but then they dimmed and his shoulders slumped. "That's not what I was talking about when I said things had gone wrong. I've hurt you terribly over the years. I shouldn't be surprised by the lengths to which you would go in order to gain something you deserved. If you had wanted this damned boardinghouse, I should have given it to you outright. As Virginia pointed out to me almost nightly, this place was nothing but a bother for me. But no, I used it to manipulate you while I doted on Emma. The same scenario has played itself out again and again over the years, and look what it got me. A daughter who is good and true who can't stand the sight of me, and another daughter who has learned to be deceitful and conniving to get what she wants—no matter who gets hurt in the process. Emma learned well from her father," he said, his voice filled with angry sarcasm that turned to a groan as if he only just remembered all that had transpired. "And many people have been hurt. Especially poor little Lou." He hesitated. "Grant's gone, you know."

"No!" Abigail gasped. "Where?"

"Don't know. Left right after the burial. Can't say that I blame him either after what Emma has done." He pressed his fingers to the bridge of his nose. "How could she have done such a thing?"

Abigail watched her father. No matter how she felt about her father, she had always seen him as all powerful, infallible. Now she had learned differently. How was it possible that the person who had taught her everything she knew didn't know everything? Abigail wondered.

It was a strange feeling. Disappointing, yes, but strangely freeing at the same time. If he was wrong about some things, perhaps he was wrong about others as well. Perhaps he had been wrong about her all along. She nearly staggered at the thought.

"My children are lost to me," he said, breaking into her reverie.

"Father," she replied, reaching out and placing her hand on top of his. No matter how he had treated her in the past, she hated to see her father in such pain. "You haven't lost me. I'll always be here, just as I always have been."

Sherwood met her gaze.

"Yes, Father, but more importantly, you still have Adam, sweet little Adam who desperately wants your attention and approval." She saw her father wince. "It may be too late to make any real difference with Emma and me, we are full grown and molded, but you can make a huge difference with Adam. He loves you very much. Just as Virginia does." She squeezed his hand. "Don't be afraid to admit your failures, then move on and try to do better."

Her father looked at her, his silver eyes blurry with pain. "How is it that you have become so wise?"

Thoughts of Noah loomed and she bit back the need to cry. "Noah taught me a great deal in the short time he was here."

This time her father reached out. One strong finger found her chin and forced her to look at him. "Noah is a good man, but a fool. And I certainly know about being a fool."

"Father—"

"No, you've excused my faults for too long. You are a wonderful person, Abigail. You're good and kind," he shook his head, "and forgiving. Noah Blake couldn't find a better woman if he tried. The man indeed is a fool to have left you." Taking a deep breath he stood. "I love you, Abigail. And I'm sorry it has taken me twenty-nine years to tell you."

She did not know how to answer. Her throat was tight and she was on the verge of tears. So instead of words, she stood up and wrapped her arms around him as she had longed to do so often over the years. "I love you, too, Father," she finally whispered before she let him go, then added, "Now you better get back home and say those very same words to Virginia and Adam."

Sherwood left, leaving Abigail alone with her thoughts. She felt light-headed from the unexpected attention and support from her father. Glasses of the finest champagne could not have come close to giving her that feeling. And she realized with a start that just as it wasn't too late for her father, it wasn't too late for her either. Noah Blake loved her. She felt it in her bones. And just like she'd had to learn over the last several weeks, she had to fight for what she wanted. She had to take to heart what Noah Blake had taught her and fight for him—just as Wanderer had predicted she would have to do.

She couldn't be afraid of life or living. She couldn't sit back and wish her life was different. She had to make her life what she wanted. Which meant going after Noah and forcing him to admit his love for her. But more importantly, she had to force him to tell her about the dark place in his soul, for surely that was what held them apart.

Purpose as she had never felt before pounded through

her veins. And this time experience had taught her that she could follow through.

"Noah Blake is a fool for leaving me," she suddenly blurted out to the empty kitchen. "And I'm going to find him and tell him just that."

With a good bit of effort, she dressed in layers of woolens to keep warm, and then borrowed a horse from the livery. She didn't like going out into the cold any more than the horse did, but she was determined to persevere. She rode for hours, following the trail that would take her into the mountains, that sacred place that Noah said he couldn't live without. She knew if she continued, soon enough she would overtake him. He would be traveling with the wagonload of supplies. She remembered the day he brought them home—the day that Lou came running up the steps and pleaded with her to help the mama. The memory tore at her. Her sweet Lou was gone. She would not lose Noah as well.

It was nightfall when she finally made out Noah's wagon in the distance outlined by long rays of silver moonlight. She didn't give a thought to the dangers of outlaws and Indians, much less the dangers of riding at night. Her only thoughts were of what she would say when she came face to face with Noah once again.

But all her gloriously rehearsed speeches fell by the wayside when she came up next to Noah. There were no relieved or heartfelt embraces awaiting her, no declarations or avowals of love and happiness. It was plain to anyone with a lick of sense that this man was furious.

"What the hell are you doing out here, woman?" he shouted at her.

Her cheeks burned. She was barely aware of Wanderer riding next to him on the wagon bench. "Well, I—"

"You could have been killed or maimed or captured or any one of a hundred different things just as bad riding out here alone!"

All traces of the Noah she had known were gone. She felt uncertain, and oddly enough, fear for this man who had taken his place. This was the man who hunted and killed, not the teasing man back in El Paso who now and again lost his temper. But more than anything she felt a mortifying dread, worse than her fear of harm, that she had been wrong about Noah—that she had been wrong and he didn't love her at all. She had assigned him feelings that were nothing more than a figment of her overactive imagination. She had wrapped herself up in the make-believe world she spent so much time in. Noah Blake didn't love her. He hardly liked her, and that point was being brought home most effectively just then by his towering rage. How could she have been so wrong.

"What are you doing here?" he demanded once again.

"I thought . . . I thought you loved me," she said without thinking.

The words clearly surprised him. The rage wavered on his face and Abigail saw it. In that second an inkling of hope rekindled in her breast. "You do love me, don't you?"

She noticed that Wanderer looked away.

"Go home, Abigail," Noah said through clenched teeth. "You're playing at games that aren't really games. I'm not a civilized man like Walter or your father. I'm more than capable of hurting you."

His words didn't move her. And she wouldn't give up. "Tell me that you don't love me, Noah Blake, then I'll go."

Their eyes locked and held in a deadly stare. Each of their lives seemed to depend on his answer.

"Sentiments don't matter in this world, Abby. Now turn around and go." His voice was taut, strained.

But Abigail merely sat in the saddle, her fingers clutching the reins. "No, Noah. I won't go until you tell me you don't love me. Tell me you don't care. Tell me that you don't want me to be your wife."

With that he snapped. "You're damn right I don't want you to be my wife! I've already had a wife . . . and a child!" He leaned closer. "And you know what happened to them?"

His venomous words washed over her. Her mind froze at the import. He already had a wife, and a child. Her head swam with denial and the pain of betrayal from the one person she had believed, had sworn, would never betray her. "A wife . . . and a child?" she whispered.

"That's right, Abigail. And don't you want to know where they are now?" His eyes were crazed and angry and hurt. "They're dead, Abigail. And do you want to know what I see in that dark place inside of me? It's their dead and mutilated bodies. They died alone and miserable at the hands of marauding Indians. And they wouldn't have been alone had I not been a mountain man. Yes, Abigail. A mountain man through and through. So I was gone. Had left them alone to go and trap. They were butchered. And I found them. So no, Abigail, I don't want you for a wife. And I don't want you here. So turn that horse around and get the hell out of my life."

Abigail sucked in her breath. There was too much to take in. But one thing became quite clear to her as anger seeped back into her, filling the cracks in her heart. "You aren't a mountain man, Noah Blake." Her words were laced far stronger with venom than Noah's had been. "You're a hypocrite."

Noah's eyes widened.

"That's right, Mr. Blake. You are a hypocrite of the worst kind, because you are not first and foremost a mountain man. You are a man who is afraid of living under the restraints of society so you hide in the wild, missing out on what society can give you—like love and sharing and children and a home. And most shameful of all, you hide behind the death of a woman and a child to provide you with reason not to change. You said I was afraid to live. Life, Noah Blake, does not have to mean living on the edge. Life means living and loving each day as best you can." Her manic laugh wafted through the nighttime darkness, swirling with the silver moonlight. "Admit that you loved and lost, then be brave enough to go on with your life."

And with that, she snapped the reins, and horse and rider raced off in a cloud of churned up dust and gravel.

Noah watched her go, his fingers curled around the wagon reins, forcing himself not to go after her.

"She is very wise," Wanderer said into the cold night air.

Noah's hands clenched tighter.

"You have thrown yourself into the wild for many years," Wanderer continued. "You have known no other life. Rosemary knew that when she married you. It is not your fault that she and your child were killed."

"But I left them alone!" Noah cried out.

"No," Wanderer said firmly. "Not alone, but in the village she was from, with many families. All were killed. You would have been killed, too, had you been there. There was nothing anyone could have done. But now you have sent away an innocent woman who barely knows how to ride—alone—a woman you love."

Noah flung back his head and roared into the heavens like a wounded lion. And he knew then that no matter what, he had to find Abigail and admit his love, not only to save her, but to save himself as well.

He jumped down from the wagon and untied his horse that trailed along behind them. Only minutes after Abigail had raced off, he was chasing after her, praying it was not too late.

21

SHE RODE LIKE THE WIND, UNAWARE OF ANY DANGER, simply holding on for dear life as her mount raced across the countryside. Her mind raced as well, staggering on Noah's words as they played over and over again in her head.

He already had a wife, and a child. How could she not have known something so essential about the man she married—a man with whom she had shared the most intimate experience two people can share? She had thought she knew him. Had been sure he loved her. She had felt it in her bones. Certainly he had surprised her on occasion, but still she would have sworn she knew his soul.

She threw her head back and laughed up into the dark heavens, ignoring the beauty of the stars and long rays of silver moonlight. What a fool she had been. She hadn't known Noah Blake at all.

Suddenly, no more than a few miles away Abigail felt the steed lurch forward. The steady rhythm ceased, and she was thrown into the night. But oddly she found she didn't care what befell her. For one searing moment she only felt the freedom of letting loose, of not caring what happened. Her limbs relaxed and her mind soared as her body hurtled through the air. She was aware of the cold night air on her face, and the landscape seemed to be carved out of the night by moonlight. She felt nothing more than intense awareness. And freedom.

But then she landed in a heap on the rock strewn ground and another kind of intense awareness wrapped around her. With the hard contact of reality, her sense of freedom evaporated as pain seared through her body. She lay in the dirt and sand, her breath knocked clean from her lungs. Panic threatened. Though only for the sudden thought that she didn't want to die. She had only just begun to live—with or without Noah Blake.

And then air surged back, filling her, and with it came the same raging anger she had felt before. Yes, anger. She nearly screamed it out loud. She was mad. Madder'n hell, she thought to herself, bringing a wry smile to her lips. She was fighting mad.

The sound of hooves pounding against the hard earth gained her attention. Seconds later, she glanced up just in time to witness Noah Blake appear out of the black night, a portrait of towering fury. Her mind reeled. He was still angry that she had followed him! Did he think to ride after her just to vent his spleen on her a bit more—did he think his point was not well taken? If so he was more boorish and obnoxious than she ever gave him credit for. How had she ever fallen in love with this man? she wondered.

But her traitorous mind flashed all of his caring deeds in front of her mind's eye. And that made her all the angrier. She was tired of her mind continually deceiving her with fictitious pictures of Noah Blake. He was a beast, and she relished his arrival. Her spleen was in need of venting, too.

Noah leaped down from his horse before it had stopped completely. Abigail had yet to pull herself up from the rock and cactus strewn ground. She still lay in a heap, pressing her eyes closed, not because of the pain that seared her body, but because she was churning with all she wanted to say to this beast.

"Abby," he said, the word a demand, when she failed to speak. "Abigail, say something!"

Her eyes snapped open in a flash. "You're damned right I'm going to say something, you bullheaded, boorish lout of a man!"

Noah jerked back in surprise. "Abby—"

"Don't you Abby me. And if I don't hear another word out of you the rest of my life it will be none too soon. 'Playing at games that aren't really games.' Threatening me! How dare you! I haven't been playing games. I have loved you. And what's more, I've been working, hard. And you damn well know it. And I've done a good job, better than most would have done in the same circumstances. No, I haven't been playing games, though I've been a pawn in all too many men's schemes. My father's scheme to get me married, Walter's to get at my father's money, and yours . . ." She could think of no particular game he had tried to play with her unless it was sexual. And even she couldn't deny that she had been more than willing to play that game.

Embarrassment and shame washed over her and with it came remembered fury. "Well, I'm tired of it! I don't have to be anyone's pawn any longer. Furthermore, I don't need anyone's help, either. Do you understand me? And I especially don't need the likes of you lecturing me. I can survive—on my own!" Her diatribe ceased abruptly. Her eyes narrowed as if suddenly the meaning of her words, the import of them, just then came clear to her.

Her head swayed. She *didn't* need anyone, she realized. She *could* do it by herself. And she believed it.

Her anger evaporated into the night.

"Are you finished?" Noah demanded, unaware of the change that had taken place.

Slowly she met his heated gaze.

His eyes narrowed further. "You make me so mad that you make me say things I don't mean. Yes, you have done a good job and you don't need anyone else! You are an independent woman of means," he said, practically shouting. Then he pressed his fingers to his temples and closed his eyes. When he looked at her again he finally noticed her rage had disappeared. The anger and frustration in his blue eyes melted away, and he shook his head. "And though I might not sound like it, I'm proud of you—very, very proud of you."

She took a deep breath then let it out slowly. A tentative smile found her lips. "Yeah," she said softly. "I guess I'm proud of me, too."

He chuckled though the sound held no mirth. "You

should be proud. For years I've boasted about being brave. I realize now I didn't know the first thing about bravery. I was the coward you accused me of being. Afraid to live life on any other terms than the ones I had lived for a lifetime."

"Better safe and well fed than adventuresome and dead," she whispered.

"What?" He looked confused by her words.

"My lifelong motto. I have lived my whole life by that. You gave me the courage to change."

He looked away and repeated the words. "Obviously I have lived by that motto for decades without realizing it. I was safe and well fed in the wilderness I knew like the back of my hand. To venture into town and try to make a new life was adventuresome to me. And I was afraid. What if I couldn't make it?"

He turned back to her then, fiercely. "But know that I'm going to take my own advice, and follow your actions. I'm going to make a new life for myself. I'm going to take all that money of mine that your father has been badgering me about and use it to find a way to exist day to day in society." He hesitated. "And I'm not going to run away even if at first I fail. Because you have shown me that with practice a person will learn. Surely there is something in El Paso that I can do to make a living."

"I believe you were the man who said that a person can do anything he puts his mind to."

He took her hand in his and met her gaze. "Damn, was that me?"

Her lips twitched. "Yes, you."

"Well, as I said, I guess there is no help for it. I'm going to have to take my own advice."

She took a deep breath. "Only if you want to."

He dropped his gaze and stared at her hand. With great care he stroked her fingers and circled her knuckles. Finally he looked back at her. His blue eyes were stormy. "I love you, Mrs. Blake. And if you will give me a second chance, I'd like you to stay Mrs. Blake. Forever."

She studied him, her face still and expressionless. "Just

like that? You expect me to forget what a boorish lout you've been to me."

His eyes opened wide for a second. But then he noticed the smile that threatened on her beautiful lush lips. "My declaration's not good enough?"

His expression grew devilish while hers grew decidedly leery. She was still on the ground and he crouched before her. At the look that grew more devilish by the second, she scooted back a few inches. He scooted forward.

"All right," she said, inching further back. "I was wrong. I agree. Mrs. Blake. Forever."

Scrabbling backwards, she managed to put a few feet between them. Just when she decided it was time to jump to her feet and run for it, he grabbed her ankle with lightning quickness.

"Too late for that, my sweet." With feigned menace, he pulled her toward him.

"Noah, what are you doing?"

"I'm going to do a better job of making my declaration, my love, in hopes of getting you to reevaluate your opinion of me." Slowly, he raised her booted foot to his lips. "I love you, Mrs. Blake," he whispered, his eyes locked with hers.

"Okay, I believe you," she responded, trying to pull her foot away.

Noah only smiled and held firm. He kissed the stocking above her boot, then higher until he reached her knee. "I want you at my side, Mrs. Blake. Until we are old, and gray, and can no longer hear so well." His hand strayed higher on her leg.

"You've got it," she said, her voice growing breathless. "Now let me go."

"Not until you reassess my personality," he stated as he kissed her stockinged thigh.

"You're not boorish."

"I'm happy to hear it." He pushed the stocking aside and nipped at her bare skin. "What about the lout?"

"I was mistaken," she said as her head fell back.

"Good," he said simply, dropping her leg, then leaping to his feet.

Moments passed before Abigail realized the kisses had ceased. Her eyes flew open. "You beast!"

"Calling me names again so soon. Tut, tut. How soon we forget."

He stood over her, his arms akimbo, his feet spread wide. He was the most devastatingly handsome man she had ever seen, and she realized with a start that he was hers—not temporarily, not on loan, but forever. And she wanted him. Shamelessly.

"If you're not careful," he added, "I'll have to punish you once again."

The corner of her mouth tilted in a sly smile. "You cad."

He stared at her, not sure if he believed what he heard. "Pardon?"

"You lout. You knave." She reached down and inched her skirt up higher. "Looks like you're going to have to punish me now."

He threw his head back and laughed. "You little imp. I'll show you punishment," he said as he came down beside her.

"I'm counting on it."

He kissed her then, long and slow. "You've certainly learned how to live, my sweet, sweet Abby. How could I ever live without you?"

"You can't." She grabbed his shirt and pulled him close. "Just as I can't live without you."

RED. BRIGHT, VIBRANT RED. MIXED WITH A SPECTRUM of other colors, streaming through the line of jars filled with various jellies in the front, mullioned window. Abigail reached out and moved her hand through the colored ribbons of light. Slowly she turned, following the multicolored prism to its end. And there she found Noah. As she knew she would.

He sat at a small desk, his head bent over the General Store's massive ledgers. The only sounds that came from his corner were the scratching of pencil on paper and the all too frequent curse when he made a mistake. With a smile Abigail turned away to head back to the boardinghouse, which thankfully ran as smooth as clockwork now.

Weaving her way through the bins of flour and locked boxes of sugar that crowded the floor, she marveled at how her life had changed.

Emma had gone to live with their aunts in St. Louis. Walter had traveled west in search of better opportunities. Hester Smith had followed him, though it was unclear if he had asked her to go or if she had simply gone. Myrtle Kent had sold the store to Noah, then with a hug and profuse thanks, headed for Houston the following morning to live with her sister. Grant hadn't been seen since the day they buried little Lou.

Oh, Lou, Abigail thought, are you in heaven now? Did you find the Angel Mama?

There wasn't a day that went by that Lou wasn't in Abigail's thoughts. For Lou had played a significant part in that time when Abigail learned to break free of self-doubt and fear. It was Lou who first called Abigail pretty that day on the steps outside the General Store. And had she not taken the time with Lou that day she would have been long past the Red Dog Saloon when Noah burst through the doors.

Noah. His name drifted through her mind like a caress.

The bell over the door jingled, announcing a customer. A light gust of summer breeze drifted through the store, stirring up the smell of herbs and spices, dried chilies and coffee beans. And with the gust came Sherwood Ashleigh.

"How is everyone on this glorious morning?" he asked as he walked over and kissed Abigail on the cheek.

Even after all these months Abigail still marveled at the change in her father. And more than that, she marveled at the relationship that had grown between them. Had someone predicted this turn of events a year ago or even six months ago she would have called them a fool.

"I'm fine, Father—"

"Damn!"

Both Sherwood and Abigail turned to the back corner.

"Noah, it would appear," her father said, "isn't faring so well."

"The books," Abigail added with a shrug, as if that was explanation enough. And of course it was. The books had been a problem since Noah took over the store.

"Son, I've told you to take those darned things over to the bank. Just let my clerk help you until you learn."

Noah cursed and grumbled.

Sherwood held up his hands. "But do what you want. I know you will. Just like my daughter here. Stubborn as any mule this side of the Mississippi."

The bell jingled again.

"Papa! Look what Mama found!" Adam bounded into the store, Virginia close behind him.

Everyone looked.

Virginia stood at the door, her hands behind her back, red staining her cheeks. "Adam, really."

"Well, come on," Abigail said with a smile. "You've got to show us now."

"It's just a hat."

"If it's just a hat, sweetie," Sherwood said, placing his hand on Adam's shoulder while he smiled at his wife, "then why are you hiding it."

"Well, it's one of Millie's newest creations."

At this, Sherwood groaned. "Not more of Millie's haute couture. This town has never seen so many feathers and foofs in all its days."

"But isn't it all so lovely," Virginia said, her voice like a child's, as she whipped the hat from behind her back and placed it over her blond curls. "What do you think?"

Adam burst out laughing as Noah's and Sherwood's eyes widened at the sight of the befeathered concoction that was a good ten times the size of her dainty head.

Abigail tried to hide her smile. "Well, Virginia," she ventured. "It's . . ."

"Big," Noah finished for her.

"True," Virginia said. "But I loved it and I didn't want to hurt Millie's feelings. She is such a dear. And since the townspeople seem to follow our lead, like Abigail, I wanted to be sure and support her attempts at branching out from making clothes to making hats."

"Yes, Abby certainly has helped Millie," Noah said, looking at his wife with pride and love.

Virginia reached across and squeezed Abigail's hand. "She has helped us all."

This time Abigail blushed. "It was nothing."

Noah put his arm around her shoulder and pulled her close. "Yeah, nothing at all. Just got the whole town to start buying clothes and now hats from a soiled dove, and whipped a bunch of pig-headed men into shape is all. Just another day's work in my sweet Abigail's life."

Sherwood laughed. "Pig-headed? Speak for yourself. I prefer to think of myself as determined." He turned to Abigail and smiled. "You whipped determined men into shape."

"Pig-headed," Virginia clarified with a teasing smile, "seems more the appropriate adjective to me."

With that they all laughed, for whether it was pig-headedness or determination, the result was the same.

"We're on our way to Holloway's Restaurant," Sherwood said. "We just came by to see if anyone wants to join us?"

"Thanks, but I've got to get back to the boardinghouse," Abigail said.

"Fine, we'll see you all later then."

The bell jingled to a halt over the door, leaving Abigail and Noah alone.

"I'd best be going home now," Abigail said as she headed toward the door. "I need to start supper."

"Not so fast, darlin'." Noah reached out and pulled Abigail back to him. "Have I told you how much I love you today, Mrs. Blake?"

Abigail smiled. "Yes, Mr. Blake, at least a dozen times."

Noah's answering chuckle rumbled deep in his chest. "Well count on hearing it at least a dozen more before the day is out." He glanced over at the ledgers that waited for him and groaned. "For now, however, duty calls." He kissed her again. "But first . . ." He pulled away and walked to the back room. "Close your eyes."

"What is this all about?"

"Just close your eyes, Abigail."

Excitement bubbled up and she closed her eyes.

"Are they closed?" he bellowed from the back.

"Yes, Noah, they're closed."

"Good, I have a little surprise for you."

She stood very still. She could hear his pounding footsteps grow close, then she heard rustling just in front of her. It was all she could do to keep her eyes shut.

"The next Saturday Social is in a week," he said simply.

Then she could feel him drape something soft and shimmery about her shoulders. "Noah?"

"And you are going to be the most beautiful woman there."

Without opening her eyes she reached up and touched

the fabric. Her breath caught in her throat. And she knew what it was.

"What do you think?" he asked as he stood back.

She opened her eyes and took in the length of red satin draped across her shoulders. "Oh Noah," she breathed. "It seems I've waited for this for a lifetime."

He took hold of her shoulders and pulled her in front of an oval mirror that was for sale in the corner. "I take it you approve?"

A smile tilted on her lips. "I don't know that I approve," she said as she reached up and slipped her fingers beneath the edge of the red satin and the cotton of her dress. "But that seems to make it all the more beautiful."

His smile turned to a groan. "Your heart is wild, my love," he murmured as he nipped at the fine line of her shoulder, "but I'd have you no other way."

With that his fingers entwined with hers, gently pushing, until cool, dry air whispered against her skin as the red satin finally fell free.

Diamond Wildflower Romance

*A breathtaking new line of spectacular novels set in the untamed
frontier of the American West. Every month, Diamond Wildflower
brings you new adventures where passionate men and women
dare to embrace their boldest dreams. Finally, romances that
capture the very spirit and passion of the wild frontier.*

__RUNAWAY BRIDE by Ann Carberry
   0-7865-0002-6/$4.99

__TEXAS ANGEL by Linda Francis Lee
   0-7865-0007-7/$4.99

__FRONTIER HEAT by Peggy Stoks
   0-7865-0012-3/$4.99

__RECKLESS RIVER by Teresa Southwick
   0-7865-0018-2/$4.99

__LIGHTNING STRIKES by Jean Wilson
   0-7865-0024-7/$4.99

__TENDER OUTLAW by Deborah James
   0-7865-0043-3/$4.99

__MY DESPERADO by Lois Greiman
   0-7865-0048-4/$4.99

__NIGHT TRAIN by Maryann O'Brien
   0-7865-0058-1/$4.99

__WILD HEARTS by Linda Francis Lee
   0-7865-0062-X/$4.99

__DRIFTER'S MOON by Lisa Hendrix
   0-7865-0070-0 (January)

Payable in U.S. funds. No cash orders accepted. Postage & handling: $1.75 for one book, 75¢
for each additional. Maximum postage $5.50. Prices, postage and handling charges may
change without notice. Visa, Amex, MasterCard call 1-800-788-6262, ext. 1, refer to ad # 406

Or, check above books and send this order form to:	Bill my: ☐ Visa ☐ MasterCard ☐ Amex
The Berkley Publishing Group	Card#_____ (expires)
390 Murray Hill Pkwy., Dept. B	
East Rutherford, NJ 07073	Signature_____ ($15 minimum)
Please allow 6 weeks for delivery.	Or enclosed is my: ☐ check ☐ money order
Name_____	Book Total $_____
Address_____	Postage & Handling $_____
City_____	Applicable Sales Tax $_____
State/ZIP_____	(NY, NJ, PA, CA, GST Can.) Total Amount Due $_____

AWARD-WINNING NATIONAL BESTSELLING AUTHOR

JODI THOMAS

__TO TAME A TEXAN'S HEART 0-7865-0059-x/$4.99

True McCormick needs a gunslinger to pose as Granite Westwind, a name
True uses to publish her books of the Wild West. She finds her legend in
a Galveston jailhouse–Seth Atherton. True is fooling everybody, until the
bullets start to fly and True begins to fall in love with the hero she created....

__THE TEXAN AND THE LADY 1-55773-970-6/$4.99

Jennie Munday left Iowa for Kansas to become a Harvey Girl–only to meet
Austin McCormick, the abrasive Texas marshal on her train. When the
train is held up, Jennie learns the law can be deadly... and filled with desire.

__CHERISH THE DREAM 1-55773-881-5/$4.99

From childhood through nursing school, Katherine and Sarah were best
friends. Now they set out to take all that life has to offer–and are swept up
in the rugged, positively breathtaking world of two young pilots, men who
take to the skies with a bold spirit. And who dare them to love.

__THE TENDER TEXAN 1-55773-546-8/$4.95

Anna Meyer dared to walk into a campsite full of Texan cattlemen and offer
one hundred dollars to the man who'd help her forge a frontier homestead.
Chance Wyatt accepted her offer and they vowed to live together for one
year...until the challenges of the savage land drew them closer together.

__PRAIRIE SONG 1-55773-657-X/$4.99

Maggie is Texas born and bred. When this beautiful Confederate widow
inherits a sprawling house of scandalous secrets, she also is left with a
newfound desire–for a Union Army soldier.

__NORTHERN STAR 1-55773-396-1/$4.50

Hauntingly beautiful Perry McLain is desperate to escape the cruel,
powerful Union Army captain who pursues her, seeking vengeance for her
rebellion. Yet, her vow to save an ailing soldier plunges her deep into
enemy territory...and into the torturous flames of desire.

Payable in U.S. funds. No cash orders accepted. Postage & handling: $1.75 for one book, 75¢
for each additional. Maximum postage $5.50. Prices, postage and handling charges may
change without notice. Visa, Amex, MasterCard call 1-800-788-6262, ext. 1, refer to ad # 361

Or, check above books Bill my: ☐ Visa ☐ MasterCard ☐ Amex	
and send this order form to:	(expires)
The Berkley Publishing Group	Card#_____
390 Murray Hill Pkwy., Dept. B	($15 minimum)
East Rutherford, NJ 07073	Signature_____
Please allow 6 weeks for delivery.	Or enclosed is my: ☐ check ☐ money order
Name_____	Book Total $_____
Address_____	Postage & Handling $_____
City_____	Applicable Sales Tax $_____
	(NY, NJ, PA, CA, GST Can.)
State/ZIP_____	Total Amount Due $_____

If you enjoyed this book, take advantage of this special offer. Subscribe now and...

Get a Historical

No Obligation

If you enjoy reading the very best in historical romantic fiction...romances that set back the hands of time to those by-gone days with strong virile heros and passionate heroines ...then you'll want to subscribe to the True Value Historical Romance Home Subscription Service. Now that you have read one of the best historical romances around today, we're sure you'll want more of the same fiery passion, intimate romance and historical settings that set these books apart from all others.

Each month the editors of True Value select the four *very best* novels from America's leading publishers of romantic fiction. We have made arrangements for you to preview them in your home *Free* for 10 days. And with the first four books you

receive, we'll send you a FREE book as our introductory gift. No Obligation!

FREE HOME DELIVERY

We will send you the four best and newest historical romances as soon as they are published to preview FREE for 10 days (in many cases you may even get them before they arrive in the book stores). If for any reason you decide not to keep them, just return them and owe nothing. But if you like them as much as we think you will, you'll pay just $4.00 each and save at *least* $.50 each off the cover price. (Your savings are *guaranteed* to be at least $2.00 each month.) There is NO postage and handling—or other hidden charges. There are no minimum number of books to buy and you may cancel at any time.

FREE
Romance
(a $4.50 value)

Send in the Coupon Below

To get your FREE historical romance and start saving, fill out the coupon below and mail it today. As soon as we receive it we'll send you your FREE Book along with your first month's selections.

Mail To: **True Value Home Subscription Services, Inc.** P.O. Box 5235
120 Brighton Road, Clifton, New Jersey 07015-5235

YES! I want to start previewing the very best historical romances being published today. Send me my FREE book along with the first month's selections. I understand that I may look them over FREE for 10 days. If I'm not absolutely delighted I may return them and owe nothing. Otherwise I will pay the low price of just $4.00 each: a total $16.00 (at *least* an $18.00 value) and save at least $2.00. Then each month I will receive four brand new novels to preview as soon as they are published for the same low price. I can always return a shipment and I may cancel this subscription at any time with no obligation to buy even a single book. In any event the FREE book is mine to keep regardless.

Name _____

Street Address _____ Apt. No. _____

City _____ State _____ Zip Code _____

Telephone _____

Signature _____
(if under 18 parent or guardian must sign)

Terms and prices subject to change. Orders subject
to acceptance by True Value Home Subscription
Services. Inc.   **0062-X**